D0225769

A SON OF THE SUN

THE ADVENTURES OF CAPTAIN DAVID GRIEF

Jack and Charmain London plan their voyage on the *Snark*.

A SON OF THE SUN

THE ADVENTURES OF
CAPTAIN DAVID GRIEF
by
JACK LONDON

WITH INTRODUCTIONS AND NOTES BY
Thomas R. Tietze AND Gary Riedl

UNIVERSITY OF OKLAHOMA PRESS · Norman

Library of Congress Cataloging-in-Publication Data

London, Jack, 1876–1916.
A son of the sun: the adventures of Captain David Grief /
by Jack London ;
with introductions and notes by Thomas R. Tietze and Gary Riedl.
p. cm.
Includes bibliographical references (p.) and index.
Contents: A son of the sun—The proud goat of Aloysius Pankburn
—The devils of Fuatino—The jokers of New Gibbon—A little
account with Swithin Hall—A Goboto night—The feathers of the
sun—The pearls of Parlay.
ISBN 0-8061-3362-7 (alk. paper)
1. Oceania—Social life and customs—Fiction. 2. Autobiographical
fiction, American. 3. Americans—Oceania—Fiction. 4. Adventure
stories, American. 5. Ship captains—Fiction. 6. Sea stories,
American. I. Tietze, Thomas R. II. Riedl, Gary III. Title.

PS3523.O46 S64 2001
813'.52—dc21

2001023410

The paper in this book meets the guidelines for permanence and
durability of the Committee on Production Guidelines for Book
Longevity of the Council on Library Resources, Inc. ∞
Copyright © 2001 by the University of Oklahoma Press, Norman,
Publishing Division of the University. All rights reserved.
Manufactured in the U. S. A.

1 2 3 4 5 6 7 8 9 10

The editors wish to
dedicate their work on this volume to

WINNIE KINGMAN,

EARLE LABOR

and

I. MILO SHEPARD.

CONTENTS

A SON OF THE SUN
THE ADVENTURES OF CAPTAIN DAVID GRIEF

ILLUSTRATIONS

DRAWINGS

All drawings are from the 1911 *Saturday Evening Post* serialization of *A Son of the Sun*.

PHOTOGRAPHS

All photographs are from the Jack London Collection,
copyright California State Parks, 2000.

MAPS

All maps are from the Jack London State Park Archives,
Glen Ellen, California.

ACKNOWLEDGMENTS

To Earle Labor, our friend and mentor, who first shared with us his passion for Jack London.

To I. Milo Shepard, London's grandnephew, at whose home we have shared many a smoky scotch and enjoyed happy times.

To the National Endowment for the Humanities for providing us with generous grants that have enabled both of us to study Jack London's life and works.

To the many members the American Literature Association who have given us the gift of friendship and encouragement, especially Donna Campbell, Jesse Crisler, Dan Dyer, Sara S. Hodson, Gail Jones, Richard Kopley, Joseph McCullough, Joseph McElrath, Susan Nuernberg, Jeanne Campbell Reesman, Jacqueline Tavernier-Corbin, James Williams, and of course, Lawrence I. Berkove and his long-suffering wife, Gail.

To Winnie Kingman, wonderful friend, Director of the Jack London Foundation, owner of the Jack London Bookstore, and the repository of every possible fact concerning Jack London. And to the late Russ Kingman, beloved husband of Winnie and an inspiration to all London scholars.

To Raleigh Patterson, Roy Tennant, and Waring Jones.

To Kimberly Wiar and Karen Wieder, our editors.

To Ranger Greg Hayes and Debra Rawlings at the Jack London State Park for help in making available London's maps and charts.

To Glenn Burch, Historian of the California Department of Parks and Recreation, for his assistance in preparing the photographs for this volume and to the California Department of Parks and Recreation, Silverado District, for permission to use the photographs in this volume.

To the members of the Jack London Society and the Jack London Foundation.

To our fellow members in the 1990 and 1993 NEH seminars on Jack London for sharing good times in California.

To our teachers, particularly David Haley, Calvin Kendall, John Loegering, Jerry Reedy, and Marty Roth, for their inspiration and encouragement.

To the English Department of Wayzata Senior High School in Plymouth, Minnesota, respected colleagues and close friends who share our days and keep us laughing, particularly our nearest neighbors: Barb Johnson, Tiffany Joseph, Janice Korstange, Elizabeth Smith, and our spiritual leader, Marc Terrass. We also thank Don Anderson, Darrel Danner, Phil and Marion Fraser, and Jim Lewis. And of course, Mrs. Jewell.

To other members of the teaching staff at Wayzata High School, particularly Bill Miles, Maralynn Rye, and Larry Tuura, for their assistance in finding arcane pieces of information.

To Vera Johnson, our indefatigable secretary.

To our friends Bob and Mari Schestak, Tim and Lauri Carlson, and R. Dixon Smith.

And finally to our loving and lovely wives, Corinne and Kathryn, and our wonderful children, Renneca, John, Sam, and Hugh.

EDITORS'
INTRODUCTION

I

Jack London grabbed hold of life with both hands. Perhaps no other modern writer so identified his life with the adventures he described in his fiction. From the frozen Klondike to the sultry tropic seas, from the slums of London to the battlefields of Asia, Jack packed several lifetimes' worth of adventure into his own brief span of forty years. Born on January 12, 1876, in San Francisco, London grew up struggling against a hardscrabble environment that toughened him physically but scarred his sensitive spirit. It also inspired a determination to raise himself out of poverty and to reach for the American dream of financial success and independence. Charged with the responsibility to help the family's unstable financial situation, young Jack London dropped out of school to go to work.

"By the time he was ten," says London biographer Russ Kingman, "he was a work beast." His only relief from the relentless drudgery of his squalid life came when he discovered the world of books. Jack developed a habit of reading anything and everything he could find, a practice that effectively substituted for his lack of formal schooling and stimulated his thoughts for the rest of his life. Between the ages of fifteen and twenty-three, Jack threw himself into a bewildering array of jobs, including a stint as an oyster pirate in San Francisco Bay, followed quickly by another as a member of the Fish Patrol—the police who were supposed to arrest such pirates.

In 1893 he signed on aboard the *Sophia Sutherland* as able-bodied seaman for an eight-month, rough-and-tumble sealing voyage that took him as far as Japan. When he returned, frustrating efforts at hard labor caused him in the following year to give up and become a hobo. After riding the rails across America, Jack found himself flung into the Erie County Penitentiary in Buffalo, New York, sentenced to thirty days for vagrancy. On his return home to Oakland, Jack, at the age of nineteen, tried to finish high school and wrote for the school's literary magazine, the *Aegis*.

Another flirtation with formal education—one semester in Berkeley at the University of California—was permanently broken off by the great adventure of the 1897 gold rush in the Klondike. Jack found no gold during his year in the northland, but perhaps to his surprise, he did discover his "perspective." His experiences in Alaska furnished material for his fiction for the rest of his life. By this time, Jack London had determined to make his fortune not with his brawn but with his brain: he would become a writer.

Scores of essays, short fiction, a novel, a book of undercover reportage, and an extended discussion of human love found publication from 1898. After several years of struggle, London gained worldwide fame and success in 1903 with the publication of his most famous book, *The Call of the Wild*. Although this classic story of a dog in the Klondike followed the publication of several volumes of his work and preceded the appearance of more than forty more books, London's claim to popular literary prominence has rested on his masterpiece, supplemented by *The Sea-Wolf* (1904) and his other great dog story, *White Fang* (1906). Jack's early, bitter experiences with manual labor turned his political sympathies to socialism and his literary identification to the outcast and the underdog, but as his career flourished and his fame spread, Jack London became a millionaire through the income from his pen. With a set "stint" of writing a thousand words every morning—rain or shine, in sickness or in health, on land or at sea—London made enough money to buy up large tracts of land in order to create his fabulous Beauty Ranch, near Glen Ellen in the Sonoma Valley in northern California. However, his ambitious investments caused him, more often than not, to need cash in hand. Fortunately, such was the strength of his sales that he could ask for and obtain advances from publishers even for works he had not yet composed.

Though his three best-selling novels have retained worldwide popularity, many of his most interesting books have gone out of print and are no longer available. One such group of neglected short stories grew out of a daring adventure London and his wife, Charmian, designed for themselves: Between 1907 and 1909, they sailed the then little-explored waters of the South Pacific in the *Snark*, a fifty-five-foot sailing vessel Jack had built for the occasion. Risking death in the often treacherous seas, wracked with tropical diseases, sometimes lost, once nearly dying of thirst, occasionally threatened by cannibal islanders, the Londons nevertheless had the time of their lives. In the fiction that emerged from his adventures in the South Seas, London reworked some of his earlier ideas about the human condition.

After the South Seas adventure, London returned to his beloved Beauty Ranch. Always proud of his youthful physical strength but now suffering from a variety of ailments, some encountered on his ocean voyage and others made worse by it, London nevertheless managed to maintain an active and cheerful social life, to follow a disciplined writing regimen, and to work his ranch using the latest in scientific farming advances. He was deeply affected by the loss of his massive dream home, Wolf House, which burned to its foundations through an accidental fire in 1913, shortly before the Londons were to move in. On November 22, 1916, while his work continued to draw a worldwide readership and his mind was still filled with projects yet to be written, Jack London died of uremic poisoning.

Though the staples of his work have continued to be widely available since their original publication, by far the greatest proportion of his writings, and some of his most intriguing, has been allowed to go out of print. Because of this, few casual readers know that London authored more than merely boys' dog stories, even though in his short life he wrote many nonfiction essays, plays, poems, scores of books, and over two hundred short stories. *A Son of the Sun* appeared in 1912 and marked a new direction in London's thinking. It is a particularly interesting example of the sort of work he was doing in the later part of his career, which the critic Lawrence I. Berkove has called London's period of "second thoughts" (see Berkove, "Les derniers" and "London's Developing Conceptions"). Berkove has noticed London's habit of revisiting themes and ideas the author had worked with in earlier stories, and the relationship of this series to his other fiction will support that insight. Unseen by the general public for decades, the adventures of Captain David Grief are atmospheric, exciting, humorous, action-packed yarns as well as material that will richly reward scholarly examination.

II

When London needed to get an advance in order to make improvements on his California ranch in 1911, he promised the editor of *Red Book* a series of "ripping stories" about a "strong hero"; the only detail he offered was that these tales would be set in the South Seas (London, *Letters*, 971–72). After *Red Book* turned the idea down, the *Saturday Evening Post* picked it up, and London composed a group of adventure stories that would take as its theme a new kind of hero—the macho David Grief, who appears in the eight tales ultimately collected in *A Son of the Sun* (Doubleday, Page, 1912).

Throughout his writing career, London planned two levels of reading experience for those who read his books: for the ordinary reader, a fast-paced adventure story would hold the attention while it impelled one forward toward the exciting conclusion; and for the more thoughtful reader, deeper themes would demand a more careful response. One such complex book was *The Sea-Wolf*, which on the surface tells the story of a weak, intellectual, city-bred man who finds himself shanghaied aboard a seal-hunting ship in the command of a monster captain, Wolf Larsen. This character, which London's fellow American writer Ambrose Bierce considered one of most remarkable achievements in literature, is a compelling combination of brute and genius, of flesh and spirit, of physical perfection and moral depravity. But beneath the surface of the adventure and beyond the fascination of the main character lurk many other layers of meaning, one of the most important of which is London's attempted examination of the ideas of the German philosopher Friedrich Nietzsche (1844–1900).

London first read Nietzsche in an English translation in the autumn of 1904, although he almost certainly had heard about Nietzsche's main ideas at the time of the worldwide reporting of the philosopher's death in 1900. London also had had spirited discussions with his friend Frank Strawn-Hamilton, an amateur philosopher and hobo, before having read Nietzsche. Never a deep student, as his daughter Joan admits, London's approach to Nietzsche was emotional and enthusiastic, not scholarly (Joan London, *Jack London,* 209). As Jack London understood him, Nietzsche taught that there were some people for whom ordinary moral boundaries did not exist. These superior people were called "supermen," and they would naturally emerge as leaders. Wolf Larsen assumes such a role, though the Nietzsche scholar Patrick Bridgwater points out that the character "is close to the popular misconception of the Superman, but far indeed from embodying Nietzsche's essentially spiritual ideal" (*Nietzsche,* 165). As captain of the *Ghost,* Larsen leads a crew of human brutes solely by the force of his personal strength. When he is no longer strong, his crew deserts him and he dies. For most critics this depiction of the Nietzschean disposition and attitude has been imagined to be London's final position. The critic F. W. Parkay suggests, for example, that *The Sea-Wolf*'s assault on Nietzsche's ideas represents London's permanent views: "London ultimately found [them] disillusioning and sterile" ("Influence," 23). In *Martin Eden,* which followed in 1909, London turned again to the study of a Nietzschean personality who finds his dream of success unfulfilling and meaningless. Just as happened with Wolf Larsen, however, Martin was such a compellingly intriguing personality that London's critique of the individualist philosophy was missed by readers.

More than any other philosopher of the previous century, Friedrich Nietzsche has been popularly celebrated, condemned, and largely misunderstood owing in part to his own ambiguities and extravagances. Even in his original German, Nietzsche's language is playful, ambiguous, and often obscure and contradictory. Nietzsche warns, "Imperturbable is my depth—it glitters with swimming riddles and laughter" (*Thus Spoke Zarathustra,* 139). Together, the challenging style and the unreliable early translations naturally make misreading likely (Kaufmann, *Portable Nietzsche,* 3). Although London's understanding of Nietzsche's ideas was not profound, it was enthusiastic, and the author's 1904 immersion in Nietzsche's work was the beginning of a lifelong attraction, mixed with an enduring political repulsion. "I . . . am in the opposite intellectual camp from that of Nietzsche. Yet no man in my own camp stirs me as does Nietzsche," London wrote on February 21, 1912 (*Letters*, 1072).

Another connection with the colorful German philosopher, perhaps psychologically closer to home, is London's 1905 sense of identification with Nietzsche's "long sickness" (*Letters*, 500). Apparently afflicted during this critical time in his life by a deep depression rather like that of his autobiographical alter ego, Martin Eden, Jack felt a strong sympathy with the brilliant and misunderstood German philosopher. Even though by 1909 he announced his recovery, saying, "I am no longer sick" (*Letters*, 847), London's sympathy for the philosopher's own emotional decline could not overcome his aversion to what he understood to be Nietzsche's main point. London, along with many of his contemporaries, thought that Nietzsche advocated the ruthless manipulation of those who were less than superior: "I like Nietzsche tremendously," he wrote, "but I cannot go all the way with him" (*Letters*, 584).

London added in 1915 to another correspondent, "I have been more stimulated by Nietzsche than by any other writer in the world. . . . Both *Martin Eden* and *The Sea-Wolf* were indictments by me of the Nietzschean philosophy of the super-man" (*Letters*, 1485). In fact, *The Sea-Wolf* is, says Charles N. Watson Jr., "the book that contains the first full elaboration of the Superman philosophy" ("Nietzsche," 34), and Patrick Bridgwater claims, "The Nietzschean Superman was introduced into American literature in the novels of Jack London" (163). In *The Sea-Wolf*, years before the appearance of the noble David Grief, London expressed his interest in the idea of an ultimate individualist who would rise in scorn above the efforts of the indifferent and less talented masses. It is fair to add that London's grasp of Nietzsche was superficial and based on popular misconceptions of what the philosopher meant. A result is that Wolf Larsen's superiority over the crew members is stressed throughout the novel, perhaps most clearly in the scene in chapter 14. It seems impossible not to see both Darwin and Nietzsche symbolically represented in that dramatic fight in the forecastle of the *Ghost*, in which the superhuman yet brutish Wolf Larsen manages to shake the mutinous crew from his legs as he pulls himself rung by rung up to the deck. This scene is a microcosmic representation of the range of ideas embraced in London's creative imagination—a habit of thought his critics have frequently characterized as contradictory.

Nietzsche's attitude toward socialism was antagonistic, and Jack London felt the tension between the muscular assertion of individual will that he drew from Nietzsche and the selfless devotion to the rights of man that he found in American socialist thought. When he thought of himself as a "Nietzsche-man" it troubled him, yet the idea of the superman irresistibly attracted him as well. On the one hand, Jack London seems nowhere to have ignored or denied with false modesty the fact of his own gifts, his own personal superiority. On the other hand, his life had often cast him into friendships with people of all classes, and his political beliefs made repugnant to him the idea of shaking himself away from the masses to which he felt he belonged. Therefore, in the creation of Wolf Larsen, the superman is shown at its most amoral, selfish, and brutal realization; yet the power of the idea of the transcendent man—combined with the excellence of London's urgent and evocative style—caused this tormented, romantic monster to be interpreted by many readers as an endorsement of Nietzsche's ideas.

Michael Qualtiere notes the dark ubiquity of dangerous waters running through Nietzsche's work, indicating "psychological turmoil" and the sense of the self resembling "a small ship far removed from the security of land, tossed about on stormy and uncharted seas" ("Nietzschean Psychology," 263). This is definitely the psychological pattern for Wolf Larsen, but there is another voice—lyrical, rhapsodic, and even optimistic—in Nietzsche, and it seems that by 1911 London did take note of the exotic values to be found in Zarathustra's thoughts and images, perhaps suggesting ways in which his new hero could be sketched.

James Baird, in his 1956 study, *Ishmael*, was apparently the first to suggest (37n) that it was the author's interest in Nietzsche that led him to create this "strong hero," Captain David Grief, the embodi-

ment of the notion of the adventurer as entrepreneur and the truest
of all London's Nietzschean characters. For his title and main theme,
London's imagination may well have been caught by the prophet's
identification of himself with a "sun," by references to "the Blissful
Islands where my friends are waiting," by the exciting suggestions
that "there are a thousand paths that have never been trodden, a
thousand forms of health and hidden islands of life," and by the
reminder that "it is fine to gaze out upon distant seas from the midst
of superfluity" (Nietzsche, *Thus Spoke Zarathustra,* 130, 108, 109,
103, 109). Adventure might be profitably coupled with entrepre-
neurship, as Zarathustra urges his new view of morality: "Truly, I
did this and that for the afflicted; but it always seemed to me I did
better things when I learned to enjoy myself better" (112), words
that are paraphrased by Captain Grief in the title story.

However problematic the relationship between London and Nietzsche might be, it is impossible for a reader of *A Son of the Sun* not to
notice the relevance of the following passage from Nietzsche's *The
Gay Science*:

> We now need many preparatory valorous . . . men who are bent
> on seeking for that aspect in all things which must be overcome;
> men characterized by cheerfulness, patience, unpretentiousness,
> and contempt for all great vanities, as well as by magnanimity in
> victory and forbearance regarding . . . the vanquished; men pos-
> sessed of keen and free judgment concerning all victors and the
> share of chance in every victory and every fame; men . . . who are
> accustomed to command with assurance and are no less ready to
> obey when necessary, in both cases equally proud and serving
> their own cause; men who are in greater danger, more fruitful,
> and happier! For, believe me, the secret of the greatest fruitful-
> ness and the greatest enjoyment of existence is: to live danger-
> ously! Build your cities under Vesuvius! Send your ships into un-
> charted seas! (Kaufmann, *Portable Nietzsche,* 97)

Thus, Captain David Grief becomes another of London's carica-
tures of a Nietzschean hero who might be used to reexamine the
negative impression presented by Wolf Larsen. Wolf Larsen's despair
over the struggles of life would be replaced by David Grief's existential joy in adventure. Larsen's selfish power to dominate others

would be replaced by Grief's cheerful and overarching power to help others at the same time that he sets all to rights and promotes his own financial expansion. Where Wolf Larsen and Martin Eden were unable to shed the terrifying responsibilities of superiority, David Grief would perfectly represent the easygoing ideals of the "preparatory men" of Nietzsche's vision. London was aware of the irony that, though he meant his depiction of Larsen to be an "indictment," the sheer power of the presentation had resulted in one of the most ambivalently attractive characters in American literature. David Grief would be all that Wolf Larsen might have been, had he been strong enough—big enough—to be what London understood to be a true superman. Grief would reflect the adventurous capitalist but with a responsible and loving soul. And Grief's seemingly altruistic acts would reflect Nietzsche's moral position of egoism in its most positive light.

Such a character would have had a natural appeal to London for yet another reason—one strong enough for London to allow his emotional attraction to overcome his philosophical hesitancy about Nietzsche. London, the two-fisted businessman, determined to make a lasting place in the world, was increasingly occupying the fantasies of his own self-image. In Jack's case, there was no significant gap in the author's mind between art and commerce—any more than there could be in his creative imagination a gap between adventure and art. During his life of adventure, London picked up ideas for his stories, which in turn he sold to magazines to pay for equipment and livestock for his Beauty Ranch. For example, before the *Snark* was even completed, London formalized a relationship with *Woman's Home Companion*, promising to use his adventurous voyage as material for a series of articles (London, "Preliminary Letter," 19).

Though some critics have condemned his later stories as hack work because of this commercialism, for London, a three-point practical life made perfect sense: life, literature, and business. As London explained in September 1911 to the editor of *Sunset*: "A writer may also be a businessman. . . . This writer is a businessman" (*Letters,* 1027). An examination of his other letters in the autumn of 1911 reveals London caught up in a flurry of business interests and film-producing deals. Nevertheless, James Williams has argued persuasively that Grief was "a project London was engaged in for both money and pleasure" ("Composition," 71). Furthermore, lest his contradictory attraction to both Marx and Nietzsche seem insurmountably paradoxical, it should be remembered that London's socialism was of a peculiar sort. As he worked faithfully for the party one morning on an essay advocating political revolution, a week later he would experience no qualms as he wrote a David Grief story for the ultra-bourgeois *Saturday Evening Post* that would net him $750. Meanwhile, he instructed his sister Eliza Shepard, who managed the ranch, to buy ten acres from the California Wine Association for $1,500, which would add to his ranch several buildings as well as land, all paid for by his earnings as a writer (Kingman, *Chronology*, 126–36).

In many of London's tales, the hero is a kind of fantasy extension of one or more aspects of the author's view of his own persona: Ernest Everhard of *The Iron Heel*, Elam Harnish of *Burning Daylight*, Martin Eden, Dick Forrest of *Little Lady of the Big House*, the narrator of *John Barleycorn*, and perhaps even Joan Lackland of *Adventure* are examples of characters based to some extent on Jack himself, filled with his own vitality and drive, muscle and brawn, ambition and anxieties, successes and failures, erotic magnetism and intellectual confidence. The flaws of London's characters—attraction to alcohol, liability to clinical depression—tend to be the author's flaws, exaggerated in some cases (though, unlike Jack himself, none of them have bad teeth). It is therefore something of a departure, but perhaps no surprise that the virtues of Captain David Grief combine the larger-than-life virtues London possessed and others he could only wish he possessed. Grief radiates a great joy in life, is fair-minded, honest, and magnanimous. He is physically perfect, highly intelligent, and famous throughout the Pacific for various exploits; every business venture he undertakes is fabulously successful. Though unflawed animal characters and admirable human heroines appear in London's other fiction, David Grief is Jack London's only unflawed hero, one of the few main characters who never develops or degenerates—because he is already what he needs to be. If Jack's expressed wish was that *The Sea-Wolf* ought to be read as an attack on Nietzsche's philosophy, *A Son of the Sun* is both a rethinking of that attack and a celebration of a hero who reflects the zeal and the joy and the power London found in his reading of *Thus Spake Zarathustra*.

III

Though by 1911, beneath his well-muscled body, London himself was riddled with exotic ailments garnered in part from his extraordinary travel adventures, David Grief is a picture of both strength and health. At the height of the popular physical culture movement, and in the year before the first appearance of Edgar Rice Burroughs' *Tarzan of the Apes*, London describes Grief in 1911's "A Son of the Sun":

> As he swung over the rail and stepped on deck a hint of catlike litheness showed in the apparently heavy body. . . . The cheap undershirt and white loin-cloth did not serve to hide the well put up body. Heavy muscled he was, but he was not lumped and hummocked by muscles. They were softly rounded, and, when they did move, slid softly and silkily under the smooth, tanned skin. Ardent suns had likewise tanned his face till it was swarthy as a Spaniard's. . . .
>
> Unlike other white men in the tropics, he was there because he liked it. He had been born to the sun. One he was in ten thousand in the matter of sun-resistance. The invisible and high-velocity light waves failed to bore into him. Other white men were pervious. The sun drove through their skins, ripping and smashing tissues and nerves, till they became sick in mind and body, tossed most of the Decalogue overboard, descended to beastliness, drank themselves into quick graves, or survived so savagely that war vessels were sometimes sent to curb their license.

In this story, as elsewhere in his work, London takes a grim look at the terrors of alcohol, showing its role in the degeneration of mental and physical health. It is not widely enough appreciated that London, though a drinking man himself, was actively involved in support of the turn-of-the-century prohibition movement (Kingman, *Pictorial Life*, 242). Grief's strong character is here stressed by showing his control over excessive drink, as well as showing him to be physically and morally superior to other white traders. In "The Proud Goat of

Aloysius Pankburn" the alcoholic title character has started drinking again. Pankburn asks Grief for help. David Grief's cure for alcoholism is a far cry from today's twelve-step AA program. He simply
beats the desire for alcohol out of Pankburn:

> Grief struck him, with bare knuckles, punched him and punished
> him—gave him the worst thrashing he had ever received. "For
> the good of your soul, Pankburn," was the way he emphasized
> his blows. "For the good of your mother. For the progeny that
> will come after. For the good of the world, and the universe, and
> the whole race of man yet to be. And now to hammer the lesson
> home, we'll do it all over again."

Grief's physical prowess is evident in many places and takes many
forms. In "A Son of the Sun," Grief must overpower the villain Griffiths after Griffiths has threatened him with a gun. Instead of shooting Griffiths, he bodily carries him up on deck and, "with two jumps,
still holding the helpless Griffiths, Grief leaped to the rail and overboard."

After diving overboard with the hapless Griffiths, Grief must avoid
pistol shots from Griffiths's mate, Jacobsen, by diving beneath the
surface and swimming underwater to a waiting canoe. London's love
of physical culture and swimming is well known, so it comes as no
surprise to find Grief an excellent swimmer. But in "The Devils of
Fuatino" Grief joins the archetypal ranks of Beowulf as he and a
comrade must swim away from the shots of vicious pirates for over
an hour to reach the relative safety of Big Rock; they then must dive
for fresh water fifty feet down in the lagoon while sharks loom above
them. Also in this story, Grief displays a remarkable rock-climbing
ability.

IV

But more significant than his physical strengths and talents, David
Grief's mental gifts allow him not only to defeat his opponents clev-
erly but also to enjoy himself mightily in the process. His acuity is
demonstrated first through his business expertise. A keen entrepreneur, Grief has amassed a fortune in the South Seas and in the effort
has learned many details about the environment and the people of

the area. Although many London heroes experience a tension between financial success and personal happiness, David Grief is an
enthusiastic capitalist with interests in every imaginable natural re-
source in the South Seas. Copra, tortoiseshell, pearls, and coconuts
are gathered or harvested and the profits invested in the purchase of
yet another promising little island Grief deems worthy of clearing
and planting for long-range plans. The environment is not to be pre-
served in its natural form if its cultivation can be turned to cash
someday; in the minds of turn-of-the-century Americans, this attitude—of turning what was "wasted" in nature's profligacy into something profitable—was entirely laudable.

In fact, Grief's practices mirror London's own activity of buying
California land to add to his ranch as it became available and turning wasted or worn-out acreage into profitable property (*Letters,*
1377–78). Grief's capitalistic sense of enterprise and his long-range
economic vision are celebrated throughout the tales as evidence of
his personal superiority over others, and that excitement about the
achievement of business success grows naturally into a romantic sense
of the adventure and the charm of the South Seas:

> As the golden tint burned into his face it poured molten out of
> the ends of his fingers. His was the golden touch, but he played
> the game, not for the gold, but for the game's sake. It was a man's
> game, the rough contacts and fierce give and take of the adven-
> turers of his own blood and of half the bloods of Europe and the
> rest of the world, and it was a good game; but over and beyond
> was his love of all the other things that go to make up a South
> Seas rover's life—the smell of the reef; the infinite exquisiteness
> of the shoals of living coral in the mirror-surfaced lagoons; the
> crashing sunrises of raw colors spread with lawless cunning; the
> palm-tufted islets set in turquoise deeps; the tonic wine of the
> trade-winds; the heave and send of the orderly, crested seas; the
> moving deck beneath his feet, the straining canvas overhead; the
> flower-garlanded, golden-glowing men and maids of Polynesia,
> half-children and half-gods; and even the howling savages of
> Melanesia, head-hunters and man-eaters, half-devil and all beast.
> ("A Sun of the Sun")

Grief's mental alertness becomes at once a survival necessity, a
commercial strength, and a romantic magnet: Grief's "quick eye for

the promise of adventure [is] prepared always for the unexpected to leap out at him from behind the nearest coconut tree." In "A Sun of the Sun" he explains to someone who asks why he does it that his motivation for his capitalist drive as well as his love of adventure is frankly existential: "I just want to, I suppose," says Grief. "And can you give any better reason for anything you do?"

David Grief's physical, moral, and economic mastery over others is legendary. When he turns up, it is always a surprise to those who fear him. Sometimes crooked entrepreneurs try to keep track of his whereabouts before carrying out their schemes, but Grief's economic power allows him to be almost preternaturally ubiquitous. "He's loaded with money, he's stuffed with money, he's busting with money," says one awe-stricken villain about to have an encounter with our hero in the title story, knowing that a crisis is about to occur that can ruin him but that would be—in financial terms—meaningless to Grief. But exact accounts, for Grief in these tales, are not meaningless at all; they are part and parcel of his principles of strict accountability, and by the story's end David Grief has employed his quick wit and superior knowledge of the islands to defeat the miscreant and force him to pay off his debt. Grief demands nothing more.

Similarly, in "The Proud Goat of Aloysius Pankburn" Grief uses his mental powers to find a viable cure for the alcoholic Pankburn, an insightful way to interpret data in order to find a hidden treasure, and an effective scheme to trick the native headhunters into turning the treasure over to him in exchange for tobacco. "The Devils of Fuatino" recounts Grief's conflict with a group of ruthless pirates. Such is Grief's formidable reputation that the natives of Fuatino have been praying for David Grief to come to deliver them, and the pirate captain himself, upon meeting Grief, expresses a wish that he wasn't up against him. In "The Jokers of New Gibbon" Grief's intelligence has allowed him to find a way to contain the violence of the headhunters of Chief Koho—a "black Napoleon"—through the administration of an inflexible system of punishment. Grief's understanding of islander psychology allows him to keep a peace that lasts until thoughtless cross-cultural confusions result in a horrifying disaster—though, of course, it's none of Grief's doing.

V

Grief's greatest asset, however, is his high sense of morality, which will not allow him to treat anyone unfairly and immediately alerts him to moral turpitude in others. Grief will not tolerate unfairness in those he encounters; in fact, it seems to give him joy to teach an object lesson in forthrightness to others in need of such a lesson. With the alacrity of a man of action and the patience to undertake a long-term scheme, Grief has earned a fearsome reputation among those who would bend the law or exploit the islanders unfairly.

For example, in "A Little Account with Swithin Hall" Grief has an opportunity to set an injustice to rights through his knowledge of business methods and through his scrupulous sense of morality. As usual, Grief's adventure is connected with business concerns, this time because Grief is looking for Leu-Leu Atoll, one of his many holdings. Grief has a chance to right a wrong done to his ship's mate, Snow, by a mysterious character known as Swithin Hall. The story makes the point that Grief is eminently fair, even to villains, and exact to the dollar in his honesty in accounting for the money.

In "A Goboto Night" Grief takes another opportunity to teach an object lesson to the thoroughly dislikable Alfred Deacon, an agent for an Australian company who has stopped at Goboto on business. The main activities of the white adventurers on Goboto are card playing and drinking—in the nearby island of Guvutu they merely drink "between drinks," we are told, but in Goboto, "no such interval of time is known." As in several of the Grief stories, drunkenness is treated as a character fault and as a cause for lack of sound business sense. The inebriated Deacon bullies the other men and makes racist comments the others do their best to ignore. By the time Grief enters the story at about the midpoint, readers are ready for Deacon to be taught a lesson. Grief uses Deacon's insistence for a game of casino to take all of his money, including the amount promised in Deacon's letter of credit. But Grief is not interested in the money; instead he uses his victory to bring Deacon to his senses and make a better businessman and man of him. Godlike even in his forgiveness, Grief hires the now repentant Deacon at a handsome salary to man-

age his holdings on nearby Karo-Karo, where Deacon vows to repeat daily the macho creed that Grief supplies for his betterment:

> "I must always remember that one man is as good as another,
> save and except when he thinks he is better.
> "No matter how drunk I am I must not fail to be a gentleman.
> A gentleman is a man who is gentle. Note: It would be better not
> to get drunk.
> "When I play a man's game with men, I must play like a man.
> "A curse, rightly used and rarely, is an efficient thing. Too
> many curses spoil the cursing. Note: A curse cannot change a
> card sequence nor cause the wind to blow.
> "There is no license for a man to be less than a man. Ten
> thousand pounds cannot purchase such a license."

The reader who is familiar with the infallible David Grief knows
that these are rules that represent a standard to which he holds himself.

In sharp contrast to other London characters involved in the commercial exploitation of the people and resources of the South Seas,
David Grief's moral rectitude results in benefits for both traders and
islanders. In the riotously funny "The Feathers of the Sun," Grief's
understanding of banking dynamics allows him to defeat the schemes
of an Irish scalawag who attempts to corner an island's economy
through the introduction of worthless paper money. While saving
the islanders from exploitation, Grief's sense of justice causes him,
at story's end, to give the disgraced rascal a clean outfit, a free passage to the next port, and a drink of "smoky Irish," all in good-hu-
mored forgiveness.

The last of the Grief stories is the richest and most troubling. A
melodramatic, eerie tale of a reclusive, embittered superman whose
life has gone horribly off course, "The Pearls of Parlay" takes our
hero, along with several other merchant seafarers, to a lonely Pau-
moto atoll for the pearl auction of a lifetime. Racism sets the plot of
this story in motion, underscores the motivation of the characters,
seems mysteriously related to the violence of nature itself, and resists
any efforts to resolve it. Though the topic appears frequently in other
Pacific tales, this is the only Grief episode that confronts the injustice

of racial bigotry so directly. Parlay, aware of the racist "rules" that operate the white islanders' world, chooses to think himself above petty restrictions; but he finds out too late that he has made an ultimately fatal miscalculation in his estimate of his own ability to rise above the notions of social propriety that operate in this strange culture clash. "The Pearls of Parlay" is a gothic tale of lost love, madness, and revenge, with a hint of the supernatural. At the same time, it reminds those who follow the adventures of Captain David Grief that not everyone can be a superman.

VI

Though "The Pearls of Parlay" assaults bigotry, in other places London shows that he himself was not able to overcome his own inclinations toward that state of mind, and it is important to confront this issue straightforwardly. London's opinions about racial differences were drawn in part from his reading of selected contemporary scientists and anthropologists. At the end of the nineteenth century, anthropologists recorded the "primitive" cultural and religious practices of the people increasingly being discovered by the agents of the European colonialist imperative. In 1911 Jack London perhaps understandably had no qualms about describing some islanders as savages and experienced little concern about the moral ambivalence of his role as a writer in the South Pacific.

That being said, it is also true—but rarely discussed—that Jack struggled often in his fiction to fight the very racism of which he is now so commonly and casually accused. In many of his Pacific stories, London created or reported adventures that featured white villains and black heroes. Though composed at the height of London's popularity, several of these stories featuring islander heroes took nearly two years to find willing magazine publishers, almost certainly in part because he refused to support the prevailing racial bias of the white, middle-class magazine-reading public. During the voyage of the *Snark*, he appears not only to have interviewed black islanders to get their stories but also to have established some degree of sympathetic fellowship with them.

Despite his unusually open-minded attitude to the islanders, it is impossible in today's culture to ignore the author's use of racist language. Throughout the David Grief stories, the word "nigger" appears not only in the dialogue of the characters but also in the authorial voice. Briefly, but importantly, London's language needs to be set into a historical context.

Perhaps surprisingly, for most white writers at the turn of the century the word itself carried little of the volatility that it carries today. Because of this insensitivity—or perhaps because of the perceived unimportance of being sensitive to the issue—racist terms and illustrations abounded in popular fiction and journalism written in English during the period between 1880 and 1920, and few magazine readers seem even to have blinked over their inclusion. For example, Mark Twain's *Huckleberry Finn* (1884) had already been accepted as an American classic when London was writing, though its casual use of racist language offends many readers today. Though the American publisher of Joseph Conrad's 1897 novel *The Nigger of the "Narcissus"* chose to change the title to *Children of the Sea*, the rest of the English-speaking world was less scandalized and retained the original title. In 1911 David Belasco, Broadway's biggest producer, mounted a hit show in which the young Henry Hull got his first big acting break in the dual role of an escaped slave and the white lawman who hunts him. Its title blazed in lights on the theater marquee: *The Nigger*. Protests against the depiction of American blacks in D. W. Griffith's 1915 epic *The Birth of a Nation* seem to have surprised President Wilson. In fact, the study of London contemporary Thomas W. Dixon, whose work inspired the Griffith film, is a useful exercise; in Dixon may be seen unashamed racism in full bloom, and the huge popularity of his novels must be seen not only as a tribute to his unquestionable gifts as a storyteller but also as evidence that he was speaking to a wide and sympathetic audience of American readers. Jack London's South Seas stories often seem in contrast to suggest a racial openness unusual in his time.

London's attitudes toward race currently constitute a topic of lively academic discussion. Some of today's literary scholars judge him heavily for his flaws, while others seem to be in denial about some of the evidence; in explaining the author's attitudes, they often seem to attempt to explain them away. The root causes, peculiarities, and contradictions of his ideas may be discussed and analyzed, for they certainly present many complexities, but nothing can make his use of racial slang palatable to modern readers. A possible solution the editors considered but rejected was to change the language of the text. We thought it best to leave the stories as London wrote them, facing the certainty that readers will wince and the possibility that teachers might find the book unusable on political grounds. Our choice to leave the text unexpurgated was finally based on the conviction that the complexities of colonialism and the unsettling power of language ought to be examined and discussed in the classroom. In an era that finds *Huckleberry Finn* censored from some schools, the editors hope that this text might bring up issues that will open, rather than close, the analysis of racism in American literature.

VII

The stories collected in *A Son of the Sun* not only praised responsible capitalism and allowed Jack London to examine in a new and positive light some ideas he took from Nietzsche, but they also helped to provide him with some of the money to build his magnificent mansion, Wolf House, and to plant thousands of eucalyptus trees on his vast estate. If the eucalyptus in the long run turned out to be both a failed investment and a long-term fire hazard in the Sonoma Valley, and if the great dream of Wolf House would end in ruins, still, these were truly expansive business ventures, larger-than-life gestures that David Grief surely would have appreciated.

A socialist intellectually, a Nietzschean emotionally, and an entrepreneur practically, London presents in David Grief a character who sheds light on the complexities of the writer's own personality. As a world-traveled adventurer, as a self-made man who rose by his own gifts to become one of the best-selling of all American writers, and— most fundamentally important to him in 1911 and 1912—as a daring and imaginative rancher-entrepreneur, the author seems to have created David Grief as a dream self-extension that celebrates business savvy, freedom, superiority, and strength.

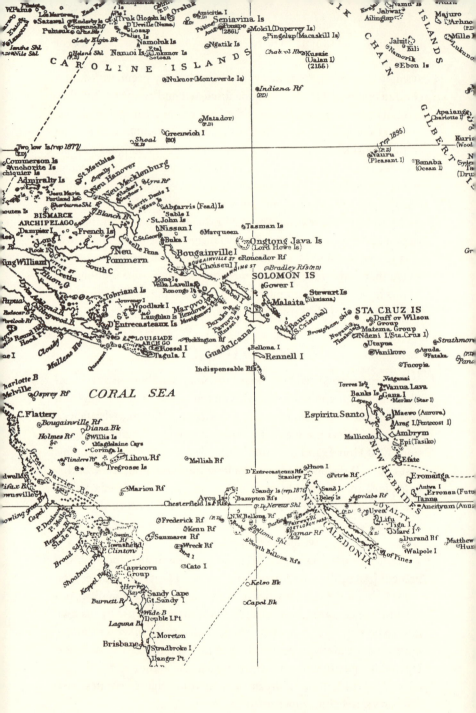

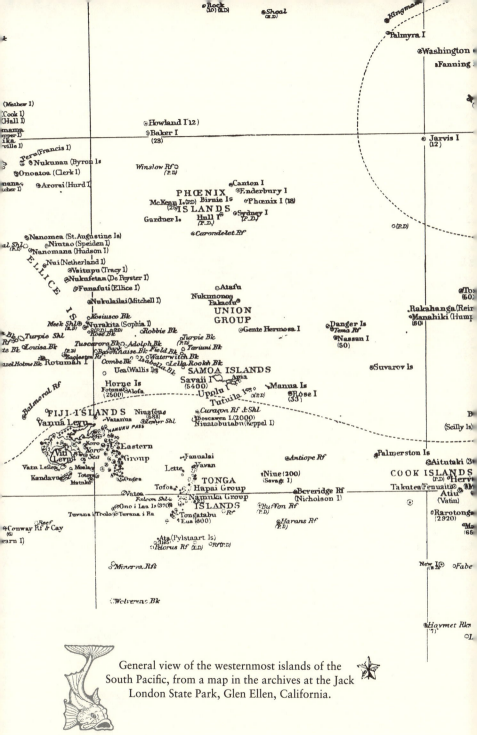

General view of the westernmost islands of the South Pacific, from a map in the archives at the Jack London State Park, Glen Ellen, California.

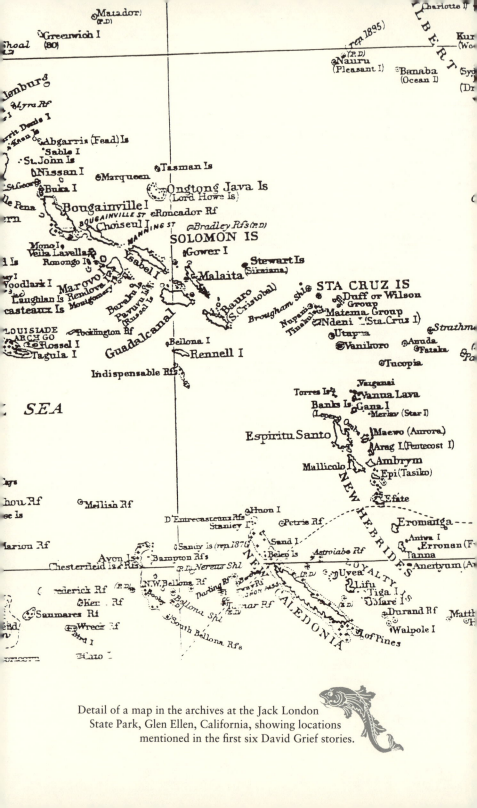

Detail of a map in the archives at the Jack London
State Park, Glen Ellen, California, showing locations
mentioned in the first six David Grief stories.

A SON OF THE SUN
THE ADVENTURES OF CAPTAIN DAVID GRIEF

A SON OF THE SUN

Captain David Grief's strengths—of body, mind, and principle—
are clearly evidenced in this opening story. Armed with an admiralty warrant, he's in hot pursuit of two scalawags named Griffiths
and Jacobsen, who have been trying to escape his cheerfully inflexible sense of justice. Handsome, blond, lithe, and well-muscled,
Grief appears in a cheap undershirt and loincloth, with a gun belt
strapped to his waist. This was the typical uniform of white sailors
in the sultry Solomon Islands, as Jack London personally observed
during his 1908 voyage on the Snark.

As in many of his stories, London drew some of these characters from life. The drunkard Jacobsen, for instance, was probably
based on a first mate hired to serve on the Snark. Jack had to fire
him soon afterward, when it became clear that the first mate felt
that occasional sobriety was an unreasonable expectation; Jack
exacted a second revenge by using him as a villain in the story.
Captain Jensen, who figures offstage as a good man and a trust-
worthy person who provides Grief with reliable information, is
based on a wild adventurer named Captain Jansen. Jansen was
skipper of the Minota, and Jack knew him well. (See the introduction to "A Goboto Night." Jansen also inspired the character of
Captain Woodward in the non-Grief Pacific tale "The Inevitable
White Man.") For the degenerate intellectual Griffiths, a whimsi-
cal Jack perhaps borrowed the name from a social contact in Suva:
A man named Griffiths and his wife were connected with the Fiji
Times and had taken Jack and Charmian on a pigeon-hunting ex-
pedition in June 1908. Finally, it is probable that Grief himself is

based at least in part on the extraordinary Harold Markham, the intrepid white trader of Ontong Java Atoll, whom the Londons got to know well. In 1917 Martin Johnson's teenage bride, Osa, met Markham; here is how Osa pictured him in A Bride in the Solomons, her 1944 reminiscence of what is without doubt one of the Western world's most bizarre honeymoon trips:

> "One of my best friends, Harold Markham," [the Governor at Tulagi] said, "is due here any time now. He has just the ship you need and knows more about the islands than any of us. And he has more personality than any man I know. We all love him and so will you." [Later, the Governor continued:] "Even if you had the finest ship made, you couldn't prowl around these islands alone. . . . The rocks and coral reefs stick up everywhere and in a heavy sea or a storm, you would be cracked to bits. But with Markham, I will know you are all right—he knows every nook in the islands, almost every rock in the sea, and all the treacherous channels. . . . The natives love him. . . . Along with being the best navigator in the Solomons, he has enormous luck and rides through adversities that would kill any other human being. We are just sure that he has been lost, when there he is, sailing into the harbor, as calmly as you please, ready for the next calamity" [Another person told her:] "I have seen him in Sydney spend a year's income in a week. . . . He took me to dinner at the Australia Hotel and ordered food and wines like a Parisian connoisseur. He drank bottles of champagne and was still as sober as an owl. He was the most perfect and natural host I've ever seen. . . . He must have had money in his youth, for he can spend it like a veteran." (116–119)

As the title suggests, David Grief is born to resist the many negative effects of being a white man in the Pacific. He thrives while lesser men stumble and fall. The villain Griffiths, who represents perhaps the all-too-common flaws of many of these opportunistic adventurers, provides himself with a naturalistic excuse—certainly a defensive rationalization as well—for his intransigent wickedness: loneliness, alienation, malaria, drink, and (always) the relentless sun: "'Oh, I don't mind being caught in a dirty trick,' Griffiths was saying defiantly. 'I've been in the tropics too long. I'm a sick man, a damn sick man. And the whiskey, and the sun, and the fever have made me sick in morals, too. Nothing's too mean and low for me now, and I can understand why the niggers eat each other, and take heads, and such things. I could do it myself.'"

The abuse of alcohol, represented here in Jacobsen and Griffiths, was a very real concern in this wild and greedy exploitation undertaken by the self-exiled eccentrics often drawn to the enterprise of colonialism. No fewer than five of the eight David Grief stories revolve around alcohol, whose depredations fascinated London throughout his life. His personal fondness for drink did not alter his support for national prohibition, and there can be no doubt that Jack's voyages in the South Seas deepened his awareness of this systemic evil.

"A Son of the Sun" provides readers with their first glimpse of the heroic David Grief, and it's a hell-for-leather sea-going Western, complete with a quick-draw pistol showdown and a break-neck battle between right and wrong. Here we first get the thrill of the romance and adventure that David Grief seeks out and of the challenges he overcomes in the act of defining himself.

The *Willi-Waw* lay in the passage between the shore-reef and the outer-reef. From the latter came the low murmur of a lazy surf, but the sheltered stretch of water, not more than a hundred yards across to the white beach of pounded coral sand, was of glass-like smoothness. Narrow as was the passage, and anchored as she was in the shoalest place that gave room to swing, the *Willi-Waw's* chain rode up-and-down a clean hundred feet. Its course could be traced over the bottom of living coral. Like some monstrous snake, the rusty chain's slack wandered over the ocean floor, crossing and recrossing itself several times and fetching up finally at the idle anchor. Big rock-cod, dun and mottled, played warily in and out of the coral. Other fish, grotesque of form and colour, were brazenly indifferent, even when a big fish-shark drifted sluggishly along and sent the rock-cod scuttling for their favourite crevices.

On deck, for'ard, a dozen blacks pottered clumsily at scraping the teak rail. They were as inexpert at their work as so many monkeys. In fact they looked very much like monkeys of some enlarged and prehistoric type.[1] Their eyes had in them the querulous plaintiveness of the monkey, their faces were even less symmetrical than the monkey's, and, hairless of body, they were far more ungarmented than any monkey, for clothes they had none. Decorated they were as no monkey ever was. In holes in their ears they carried short clay pipes, rings of turtle shell, huge plugs of wood, rusty wire nails, and empty rifle cartridges. The calibre of a Winchester rifle was the smallest hole an ear bore; some of the largest holes were inches in diameter, and any single ear averaged from three to half a dozen holes. Spikes and bodkins of polished bone or petrified shell were thrust through their noses. On the chest of one hung a white door-knob, on the chest of another the handle of a china cup, on the chest of a third the brass cog-wheel of an alarm clock. They chattered in queer, falsetto voices, and, combined, did no more work than a single white sailor.

Aft, under an awning, were two white men. Each was clad in a sixpenny undershirt and wrapped about the loins with a strip of cloth.[2] Belted about the middle of each was a revolver and tobacco pouch. The sweat stood out on their skin in myriads of globules. Here and there the globules coalesced in tiny streams that dripped to the heated deck and almost immediately evaporated. The lean, dark-eyed man wiped his fingers wet with a stinging stream from his forehead and flung it from him with a weary curse. Wearily, and without hope, he gazed seaward across the outer-reef, and at the tops of the palms along the beach.

"Eight o'clock, an' hell don't get hot till noon," he complained. "Wisht to God for a breeze. Ain't we never goin' to get away?"

The other man, a slender German of five and twenty, with the massive forehead of a scholar and the tumble-home chin of a degenerate, did not trouble to reply. He was busy emptying powdered quinine into a cigarette paper. Rolling what was approximately fifty grains of the drug into a tight wad, he tossed it into his mouth and gulped it down without the aid of water.

"Wisht I had some whiskey," the first man panted, after a fifteen-minute interval of silence.

Another equal period elapsed ere the German enounced, relevant of nothing:

"I'm rotten with fever. I'm going to quit you, Griffiths, when we get to Sydney. No more tropics for me. I ought to known better when I signed on with you."

"You ain't been much of a mate," Griffiths replied, too hot himself to speak heatedly. "When the beach at Guvutu heard I'd shipped you, they all laughed. 'What? Jacobsen?' they said. 'You can't hide a square face of trade gin or sulphuric acid that he won't smell out!' You've certainly lived up to your reputation. I ain't had a drink for a fortnight, what of your snoopin' my supply."

"If the fever was as rotten in you as me, you'd understand," the mate whimpered.

"I ain't kickin'," Griffiths answered. "I only wisht God'd send me a drink, or a breeze of wind, or something. I'm ripe for my next chill to-morrow."

The mate proffered him the quinine. Rolling a fifty-grain dose, he popped the wad into his mouth and swallowed it dry.

"God! God!" he moaned. "I dream of a land somewheres where they ain't no quinine. Damned stuff of hell! I've scoffed tons of it in my time."

Again he quested seaward for signs of wind. The usual trade-wind clouds were absent, and the sun, still low in its climb to meridian, turned all the sky to heated brass. One seemed to see as well as feel this heat, and Griffiths sought vain relief by gazing shoreward. The white beach was a searing ache to his eyeballs. The palm trees, absolutely still, outlined flatly against the unrefreshing green of the packed jungle, seemed so much cardboard scenery. The little black boys, playing naked in the dazzle of sand and sun, were an affront and a hurt to the sun-sick man. He felt a sort of relief when one, running, tripped and fell on all-fours in the tepid sea-water.

An exclamation from the blacks for'ard sent both men glancing seaward. Around the near point of land, a quarter of a mile away and skirting the reef, a long black canoe paddled into sight.

"Gooma boys from the next bight," was the mate's verdict.

One of the blacks came aft, treading the hot deck with the unconcern of one whose bare feet felt no heat. This, too, was a hurt to Griffiths, and he closed his eyes. But the next moment they were open wide.

"White fella marster stop along Gooma boy," the black said.

Both men were on their feet and gazing at the canoe. Aft could be seen the unmistakable sombrero of a white man. Quick alarm showed itself on the face of the mate.

"It's Grief," he said.

Griffiths satisfied himself by a long look, then ripped out a wrathful oath.

"What's he doing up here?" he demanded . . . of the mate, of the aching sea and sky, of the merciless blaze of sun, and of the whole superheated and implacable universe with which his fate was entangled.

"White Marster stop along Gooma boy. . . ."
Drawing by H. G. Williamson.

The mate began to chuckle.

"I told you you couldn't get away with it," he said.

But Griffiths was not listening.

"With all his money, coming around like a rent collector," he chanted his outrage, almost in an ecstasy of anger. "He's loaded with money, he's stuffed with money, he's busting with money. I know for a fact he sold his Yringa plantations for three hundred thousand pounds. Bell told me so himself last time we were drunk at Guvu-tu. Worth millions and millions, and Shylocking me for what he wouldn't light his pipe with."[3] He whirled on the mate. "Of course you told me so. Go on and say it, and keep on saying it. Now just what was it you did tell me so?"

"I told you you didn't know him, if you thought you could clear the Solomons without paying him. That man Grief is a devil, but he's straight. I know. I told you he'd throw a thousand quid away for the fun of it, and for sixpence fight like a shark for a rusty tin. I tell you I know. Didn't he give his *Balakula* to the Queensland Mission when they lost their *Evening Star* on San Cristobal?—and the *Balakula* worth three thousand pounds if she was worth a penny? And didn't he beat up Strothers till he lay abed a fortnight, all because of a difference of two pound ten in the account, and because Strothers got fresh and tried to make the gouge go through?"

"God strike me blind!" Griffiths cried in impotency of rage.

The mate went on with his exposition.

"I tell you only a straight man can buck a straight man like him, and the man's never hit the Solomons that could do it. Men like you and me can't buck him. We're too rotten, too rotten all the way through. You've got plenty more than twelve hundred quid below. Pay him, and get it over with."

But Griffiths gritted his teeth and drew his thin lips tightly across them.

"I'll buck him," he muttered—more to himself and the brazen ball of sun than to the mate. He turned and half started to go below, then turned back again. "Look here, Jacobsen. He won't be here for quarter of an hour. Are you with me? Will you stand by me?"

"Of course I'll stand by you. I've drunk all your whiskey, haven't I? What are you going to do?"

"I'm not going to kill him if I can help it. But I'm not going to pay. Take that flat."

Jacobsen shrugged his shoulders in calm acquiescence to fate, and Griffiths stepped to the companionway and went below.

II

Jacobsen watched the canoe across the low reef as it came abreast and passed on to the entrance of the passage. Griffiths, with ink-marks on right thumb and forefinger, returned on deck. Fifteen minutes later the canoe came alongside. The man with the sombrero stood up.

"Hello, Griffiths!" he said. "Hello, Jacobsen!" With his hand on the rail he turned to his dusky crew. "You fella boy stop along canoe altogether."

As he swung over the rail and stepped on deck a hint of catlike litheness showed in the apparently heavy body. Like the other two, he was scantily clad. The cheap undershirt and white loin-cloth did not serve to hide the well put up body. Heavy muscled he was, but he was not lumped and hummocked by muscles. They were softly rounded, and, when they did move, slid softly and silkily under the smooth, tanned skin. Ardent suns had likewise tanned his face till it was swarthy as a Spaniard's. The yellow mustache appeared incongruous in the midst of such swarthiness, while the clear blue of the eyes produced a feeling of shock on the beholder. It was difficult to realize that the skin of this man had once been fair.

"Where did you blow in from?" Griffiths asked, as they shook hands. "I thought you were over in the Santa Cruz."

"I was," the newcomer answered. "But we made a quick passage. The *Wonder*'s just around in the bight at Gooma, waiting for wind.[4] Some of the bushmen reported a ketch here, and I just dropped around to see. Well, how goes it?"

"Nothing much. Copra sheds mostly empty, and not half a dozen tons of ivory nuts. The women all got rotten with fever and quit, and the men can't chase them back into the swamps. They're a sick crowd. I'd ask you to have a drink, but the mate finished off my last bottle. I wisht to God for a breeze of wind."

"As he swung over the rail, a hint of catlike litheness
showed in the apparently heavy body. . . . "
Drawing by H. G. Williamson.

Grief, glancing with keen carelessness from one to the other,
laughed.

"I'm glad the calm held," he said. "It enabled me to get around
to see you. My supercargo dug up that little note of yours, and I
brought it along."

The mate edged politely away, leaving his skipper to face his
trouble.

"I'm sorry, Grief, damned sorry," Griffiths said, "but I ain't got it.
You'll have to give me a little more time."

Grief leaned up against the companionway, surprise and pain depicted on his face.

"It does beat hell," he communed, "how men learn to lie in the
Solomons. The truth's not in them. Now take Captain Jensen. I'd
sworn by his truthfulness. Why, he told me only five days ago—do
you want to know what he told me?"

Griffiths licked his lips.

"Go on."

"Why, he told me that you'd sold out—sold out everything, cleaned
up, and was pulling out for the New Hebrides."[5]

"He's a damned liar!" Griffiths cried hotly.

Grief nodded.

"I should say so. He even had the nerve to tell me that he'd bought
two of your stations from you—Mauri and Kahula. Said he paid you
seventeen hundred gold sovereigns, lock, stock and barrel, good will,
trade-goods, credit, and copra."

Griffiths's eyes narrowed and glinted. The action was involuntary, and Grief noted it with a lazy sweep of his eyes.

"And Parsons, your trader at Hickimavi, told me that the Fulcrum Company had bought that station from you. Now what did he
want to lie for?"

Griffiths, overwrought by sun and sickness, exploded. All his bitterness of spirit rose up in his face and twisted his mouth into a snarl.

"Look here, Grief, what's the good of playing with me that way?
You know, and I know you know. Let it go at that. I have sold out,
and I am getting away. And what are you going to do about it?"

Grief shrugged his shoulders, and no hint of resolve shadowed itself in his own face. His expression was as of one in a quandary.

"There's no law here," Griffiths pressed home his advantage. "Tulagi is a hundred and fifty miles away.[6] I've got my clearance papers, and I'm on my own boat. There's nothing to stop me from sailing. You've got no right to stop me just because I owe you a little money. And by God! you can't stop me. Put that in your pipe."

The look of pained surprise on Grief's face deepened.

"You mean you're going to cheat me out of that twelve hundred, Griffiths?"

"That's just about the size of it, old man. And calling hard names won't help any. There's the wind coming. You'd better get overside before I pull out, or I'll tow your canoe under."

"Really, Griffiths, you sound almost right. I can't stop you." Grief fumbled in the pouch that hung on his revolver-belt and pulled out a crumpled official-looking paper. "But maybe this will stop you. And it's something for *your* pipe. Smoke up."

"What is it?"

"An admiralty warrant. Running to the New Hebrides won't save you. It can be served anywhere."

Griffiths hesitated and swallowed, when he had finished glancing at the document. With knit brows he pondered this new phase of the situation. Then, abruptly, as he looked up, his face relaxed into all frankness.

"You were cleverer than I thought, old man," he said. "You've got me hip and thigh. I ought to have known better than to try and beat you. Jacobsen told me I couldn't, and I wouldn't listen to him. But he was right, and so are you. I've got the money below. Come on down and we'll settle."

He started to go down, then stepped aside to let his visitor precede him, at the same time glancing seaward to where the dark flaw of wind was quickening the water.

"Heave short," he told the mate. "Get up sail and stand ready to break out."

As Grief sat down on the edge of the mate's bunk, close against and facing the tiny table, he noticed the butt of a revolver just projecting from under the pillow. On the table, which hung on hinges from the for'ard bulkhead, were pen and ink, also a battered log-book.

"Oh, I don't mind being caught in a dirty trick," Griffiths was saying defiantly. "I've been in the tropics too long. I'm a sick man, a damn sick man. And the whiskey, and the sun, and the fever have made me sick in morals, too. Nothing's too mean and low for me now, and I can understand why the niggers eat each other, and take heads, and such things. I could do it myself. So I call trying to do you out of that small account a pretty mild trick. Wisht I could offer you a drink."

Grief made no reply, and the other busied himself in attempting to unlock a large and much-dented cash-box. From on deck came falsetto cries and the creak and rattle of blocks as the black crew swung up mainsail and driver. Grief watched a large cockroach crawling over the greasy paintwork. Griffiths, with an oath of irritation, carried the cash-box to the companion-steps for better light. Here, on his feet, and bending over the box, his back to his visitor, his hands shot out to the rifle that stood beside the steps, and at the same moment he whirled about.

"Now don't you move a muscle," he commanded.

Grief smiled, elevated his eyebrows quizzically, and obeyed. His left hand rested on the bunk beside him; his right hand lay on the table. His revolver hung on his right hip in plain sight. But in his mind was recollection of the other revolver under the pillow.

"Huh!" Griffiths sneered. "You've got everybody in the Solomons hypnotized, but let me tell you you ain't got me. Now I'm going to throw you off my vessel, along with your admiralty warrant, but first you've got to do something. Lift up that log-book."

The other glanced curiously at the log-book, but did not move.

"I tell you I'm a sick man, Grief; and I'd as soon shoot you as smash a cockroach. Lift up that log-book, I say."

Sick he did look, his lean face working nervously with the rage that possessed him. Grief lifted the book and set it aside. Beneath lay a written sheet of tablet paper.

"Read it," Griffiths commanded. "Read it aloud."

"Now, don't you move a muscle. . . . "
Drawing by H. G. Williamson.

Grief obeyed; but while he read, the fingers of his left hand began an infinitely slow and patient crawl toward the butt of the weapon under the pillow.

"*On board the ketch Willi-Waw, Bombi Bight, Island of Anna,*

Solomon Islands," he read. *"Know all men by these presents that I do hereby sign off and release in full, for due value received, all debts whatsoever owing to me by Harrison J. Griffiths, who has this day paid to me twelve hundred pounds sterling."*

"With that receipt in my hands," Griffiths grinned, "your admiralty warrant's not worth the paper it's written on. Sign it."

"It won't do any good, Griffiths," Grief said. "A document signed under compulsion won't hold before the law."

"In that case, what objection have you to signing it then?"

"Oh, none at all, only that I might save you heaps of trouble by not signing it."

Grief's fingers had gained the revolver, and, while he talked, with his right hand he played with the pen and with his left began slowly and imperceptibly drawing the weapon to his side. As his hand finally closed upon it, second finger on trigger and forefinger laid past the cylinder and along the barrel, he wondered what luck he would have at left-handed snap-shooting.

"Don't consider me," Griffiths gibed. "And just remember Jacobsen will testify that he saw me pay the money over. Now sign, sign in full, at the bottom, David Grief, and date it."

From on deck came the jar of sheet-blocks and the rat-tat-tat of the reef-points against the canvas. In the cabin they could feel the *Willi-Waw* heel, swing into the wind, and right. David Grief still hesitated. From for'ard came the jerking rattle of headsail halyards through the sheaves. The little vessel heeled, and through the cabin walls came the gurgle and wash of water.

"Get a move on!" Griffiths cried. "The anchor's out."

The muzzle of the rifle, four feet away, was bearing directly on him, when Grief resolved to act. The rifle wavered as Griffiths kept his balance in the uncertain puffs of the first of the wind. Grief took advantage of the wavering, made as if to sign the paper, and at the same instant, like a cat, exploded into swift and intricate action. As he ducked low and leaped forward with his body, his left hand flashed from under the screen of the table, and so accurately timed was the single stiff pull on the self-cocking trigger that the cartridge discharged as the muzzle came forward. Not a whit behind was Griffiths. The muzzle of his weapon dropped to meet the ducking body, and, shot at snap direction, rifle and revolver went off simultaneously.

Grief felt the sting and sear of a bullet across the skin of his shoulder, and knew that his own shot had missed. His forward rush carried him to Griffiths before another shot could be fired, both of whose arms, still holding the rifle, he locked with a low tackle about the body. He shoved the revolver muzzle, still in his left hand, deep into the other's abdomen. Under the press of his anger and the sting of his abraded skin, Grief's finger was lifting the hammer, when the wave of anger passed and he recollected himself. Down the companionway came indignant cries from the Gooma boys in his canoe.

Everything was happening in seconds. There was apparently no pause in his actions as he gathered Griffiths in his arms and carried him up the steep steps in a sweeping rush. Out into the blinding glare of sunshine he came. A black stood grinning at the wheel, and the *Willi-Waw,* heeled over from the wind, was foaming along. Rapidly dropping astern was his Gooma canoe. Grief turned his head. From amidships, revolver in hand, the mate was springing toward him. With two jumps, still holding the helpless Griffiths, Grief leaped to the rail and overboard.

Both men were grappled together as they went down; but Grief, with a quick updraw of his knees to the other's chest, broke the grip and forced him down. With both feet on Griffith's shoulder, he forced him still deeper, at the same time driving himself to the surface. Scarcely had his head broken into the sunshine when two splashes of water, in quick succession and within a foot of his face, advertised that Jacobsen knew how to handle a revolver. There was a chance for no third shot, for Grief, filling his lungs with air, sank down. Under water he struck out, nor did he come up till he saw the canoe and the bubbling paddles overhead. As he climbed aboard, the *Willi-Waw* went into the wind to come about.

"Washee-washee!" Grief cried to his boys. "You fella make-um beach quick fella time!"

In all shamelessness, he turned his back on the battle and ran for cover. The *Willi-Waw,* compelled to deaden way in order to pick up its captain, gave Grief his chance for a lead. The canoe struck the beach full-tilt, with every paddle driving, and they leaped out and ran across the sand for the trees. But before they gained the shelter, three times the sand kicked into puffs ahead of them. Then they dove into the green safety of the jungle.

Grief watched the *Willi-Waw* haul up close, go out the passage, then slack its sheets as it headed south with the wind abeam. As it went out of sight past the point he could see the topsail being broken out. One of the Gooma boys, a black, nearly fifty years of age, hideously marred and scarred by skin diseases and old wounds, looked up into his face and grinned.

"My word," the boy commented, "that fella skipper too much cross along you."

Grief laughed, and led the way back across the sand to the canoe.

III

How many millions David Grief was worth no man in the Solomons knew, for his holdings and ventures were everywhere in the great South Pacific. From Samoa to New Guinea and even to the north of the Line his plantations were scattered. He possessed pearling concessions in the Paumotus. Though his name did not appear, he was in truth the German company that traded in the French Marquesas. His trading stations were in strings in all the groups, and his vessels that operated them were many. He owned atolls so remote and tiny that his smallest schooners and ketches visited the solitary agents but once a year.

In Sydney, on Castlereagh Street, his offices occupied three floors. But he was rarely in those offices. He preferred always to be on the go amongst the islands, nosing out new investments, inspecting and shaking up old ones, and rubbing shoulders with fun and adventure in a thousand strange guises. He bought the wreck of the great steamship *Gavonne* for a song, and in salving it achieved the impossible and cleaned up a quarter of a million. In the Louisiades he planted the first commercial rubber, and in Bora-Bora he ripped out the South Sea cotton and put the jolly islanders at the work of planting cacao. it was he who took the deserted island of Lallu-Ka, colonized it with

Polynesians from the Ontong-Java Atoll,[7] and planted four thousand acres to cocoanuts. And it was he who reconciled the warring chief-stocks of Tahiti and swung the great deal of the phosphate island of Hikihu.[8]

His own vessels recruited his contract labour. They brought Santa Cruz boys to the New Hebrides, New Hebrides boys to the Banks, and the head-hunting cannibals of Malaita to the plantations of New Georgia. From Tonga to the Gilberts and on to the far Louisiades his recruiters combed the islands for labour. His keels plowed all ocean stretches. He owned three steamers on regular island runs, though he rarely elected to travel in them, preferring the wilder and more primitive way of wind and sail.

At least forty years of age, he looked no more than thirty. Yet beachcombers remembered his advent among the islands a score of years before, at which time the yellow mustache was already budding silkily on his lip. Unlike other white men in the tropics, he was there because he liked it. His protective skin pigmentation was excellent. He had been born to the sun. One he was in ten thousand in the matter of sun-resistance. The invisible and high-velocity light waves failed to bore into him. Other white men were pervious.[9] The sun drove through their skins, ripping and smashing tissues and nerves, till they became sick in mind and body, tossed most of the Decalogue overboard, descended to beastliness, drank themselves into quick graves, or survived so savagely that war vessels were sometimes sent to curb their license.

But David Grief was a true son of the sun, and he flourished in all its ways. He merely became browner with the passing of the years, though in the brown was the hint of golden tint that glows in the skin of the Polynesian. Yet his blue eyes retained their blue, his mustache its yellow, and the lines of his face were those which had persisted through the centuries in his English race. English he was in blood, yet those that thought they knew contended he was at least American born. Unlike them, he had not come out to the South Seas seeking hearth and saddle of his own. In fact, he had brought hearth and saddle with him. His advent had been in the Paumotus. He arrived on board a tiny schooner yacht, master and owner, a youth questing romance and adventure along the sun-washed path of the tropics. He also arrived in a hurricane, the giant waves of which deposited him and yacht and all in the thick of a cocoanut grove three hundred yards beyond the surf. Six months later he was rescued by a pearling cutter. But the sun had got into his blood. At Tahiti, instead of taking a steamer home, he bought a schooner, outfitted her with trade-goods and divers, and went for a cruise through the Dangerous Archipelago.

As the golden tint burned into his face it poured molten out of the ends of his fingers. His was the golden touch, but he played the game, not for the gold, but for the game's sake. It was a man's game, the rough contacts and fierce give and take of the adventurers of his own blood and of half the bloods of Europe and the rest of the world, and it was a good game; but over and beyond was his love of all the other things that go to make up a South Seas rover's life—the smell of the reef; the infinite exquisiteness of the shoals of living coral in the mirror-surfaced lagoons; the crashing sunrises of raw colours spread with lawless cunning; the palm-tufted islets set in turquoise deeps; the tonic wine of the trade-winds; the heave and send of the orderly, crested seas; the moving deck beneath his feet, the straining canvas overhead; the flower-garlanded, golden-glowing men and maids of Polynesia, half-children and half-gods; and even the howling savages of Melanesia, head-hunters and man-eaters, half-devil and all beast.

And so, favoured child of the sun, out of munificence of energy and sheer joy of living, he, the man of many millions, forbore on his far way to play the game with Harrison J. Griffiths for a paltry sum. It was his whim, his desire, his expression of self and of the sun-warmth that poured through him. It was fun, a joke, a problem, a bit of play on which life was lightly hazarded for the joy of the playing.

IV

The early morning found the *Wonder* laying close-hauled along the coast of Guadalcanar.[10] She moved lazily through the water under the dying breath of the land breeze. To the east, heavy masses of clouds promised a renewal of the southeast trades, accompanied by sharp puffs and rain squalls. Ahead, laying along the coast on the same course as the *Wonder*, and being slowly overtaken, was a small ketch. It was not the *Willi-Waw*, however, and Captain Ward, on the *Wonder*, putting down his glasses, named it the *Kauri*.

Grief, just on deck from below, sighed regretfully.

"If it had only been the *Willi-Waw*," he said.

"You do hate to be beaten," Denby, the supercargo, remarked sympathetically.

"I certainly do." Grief paused and laughed with genuine mirth. "It's my firm conviction that Griffiths is a rogue, and that he treated me quite scurvily yesterday. 'Sign,' he says, 'sign in full, at the bottom, and date it.' And Jacobsen, the little rat, stood in with him. It was rank piracy, the days of Bully Hayes all over again."[11]

"If you weren't my employer, Mr. Grief, I'd like to give you a piece of my mind," Captain Ward broke in.

"Go on and spit it out," Grief encouraged.

"Well, then—" The captain hesitated and cleared his throat. "With all the money you've got, only a fool would take the risk you did with those two curs. What do you do it for?"

"Honestly, I don't know, Captain. I just want to, I suppose. And can you give any better reason for anything you do?"

"You'll get your bally head shot off some fine day," Captain Ward growled in answer, as he stepped to the binnacle and took the bearing of a peak which had just thrust its head through the clouds that covered Guadalcanar.

The land breeze strengthened in a last effort, and the *Wonder*, slipping swiftly through the water, ranged alongside the *Kauri* and began to go by. Greetings flew back and forth, then David Grief called out:

"Seen anything of the *Willi-Waw*?"

The captain, slouch-hatted and barelegged, with a rolling twist hitched the faded blue *lava-lava* tighter around his waist and spat tobacco juice overside.

"Sure," he answered. "Griffiths lay at Savo last night, taking on pigs and yams and filling his water-tanks.[12] Looked like he was going for a long cruise, but he said no. Why? Did you want to see him?"

"Yes; but if you see him first don't tell him you've seen me."

The captain nodded and considered, and walked for'ard on his own deck to keep abreast of the faster vessel.

"Say!" he called. "Jacobsen told me they were coming down this afternoon to Gabera.[13] Said they were going to lay there to-night and take on sweet potatoes."

"Gabera has the only leading lights in the Solomons," Grief said, when his schooner had drawn well ahead. "Is that right, Captain Ward?"

The captain nodded.

"And the little bight just around the point on this side, it's a rotten anchorage, isn't it?"

"No anchorage. All coral patches and shoals, and a bad surf. That's where the *Molly* went to pieces three years ago."

Grief stared straight before him with lustreless eyes for a full minute, as if summoning some vision to his inner sight. Then the corners of his eyes wrinkled and the ends of his yellow mustache lifted in a smile.

"We'll anchor at Gabera," he said. "And run in close to the little bight this side. I want you to drop me in a whaleboat as you go by. Also, give me six boys, and serve out rifles. I'll be back on board before morning."

The captain's face took on an expression of suspicion, which swiftly slid into one of reproach.

"Oh, just a little fun, skipper," Grief protested with the apologetic air of a schoolboy caught in mischief by an elder.

Captain Ward grunted, but Denby was all alertness.

"I'd like to go along, Mr. Grief," he said.

Grief nodded consent.

"Bring some axes and bush-knives," he said. "And, oh, by the way, a couple of bright lanterns. See they've got oil in them."

V

An hour before sunset the *Wonder* tore by the little bight. The wind had freshened, and a lively sea was beginning to make. The shoals toward the beach were already white with the churn of water, while those farther out as yet showed no more sign than of discoloured water. As the schooner went into the wind and backed her jib and staysail the whaleboat was swung out. Into it leaped six breech-clouted Santa Cruz boys, each armed with a rifle. Denby, carrying the lanterns, dropped into the sternsheets. Grief, following, paused on the rail.

"Pray for a dark night, skipper," he pleaded.

"You'll get it," Captain Ward answered. "There's no moon anyway, and there won't be any sky. She'll be a bit squally, too."

The forecast sent a radiance into Grief's face, making more pronounced the golden tint of his sunburn. He leaped down beside the supercargo.

"Cast off!" Captain Ward ordered. "Draw the headsails! Put your wheel over! There! Steady! Take that course!"

The *Wonder* filled away and ran on around the point for Gabera, while the whaleboat, pulling six oars and steered by Grief, headed for the beach. With superb boatmanship he threaded the narrow, tortuous channel which no craft larger than a whaleboat could negotiate, until the shoals and patches showed seaward and they grounded on the quiet, rippling beach.

The next hour was filled with work. Moving about among the wild cocoanuts and jungle brush, Grief selected the trees.

"Chop this fella tree; chop that fella tree," he told his blacks. "No chop that other fella," he said, with a shake of head.

In the end, a wedge-shaped segment of jungle was cleared. Near to the beach remained one long palm. At the apex of the wedge stood another. Darkness was falling as the lanterns were lighted, carried up the two trees, and made fast.

"That outer lantern is too high." David Grief studied it critically. "Put it down about ten feet, Denby."

VI

The *Willi-Waw* was tearing through the water with a bone in her teeth, for the breath of the passing squall was still strong. The blacks were swinging up the big mainsail, which had been lowered on the run when the puff was at its height. Jacobsen, superintending the operation, ordered them to throw the halyards down on deck and stand by, then went for'ard on the lee-bow and joined Griffiths. Both men stared with wide-strained eyes at the blank wall of darkness through which they were flying, their ears tense for the sound of surf on the invisible shore. It was by this sound that they were for the moment steering.

The wind fell lighter, the scud of clouds thinned and broke, and in the dim glimmer of starlight loomed the jungle-clad coast. Ahead, and well on the lee-bow, appeared a jagged rock-point. Both men strained to it.

"Amboy Point," Griffiths announced. "Plenty of water close up. Take the wheel, Jacobsen, till we set a course. Get a move on!"

Running aft, barefooted and barelegged, the rainwater dripping from his scant clothing, the mate displaced the black at the wheel.

"How's she heading?" Griffiths called.

"South-a-half-west!"

"Let her come up south-by-west! Got it?"

"Right on it!"

Griffiths considered the changed relation of Amboy Point to the *Willi-Waw*'s course.

"And a-half-west!" he cried.

"And a-half-west!" came the answer. "Right on it!"

"Steady! That'll do!"

"Steady she is!" Jacobsen turned the wheel over to the savage. "You steer good fella, savve?" he warned. "No good fella, I knock your damn black head off."

Again he went for'ard and joined the other, and again the cloud-scud thickened, the star-glimmer vanished, and the wind rose and screamed in another squall.

"Watch that mainsail!" Griffiths yelled in the mate's ear, at the same time studying the ketch's behaviour.

Over she pressed, and lee-rail under, while he measured the weight of the wind and quested its easement. The tepid sea-water, with here and there tiny globules of phosphorescence, washed about his ankles and knees. The wind screamed a higher note, and every shroud and stay sharply chorused an answer as the *Willi-Waw* pressed farther over and down.

"Down mainsail!" Griffiths yelled, springing to the peak-halyards, thrusting away the black who held on, and casting off the turn.

Jacobsen, at the throat-halyards, was performing the like office. The big sail rattled down, and the blacks, with shouts and yells, threw themselves on the battling canvas. The mate, finding one skulking in the darkness, flung his bunched knuckles into the creature's face and drove him to his work.

The squall held at its high pitch, and under her small canvas the *Willi-Waw* still foamed along. Again the two men stood for'ard and vainly watched in the horizontal drive of rain.

"We're all right," Griffiths said. "This rain won't last. We can hold this course till we pick up the lights. Anchor in thirteen fathoms. You'd better overhaul forty-five on a night like this. After that get the gaskets on the mainsail. We won't need it."

Half an hour afterward his weary eyes were rewarded by a glimpse of two lights.

"There they are, Jacobsen. I'll take the wheel. Run down the fore-staysail and stand by to let go. Make the niggers jump."

Aft, the spokes of the wheel in his hands, Griffiths held the course till the two lights came in line, when he abruptly altered and headed directly in for them. He heard the tumble and roar of the surf, but decided it was farther away—as it should be, at Gabera.

He heard the frightened cry of the mate, and was grinding the wheel down with all his might, when the *Willi-Waw* struck. At the same instant her mainmast crashed over the bow. Five wild minutes followed. All hands held on while the hull upheaved and smashed down on the brittle coral and the warm seas swept over them. Grinding and crunching, the *Willi-Waw* worked itself clear over the shoal patch and came solidly to rest in the comparatively smooth and shallow channel beyond.

Griffiths sat down on the edge of the cabin, head bowed on chest, in silent wrath and bitterness. Once he lifted his face to glare at the two white lights, one above the other and perfectly in line.

"There they are," he said. "And this isn't Gabera. Then what the hell is it?"

Though the surf still roared and across the shoal flung its spray and upper wash over them, the wind died down and the stars came out. Shoreward came the sound of oars.

"What have you had?—an earthquake?" Griffiths called out. "The bottom's all changed. I've anchored here a hundred times in thirteen fathoms. Is that you, Wilson?"

A whaleboat came alongside, and a man climbed over the rail. In the faint light Griffiths found an automatic Colt's thrust into his face, and, looking up, saw David Grief.

"No, you never anchored here before," Grief laughed. "Gabera's just around the point, where I'll be as soon as I've collected that little sum of twelve hundred pounds. We won't bother for the receipt. I've your note here, and I'll just return it."

"You did this!" Griffiths cried, springing to his feet in a sudden gust of rage. "You faked those leading lights! You've wrecked me, and by—"

"Steady! Steady!" Grief's voice was cool and menacing. "I'll trouble you for that twelve hundred, please."

To Griffiths, a vast impotence seemed to descend upon him. He was overwhelmed by a profound disgust—disgust for the sunlands and the sun-sickness, for the futility of all his endeavour, for this blue-eyed, golden-tinted, superior man who defeated him on all his ways.

"Jacobsen," he said, "will you open the cash-box and pay this—this bloodsucker—twelve hundred pounds?"

TWO

THE PROUD GOAT
OF
ALOYSIUS PANKBURN

At this tale's opening, we find Grief lounging about in Polynesia, looking for "the unexpected to leap out at him from behind the nearest cocoanut tree." London makes masterful use of narrative detail in this brilliantly atmospheric work, making it possible to sense the cobalt sky, the white beaches, the blue rolling seas, the warm salt air. The picture of Grief at his ease, lazily contemplating the horizon, waiting for the inevitable adventure, is a captivating one, and it would be a rare reader who didn't imagine leaning casually on the deck rail next to the intrepid seaman. Very soon after meeting Aloysius Pankburn, Grief becomes entangled in the task of changing an enfeebled, sobbing, shaking alcoholic into a man of physical strength and moral fiber. The second part of "The Proud Goat" is a romantic adventure story that takes the reader to a remote cannibal island in the South Seas, searching for a legendary long-lost treasure. These two interwoven ideas occupy the core of the story, both involving the reclamation of something lost.

Pankburn's losses are deeply personal, but to all but himself they appear ironically comical. Here he is on a healing cruise to rehabilitate himself when, of all things, love should rear its head. But in David Grief's experience, love rarely if ever presents positive results. In this case, love is keeping his wealthy new acquaintance perpetually broke and drunk, because the lovers in question are the personal staff appointed by Pankburn's family to be in charge of handling his money and assuring his sobriety. Instead, swin-

dling him of his "cure," Pankburn's keepers are dallying with each other while threatening the helpless drunkard with fulfilling their responsibilities if he objects. Grief is instantly intrigued by this ironic twist.

Undertaking a practical, but brutally severe, treatment of Pankburn, Grief bases his work on a commonsensical theory no longer in vogue in our post-AA era: If you make your patient fear a greater pain than the pains of withdrawal while you force him to perform hard physical work, both mind and body will grow firm. Addiction theory had yet to be elaborated in 1911, and it seems that London believed that alcoholism was essentially a moral flaw that a real man ought to be able to overcome. Grief's crew watch the punishing "treatment": "They were men of the sea. They lived life in the rough. And alcohol, in themselves as well as in other men, was a problem they had learned to handle in ways not taught in doctors' schools."

This story provides perhaps the clearest evidence that London was rethinking one of the main themes of The Sea-Wolf *in a more positive light. After Pankburn's first relapse, he tries to quit Grief's therapy, but Grief firmly orders his officer, "Mr. Carlsen, you will see that Mr. Pankburn remains on board." This inevitably recalls the moment in* The Sea-Wolf *when Humphrey Van Weyden learns that he will never be set ashore and has no choice but to join the crew of the* Ghost. *David Grief, thinking of the betterment of the species as well as honoring his whimsically existential commitment to Pankburn, gives vent to a far more joyfully Nietzschean resolution than Wolf Larsen would ever know. His promise: "I've taken you in hand, and I'm going to make a man out of you if I have to kill you to do it." Like Wolf, Grief is proudest of his human experiment when Pankburn swears to become strong enough physically to beat his master. Unlike Wolf, Grief knows that, when his subject does become strong enough physically, Pankburn will no longer want to beat him.*

The second theme of recovery of something lost involves Pankburn's knowledge of a secret treasure, which Grief has committed himself to investigate. Following coded clues supplemented by his encyclopedic knowledge of the Pacific, Grief sails to this treasure island. On his arrival, he realizes quickly that the treasure has been discovered by the treacherous cannibals of Francis Island, though of course they set a different interpretation of its value. Though the ethics of the white men's subsequent scheme to defraud the islanders of the treasure may be dubious, it is on the face of it a comical trick. Today's readers will see in it a more sinister representation of the colonial enterprise itself. Further, their plot parallels the dishonesty of Pankburn's manager and nurse: As they have exploited their charge's dependence on alcohol, Grief and a "recovered" Pankburn conspire to exploit the islanders' addiction to tobacco.

Quick eye that he had for the promise of adventure, prepared always for the unexpected to leap out at him from behind the nearest cocoanut tree, nevertheless David Grief received no warning when he laid eyes on Aloysius Pankburn. It was on the little steamer *Berthe*. Leaving his schooner to follow, Grief had taken passage for the short run across from Raiatea to Papeete.[1] When he first saw Aloysius Pankburn, that somewhat fuddled gentleman was drinking a lonely cocktail at the tiny bar between decks next to the barber shop. And when Grief left the barber's hands half an hour later Aloysius Pankburn was still hanging over the bar, still drinking by himself.

Now it is not good for man to drink alone, and Grief threw sharp scrutiny into his passing glance. He saw a well-built young man of thirty, well-featured, well-dressed, and evidently, in the world's catalogue, a gentleman. But in the faint hint of slovenliness, in the shaking, eager hand that spilled the liquor, and in the nervous, vacillating eyes, Grief read the unmistakable marks of the chronic alcoholic.

After dinner he chanced upon Pankburn again. This time it was on deck, and the young man, clinging to the rail and peering into the distance at the dim forms of a man and woman in two steamer chairs drawn closely together, was crying drunkenly. Grief noted that the man's arm was around the woman's waist. Aloysius Pankburn looked on and cried.

"Nothing to weep about," Grief said genially.

Pankburn looked at him, and gushed tears of profound self-pity.

"It's hard," he sobbed. "Hard. Hard. That man's my business manager. I employ him. I pay him a good screw.[2] And that's how he earns it."

"In that case, why don't you put a stop to it?" Grief advised.

"I can't. She'd shut off my whiskey. She's my trained nurse."

"Fire *her*, then, and drink your head off."

"I can't. He's got all my money. If I did, he wouldn't give me sixpence to buy a drink with."

This woful possibility brought a fresh wash of tears. Grief was interested. Of all unique situations he could never have imagined such a one as this.

"They were engaged to take care of me," Pankburn was blubbering, "to keep me away from the drink. And that's the way they do it, lollygagging all about the ship and letting me drink myself to death. It isn't right, I tell you. It isn't right. They were sent along with me for the express purpose of not letting me drink, and they let me drink to swinishness as long as I leave them alone. If I complain they threaten not to let me have another drop. What can a poor devil do? My death will be on their heads, that's all. Come on down and join me."

He released his clutch on the rail, and would have fallen had Grief not caught his arm. He seemed to undergo a transformation, to stiffen physically, to thrust his chin forward aggressively, and to glint harshly in his eyes.

"I won't let them kill me. And they'll be sorry. I've offered them fifty thousand—later on, of course.[3] They laughed. They don't know. But I know." He fumbled in his coat pocket and drew forth an object that flashed in the faint light. "They don't know the meaning of that. But I do." He looked at Grief with abrupt suspicion. "What do you make out of it, eh? What do you make out of it?"

David Grief caught a swift vision of an alcoholic degenerate putting a very loving young couple to death with a copper spike, for a copper spike was what he held in his hand, an evident old-fashioned ship-fastening.

"My mother thinks I'm up here to get cured of the booze habit. She doesn't know. I bribed the doctor to prescribe a voyage. When we get to Papeete my manager is going to charter a schooner and away we'll sail. But they don't dream. They think it's the booze. I know. I only know. Good night, sir. I'm going to bed—unless—er—you'll join me in a night cap. One last drink, you know."

II

In the week that followed at Papeete Grief caught numerous and bizarre glimpses of Aloysius Pankburn. So did everybody else in the little island capital; for neither the beach nor Lavina's boarding house had been so scandalized in years. In midday, bareheaded, clad only in swimming trunks, Aloysius Pankburn ran down the main street from Lavina's to the water front. He put on the gloves with a fireman from the *Berthe* in a scheduled four-round bout at the *Folies Bergères,*[4] and was knocked out in the second round. He tried insanely to drown himself in a two-foot pool of water, dived drunkenly and splendidly from fifty feet up in the rigging of the *Mariposa*[5] lying at the wharf, and chartered the cutter *Toerau* at more than her purchase price and was only saved by his manager's refusal financially to ratify the agreement. He bought out the old blind leper at the market, and sold breadfruit, plantains, and sweet potatoes at such cut-rates that the gendarmes were called out to break the rush of bargain-hunting natives. For that matter, three times the gendarmes arrested him for riotous behaviour, and three times his manager ceased from love-making long enough to pay the fines imposed by a needy colonial administration.

Then the *Mariposa* sailed for San Francisco, and in the bridal suite were the manager and the trained nurse, fresh-married. Before departing, the manager had thoughtfully bestowed eight five-pound banknotes on Aloysius, with the foreseen result that Aloysius awoke several days later to find himself broke and perilously near to delirium tremens. Lavina, famed for her good heart even among the driftage of South Pacific rogues and scamps, nursed him around and never let it filter into his returning intelligence that there was neither manager nor money to pay his board.

It was several evenings after this that David Grief, lounging under the after deck awning of the *Kittiwake* and idly scanning the meagre columns of the Papeete *Avant-Coureur,* sat suddenly up and almost rubbed his eyes. It was unbelievable, but there it was. The old South Seas Romance was not dead. He read:

> WANTED—To exchange a half interest in buried treasure, worth five million francs, for transportation for one to an unknown island in the Pacific and facilities for carrying away the loot. Ask for FOLLY, at Lavina's.

Grief looked at his watch. It was early yet, only eight o'clock.

"Mr. Carlsen," he called in the direction of a glowing pipe. "Get the crew for the whaleboat. I'm going ashore."

The husky voice of the Norwegian mate was raised for'ard, and half a dozen strapping Rapa Islanders ceased their singing and manned the boat.[6]

"I came to see Folly, Mr. Folly, I imagine," David Grief told Lavina.

He noted the quick interest in her eyes as she turned her head and flung a command in native across two open rooms to the outstanding kitchen. A few minutes later a barefooted native girl padded in and shook her head.

Lavina's disappointment was evident.

"You're stopping aboard the *Kittiwake,* aren't you?" she said. "I'll tell him you called."

"Then it is a *he?*" Grief queried.

Lavina nodded.

"I hope you can do something for him, Captain Grief. I'm only a good-natured woman. I don't know. But he's a likable man, and he may be telling the truth; I don't know. You'll know. You're not a soft-hearted fool like me. Can't I mix you a cocktail?"

III

Back on board his schooner and dozing in a deck chair under a three-months-old magazine, David Grief was aroused by a sobbing, slubbering noise from overside. He opened his eyes. From the Chilean cruiser, a quarter of a mile away, came the stroke of eight bells. It was midnight. From overside came a splash and another slubbering noise. To him it seemed half amphibian, half the sounds of a man crying to himself and querulously chanting his sorrows to the general universe.

A jump took David Grief to the low rail. Beneath, centred about the slubbering noise, was an area of agitated phosphorescence. Leaning over, he locked his hand under the armpit of a man, and, with pull and heave and quick-changing grips, he drew on deck the naked form of Aloysius Pankburn.

"With pull and heave and quick-changing grips he drew on deck the naked
form of Aloysius Pankburn. . . . " Drawing by C.W. Ashley

"I didn't have a sou-markee," he complained.[7] "I had to swim it,
and I couldn't find your gangway. It was very miserable. Pardon me.
If you have a towel to put about my middle, and a good stiff drink,
I'll be more myself. I'm Mr. Folly, and you're the Captain Grief, I
presume, who called on me when I was out. No, I'm not drunk. Nor
am I cold. This isn't shivering. Lavina allowed me only two drinks
to-day. I'm on the edge of the horrors, that's all, and I was beginning
to see things when I couldn't find the gangway. If you'll take me
below I'll be very grateful. You are the only one that answered my
advertisement."

He was shaking pitiably in the warm night, and down in the cabin, before he got his towel, Grief saw to it that a half-tumbler of whiskey was in his hand.

"Now fire ahead," Grief said, when he had got his guest into a shirt and a pair of duck trousers. "What's this advertisement of yours? I'm listening."

Pankburn looked at the whiskey bottle, but Grief shook his head.

"All right, Captain, though I tell you on whatever is left of my honour that I am not drunk—not in the least. Also, what I shall tell you is true, and I shall tell it briefly, for it is clear to me that you are a man of affairs and action. Likewise, your chemistry is good. To you alcohol has never been a million maggots gnawing at every cell of you. You've never been to hell. I am there now. I am scorching. Now listen.

"My mother is alive. She is English. I was born in Australia. I was educated at York and Yale. I am a master of arts, a doctor of philosophy; and I am no good. Furthermore, I am an alcoholic. I have been an athlete. I used to swan-dive a hundred and ten feet in the clear. I hold several amateur records. I am a fish. I learned the crawl-stroke from the first of the Cavilles.[8] I have done thirty miles in a rough sea. I have another record. I have punished more whiskey than any man of my years. I will steal sixpence from you for the price of a drink. Finally, I will tell you the truth.

"My father was an American—an Annapolis man. He was a midshipman in the War of the Rebellion. In '66 he was a lieutenant on the *Suwanee*. Her captain was Paul Shirley. In '66 the *Suwanee* coaled at an island in the Pacific which I do not care to mention, under a protectorate which did not exist then and which shall be nameless. Ashore, behind the bar of a public house, my father saw three copper spikes—ship's spikes."

David Grief smiled quietly.

"And now I can tell you the name of the coaling station and of the protectorate that came afterward," he said.

"And of the three spikes?" Pankburn asked with equal quietness. "Go ahead, for they are in my possession now."

"Certainly. They were behind German Oscar's bar at Peenoo-Pee-nee. Johnny Black brought them there from off his schooner the night he died. He was just back from a long cruise to the westward, fishing beche-de-mer and sandalwood trading. All the beach knows the tale."

Pankburn shook his head.

"Go on," he urged.

"It was before my time, of course," Grief explained. "I only tell what I've heard. Next came the Ecuadoran cruiser, of all directions, in from the westward, and bound home. Her officers recognized the spikes. Johnny Black was dead. They got hold of his mate and log-book. Away to the westward went she. Six months after, again bound home, she dropped in at Peenoo-Peenee. She had failed, and the tale leaked out."

"When the revolutionists were marching on Guayaquil,"[9] Pankburn took it up, "the federal officers, believing a defence of the city hopeless, salted down the government treasure chest, something like a million dollars gold, but all in English coinage, and put it on board the American schooner *Flirt*. They were going to run at daylight. The American captain skinned out in the middle of the night. Go on."

"It's an old story," Grief resumed. "There was no other vessel in the harbour. The federal leaders couldn't run. They put their backs to the wall and held the city. Rohjas Salced, making a forced march from Quito, raised the siege. The revolution was broken, and the one ancient steamer that constituted the Ecuadoran navy was sent in pursuit of the *Flirt*. They caught her, between the Banks Group and the New Hebrides,[10] hove to and flying distress signals. The captain had died the day before—blackwater fever."

"And the mate?" Pankburn challenged.

"The mate had been killed a week earlier by the natives on one of the Banks, when they sent a boat in for water. There were no naviga-tors left. The men were put to the torture. It was beyond interna-tional law. They wanted to confess, but couldn't. They told of the three spikes in the trees on the beach, but where the island was they did not know. To the westward, far to the westward, was all they knew. The tale now goes two ways. One is that they all died under the torture. The other is that the survivors were swung at the yard-

arm. At any rate, the Ecuadoran cruiser went home without the treasure. Johnny Black brought the three spikes to Peenoo-Peenee, and
left them at German Oscar's, but how and where he found them he
never told."

Pankburn looked hard at the whiskey bottle.

"Just two fingers," he whimpered.

Grief considered, and poured a meagre drink. Pankburn's eyes
sparkled, and he took new lease of life.

"And this is where I come in with the missing details," he said.
"Johnny Black did tell. He told my father. Wrote him from Levuka, before he came on to die at Peenoo-Peenee. My father had saved
his life one rough-house night in Valparaiso. A Chink pearler, out
of Thursday Island,[11] prospecting for new grounds to the north of
New Guinea, traded for the three spikes with a nigger. Johnny Black
bought them for copper weight. He didn't dream any more than the
Chink, but coming back he stopped for hawksbill turtle at the very
beach where you say the mate of the *Flirt* was killed. Only he wasn't
killed. The Banks Islanders held him prisoner, and he was dying of
necrosis of the jawbone, caused by an arrow wound in the fight on
the beach. Before he died he told the yarn to Johnny Black. Johnny
Black wrote my father from Levuka. He was at the end of his rope—
cancer. My father, ten years afterward, when captain of the *Perry*,
got the spikes from German Oscar. And from my father, last will and
testament, you know, came the spikes and the data. I have the island,
the latitude and longitude of the beach where the three spikes were
nailed in the trees. The spikes are up at Lavina's now. The latitude
and longitude are in my head. Now what do you think?"

"Fishy," was Grief's instant judgment. "Why didn't your father
go and get it himself?"

"Didn't need it. An uncle died and left him a fortune. He retired
from the navy, ran foul of an epidemic of trained nurses in Boston,
and my mother got a divorce. Also, she fell heir to an income of
something like thirty thousand dollars, and went to live in New Zealand. I was divided between them, half-time New Zealand, half-time
United States, until my father's death last year. Now my mother has
me altogether. He left me his money—oh, a couple of millions—but

my mother has had guardians appointed on account of the drink.
I'm worth all kinds of money, but I can't touch a penny save what is
doled out to me. But the old man, who had got the tip on my drinking, left me the three spikes and the data thereunto pertaining. Did it
through his lawyers, unknown to my mother; said it beat life insurance, and that if I had the backbone to go and get it I could drink my
back teeth awash until I died. Millions in the hands of my guardians, slathers of shekels of my mother's that'll be mine if she beats me
to the crematory, another million waiting to be dug up, and in the
meantime I'm cadging on Lavina for two drinks a day. It's hell, isn't
it?—when you consider my thirst."

"Where's the island?"

"It's a long way from here."

"Name it."

"Not on your life, Captain Grief. You're making an easy half-
million out of this. You will sail under my directions, and when we're
well to sea and on our way I'll tell you and not before."

Grief shrugged his shoulders, dismissing the subject.

"When I've given you another drink I'll send the boat ashore with
you," he said.

Pankburn was taken aback. For at least five minutes he debated
with himself, then licked his lips and surrendered.

"If you promise to go, I'll tell you now."

"Of course I'm willing to go. That's why I asked you. Name the
island."

Pankburn looked at the bottle.

"I'll take that drink now, Captain."

"No you won't. That drink was for you if you went ashore. If you
are going to tell me the island, you must do it in your sober senses."

"Francis Island, if you will have it. Bougainville named it Barbour
Island."

"Off there all by its lonely in the Little Coral Sea," Grief said. "I
know it. Lies between New Ireland and New Guinea.[12] A rotten hole
now, though it was all right when the *Flirt* drove in the spikes and
the Chink pearler traded for them. The steamship *Castor*, recruiting
labour for the Upolu plantations, was cut off there with all hands

two years ago.[13] I knew her captain well. The Germans sent a cruiser, shelled the bush, burned half a dozen villages, killed a couple of niggers and a lot of pigs, and—and that was all. The niggers always were bad there, but they turned really bad forty years ago. That was when they cut off a whaler. Let me see? What was her name?"

He stepped to the bookshelf, drew out the bulky "South Pacific Directory," and ran through its pages.

"Yes. Here it is. Francis, or Barbour," he skimmed. "Natives warlike and treacherous—Melanesian—cannibals. Whaleship *Western* cut off—that was her name. Shoals—points—anchorages—ah, Redscar, Owen Bay, Likikili Bay, that's more like it; deep indentation, mangrove swamps, good holding in nine fathoms when white scar in bluff bears west-southwest." Grief looked up. "That's your beach, Pankburn, I'll swear."

"Will you go?" the other demanded eagerly.

Grief nodded.

"It sounds good to me. Now if the story had been of a hundred millions, or some such crazy sum, I wouldn't look at it for a moment. We'll sail to-morrow, but under one consideration. You are to be absolutely under my orders."

His visitor nodded emphatically and joyously.

"And that means no drink."

"That's pretty hard," Pankburn whined.

"It's my terms. I'm enough of a doctor to see you don't come to harm. And you are to work—hard work, sailor's work. You'll stand regular watches and everything, though you eat and sleep aft with us."

"It's a go." Pankburn put out his hand to ratify the agreement. "If it doesn't kill me," he added.

David Grief poured a generous three-fingers into the tumbler and extended it.

"Then here's your last drink. Take it."

Pankburn's hand went halfway out. With a sudden spasm of resolution, he hesitated, threw back his shoulders, and straightened up his head.

"I guess I won't," he began, then, feebly surrendering to the gnaw of desire, he reached hastily for the glass, as if in fear that it would be withdrawn.

IV

It is a long traverse from Papeete in the Societies to the Little Coral Sea—from 150 west longitude to 150 east longitude—as the crow flies the equivalent to a voyage across the Atlantic. But the *Kittiwake* did not go as the crow flies. David Grief's numerous interests diverted her course many times. He stopped to take a look-in at uninhabited Rose island with an eye to colonizing and planting cocoanuts. Next, he paid his respects to Tui Manua,[14] of Eastern Samoa, and opened an intrigue for a share of the trade monopoly of that dying king's three islands. From Apia he carried several relief agents and a load of trade goods to the Gilberts. He peeped in at Ontong-Java Atoll, inspected his plantations on Ysabel, and purchased lands from the salt-water chiefs of northwestern Malaita.[15] And all along this devious way he made a man of Aloysius Pankburn.

That thirster, though he lived aft, was compelled to do the work of a common sailor. And not only did he take his wheel and lookout, and heave on sheets and tackles, but the dirtiest and most arduous tasks were appointed him. Swung aloft in a bosun's chair, he scraped the masts and slushed down. Holystoning the deck or scrubbing it with fresh limes made his back ache and developed the wasted, flabby muscles. When the *Kittiwake* lay at anchor and her copper bottom was scrubbed with cocoanut husks by the native crew, who dived and did it under water, Pankburn was sent down on his shift and as many times as any on the shift.

"Look at yourself," Grief said. "You are twice the man you were when you came on board. You haven't had one drink, you didn't die, and the poison is pretty well worked out of you. It's the work. It beats trained nurses and business managers. Here, if you're thirsty. Clap your lips to this."

With several deft strokes of his heavy-backed sheath-knife, Grief clipped a triangular piece of shell from the end of a husked drinking-cocoanut. The thin, cool liquid, slightly milky and effervescent, bubbled to the brim. With a bow, Pankburn took the natural cup, threw his head back, and held it back till the shell was empty. He drank many of these nuts each day. The black steward, a New Hebrides boy sixty years of age, and his assistant, a Lark Islander of eleven, saw to it that he was continually supplied.

Pankburn did not object to the hard work. He devoured work, never shirking and always beating the native sailors in jumping to obey a command. But his sufferings during the period of driving the alcohol out of his system were truly heroic. Even when the last shred of the poison was exuded, the desire, as an obsession, remained in his head. So it was, when, on his honour, he went ashore at Apia, that he attempted to put the public houses out of business by drinking up their stocks in trade. And so it was, at two in the morning, that David Grief found him in front of the Tivoli, out of which he had been disorderly thrown by Charley Roberts.[16] Aloysius, as of old, was chanting his sorrows to the stars. Also, and more concretely, he was punctuating the rhythm with cobbles of coral stone, which he flung with amazing accuracy through Charley Roberts's windows.

David Grief took him away, but not till next morning did he take him in hand. It was on the deck of the *Kittiwake,* and there was nothing kindergarten about it. Grief struck him, with bare knuckles, punched him and punished him—gave him the worst thrashing he had ever received.

"For the good of your soul, Pankburn," was the way he emphasized his blows. "For the good of your mother. For the progeny that will come after. For the good of the world, and the universe, and the whole race of man yet to be. And now, to hammer the lesson home, we'll do it all over again. That, for the good of your soul; and that, for your mother's sake; and that, for the little children, undreamed of and unborn, whose mother you'll love for their sakes, and for love's sake, in the lease of manhood that will be yours when I am done with you. Come on and take your medicine. I'm not done with you yet. I've only begun. There are many other reasons which I shall now proceed to expound."

The brown sailors and the black stewards and cook looked on

and grinned. Far from them was the questioning of any of the mysterious and incomprehensible ways of white men. As for Carlsen, the
mate, he was grimly in accord with the treatment his employer was
administering; while Albright, the supercargo, merely played with
his mustache and smiled. They were men of the sea. They lived life in
the rough. And alcohol, in themselves as well as in other men, was a
problem they had learned to handle in ways not taught in doctors'
schools.

"Boy! A bucket of fresh water and a towel," Grief ordered, when
he had finished. "Two buckets and two towels," he added, as he
surveyed his own hands.

"You're a pretty one," he said to Pankburn. "You've spoiled everything. I had the poison completely out of you. And now you are
fairly reeking with it. We've got to begin all over again. Mr. Albright!
You know that pile of old chain on the beach at the boat-landing.
Find the owner, buy it, and fetch it on board. There must be a hundred and fifty fathoms of it. Pankburn! To-morrow morning you
start in pounding the rust off of it. When you've done that, you'll
sandpaper it. Then you'll paint it. And nothing else will you do till
that chain is as smooth as new."

Aloysius Pankburn shook his head.

"I quit. Francis Island can go to hell for all of me. I'm done with
your slave-driving. Kindly put me ashore at once. I'm a white man.
You can't treat me this way."

"Mr. Carlsen, you will see that Mr. Pankburn remains on board."

"I'll have you broken for this!" Aloysius screamed. "You can't
stop me."

"I can give you another licking," Grief answered. "And let me tell
you one thing, you besotted whelp, I'll keep on licking you as long as
my knuckles hold out or until you yearn to hammer chain rust. I've
taken you in hand, and I'm going to make a man out of you if I have
to kill you to do it. Now go below and change your clothes. Be ready
to turn to with a hammer this afternoon. Mr. Albright, get that chain
aboard pronto. Mr. Carlsen, send the boats ashore after it. Also,
keep your eye on Pankburn. If he shows signs of keeling over or

"Ten hours a day Aloysius Pankburn pounded chain rust. . . . "
Drawing by C.W. Ashley

going into the shakes, give him a nip—a small one. He may need it
after last night."

V

For the rest of the time the *Kittiwake* lay in Apia Aloysius Pankburn pounded chain rust. Ten hours a day he pounded. And on the
long stretch across to the Gilberts he still pounded. Then came the
sandpapering. One hundred and fifty fathoms is nine hundred feet,
and every link of all that length was smoothed and polished as no
link ever was before. And when the last link had received its second
coat of black paint, he declared himself.

"Come on with more dirty work," he told Grief. "I'll overhaul
the other chains if you say so. And you needn't worry about me any
more. I'm not going to take another drop. I'm going to train up. You

got my proud goat when you beat me, but let me tell you, you only got it temporarily. Train! I'm going to train till I'm as hard all the way through, and clean all the way through, as that chain is. And some day, Mister David Grief, somewhere, somehow, I'm going to be in such shape that I'll lick you as you licked me. I'm going to pulp your face till your own niggers won't know you."

Grief was jubilant.

"Now you're talking like a man," he cried. "The only way you'll ever lick me is to become a man. And then, maybe—"

He paused in the hope that the other would catch the suggestion. Aloysius groped for it, and, abruptly, something akin to illumination shone in his eyes.

"And then I won't want to, you mean?"

Grief nodded.

"And that's the curse of it," Aloysius lamented. "I really believe I won't want to. I see the point. But I'm going to go right on and shape myself up just the same."

The warm, sunburn glow in Grief's face seemed to grow warmer. His hand went out.

"Pankburn, I love you right now for that."

Aloysius grasped the hand, and shook his head in sad sincerity.

"Grief," he mourned, "you've got my goat, you've got my proud goat, and you've got it permanently, I'm afraid."

VI

On a sultry tropic day, when the last flicker of the far southeast trade was fading out and the seasonal change for the northwest monsoon was coming on, the *Kittiwake* lifted above the sea-rim the jungle-clad coast of Francis Island. Grief, with compass bearings and binoculars, identified the volcano that marked Redscar, ran past Owen Bay, and lost the last of the breeze at the entrance to Likikili Bay. With the two whaleboats out and towing, and with Carlsen heaving the lead, the *Kittiwake* sluggishly entered a deep and narrow indentation. There were no beaches. The mangroves began at the water's edge, and behind them rose steep jungle, broken here and there by jagged peaks of rock. At the end of a mile, when the white scar on the bluff bore west-southwest, the lead vindicated the "Directory," and the anchor rumbled down in nine fathoms.

For the rest of that day and until the afternoon of the day following they remained on the *Kittiwake* and waited. No canoes appeared. There were no signs of human life. Save for the occasional splash of a fish or the screaming of cockatoos, there seemed no other life. Once, however, a huge butterfly, twelve inches from tip to tip, fluttered high over their mastheads and drifted across to the opposing jungle.

"There's no use in sending a boat in to be cut up," Grief said.

Pankburn was incredulous, and volunteered to go in alone, to swim it if he couldn't borrow the dingey.

"They haven't forgotten the German cruiser," Grief explained. "And I'll wager that bush is alive with men right now. What do you think, Mr. Carlsen?"

That veteran adventurer of the islands was emphatic in his agreement.

In the late afternoon of the second day Grief ordered a whaleboat into the water. He took his place in the bow, a live cigarette in his mouth and a short-fused stick of dynamite in his hand, for he was bent on shooting a mess of fish. Along the thwarts half a dozen Winchesters were placed. Albright, who took the steering-sweep, had a Mauser within reach of hand. They pulled in and along the green wall of vegetation. At times they rested on the oars in the midst of a profound silence.

"Two to one the bush is swarming with them—in quids," Albright whispered.

Pankburn listened a moment longer and took the bet. Five minutes later they sighted a school of mullet. The brown rowers held their oars. Grief touched the short fuse to his cigarette and threw the stick. So short was the fuse that the stick exploded in the instant after it struck the water. And in that same instant the bush exploded into life. There were wild yells of defiance, and black and naked bodies leaped forward like apes through the mangroves.

In the whaleboat every rifle was lifted. Then came the wait. A

hundred blacks, some few armed with ancient Sniders, but the greater portion armed with tomahawks, fire-hardened spears, and bone-
tipped arrows, clustered on the roots that rose out of the bay. No
word was spoken. Each party watched the other across twenty feet
of water. An old, one-eyed black, with a bristly face, rested a Snider
on his hip, the muzzle directed at Albright, who, in turn, covered
him back with the Mauser. A couple of minutes of this tableau endured. The stricken fish rose to the surface or struggled half-stunned
in the clear depths.

"It's all right, boys," Grief said quietly. "Put down your guns and
over the side with you. Mr. Albright, toss the tobacco to that one-
eyed brute."

While the Rapa men dived for the fish, Albright threw a bundle
of trade tobacco ashore. The one-eyed man nodded his head and
writhed his features in an attempt at amiability. Weapons were lowered, bows unbent, and arrows put back in their quivers.

"They know tobacco," Grief announced, as they rowed back
aboard. "We'll have visitors. You'll break out a case of tobacco, Mr.
Albright, and a few trade-knives. There's a canoe now."

Old One-Eye, as befitted a chief and leader, paddled out alone,
facing peril for the rest of the tribe. As Carlsen leaned over the rail to
help the visitor up, he turned his head and remarked casually:

"They've dug up the money, Mr. Grief. The old beggar's loaded
with it."

One-Eye floundered down on deck, grinning appeasingly and fail-
ing to hide the fear he had overcome but which still possessed him.
He was lame of one leg, and this was accounted for by a terrible scar,
inches deep, which ran down the thigh from hip to knee. No clothes
he wore whatever, not even a string, but his nose, perforated in a
dozen places and each perforation the setting for a carved spine of
bone, bristled like a porcupine. Around his neck and hanging down
on his dirty chest was a string of gold sovereigns. His ears were hung
with silver half-crowns, and from the cartilage separating his nos-
trils depended a big English penny, tarnished and green, but unmistakable.

"Hold on, Grief," Pankburn said, with perfectly assumed care-

"Black bodies leaped forward like apes through the mangroves. . . ."
Drawing by C.W. Ashley.

lessness. "You say they know only beads and tobacco. Very well. You follow my lead. They've found the treasure, and we've got to trade them out of it. Get the whole crew aside and lecture them that they are to be interested only in the pennies. Savve? Gold coins must be beneath contempt, and silver coins merely tolerated. Pennies are to be the only desirable things."

Pankburn took charge of the trading. For the penny in One-Eye's nose he gave ten sticks of tobacco. Since each stick cost David Grief a cent, the bargain was manifestly unfair. But for the half-crowns Pankburn gave only one stick each. The string of sovereigns he refused to consider. The more he refused, the more One-Eye insisted on a trade. At last, with an appearance of irritation and anger, and as a palpable concession, Pankburn gave two sticks for the string, which was composed of ten sovereigns.

"I take my hat off to you," Grief said to Pankburn that night at dinner. "The situation is patent. You've reversed the scale of value. They'll figure the pennies as priceless possessions and the sovereigns as beneath price. Result: they'll hang on to the pennies and force us to trade for sovereigns. Pankburn, I drink your health! Boy!—another cup of tea for Mr. Pankburn."

VII

Followed a golden week. From dawn till dark a row of canoes rested on their paddles two hundred feet away. This was the deadline. Rapa sailors, armed with rifles, maintained it. But one canoe at a time was permitted alongside, and but one black at a time was permitted to come over the rail. Here, under the awning, relieving one another in hourly shifts, the four white men carried on the trade. The rate of exchange was that established by Pankburn with One-Eye. Five sovereigns fetched a stick of tobacco; a hundred sovereigns, twenty sticks. Thus, a crafty-eyed cannibal would deposit on the table a thousand dollars in gold, and go back over the rail, hugely satisfied, with forty cents' worth of tobacco in his hand.

"Hope we've got enough tobacco to hold out," Carlsen muttered dubiously, as another case was sawed in half.

"Five sovereigns fetched a stick of tobacco; a hundred sovereigns, twenty sticks. . . . " Drawing by C. W. Ashley.

Albright laughed.

"We've got fifty cases below," he said, "and as I figure it, three cases buy a hundred thousand dollars. There was only a million dollars buried, so thirty cases ought to get it. Though, of course, we've got to allow a margin for the silver and the pennies. That Ecuadoran bunch must have salted down all the coin in sight.

Very few pennies and shillings appeared, though Pankburn continually and anxiously inquired for them. Pennies were the one thing he seemed to desire, and he made his eyes flash covetously whenever one was produced. True to his theory, the savages concluded that the gold, being of slight value, must be disposed of first. A penny, worth fifty times as much as a sovereign, was something to retain and treasure. Doubtless, in their jungle-lairs, the wise old gray-beards put their heads together and agreed to raise the price on pennies when the worthless gold was all worked off. Who could tell? Mayhap the strange white men could be made to give even twenty sticks for a priceless copper.

By the end of the week the trade went slack. There was only the slightest dribble of gold. An occasional penny was reluctantly disposed of for ten sticks, while several thousand dollars of silver came in.

On the morning of the eighth day no trading was done. The gray-beards had matured their plan and were demanding twenty sticks for a penny. One-Eye delivered the new rate of exchange. The white men appeared to take it with great seriousness, for they stood together debating in low voices. Had One-Eye understood English he would have been enlightened.

"We've got just a little over eight hundred thousand, not counting the silver," Grief said. "And that's about all there is. The bush tribes behind have most probably got the other two hundred thousand. Return in three months, and the salt-water crowd will have traded back for it; also they will be out of tobacco by that time."

"It would be a sin to buy pennies," Albright grinned. "It goes against the thrifty grain of my trader's soul."

"There's a whiff of land-breeze stirring," Grief said, looking at Pankburn. "What do you say?"

Pankburn nodded.

"Very well." Grief measured the faintness and irregularity of the wind against his cheek. "Mr. Carlsen, heave short, and get off the gaskets. And stand by with the whaleboats to tow. This breeze is not dependable."

He picked up a part case of tobacco, containing six or seven hundred sticks, put it in One-Eye's hands, and helped that bewildered savage over the rail. As the foresail went up the mast, a wail of consternation arose from the canoes lying along the dead-line. And as the anchor broke out and the *Kittiwake*'s head paid off in the light breeze, old One-Eye, daring the rifles levelled on him, paddled alongside and made frantic signs of his tribe's willingness to trade pennies for ten sticks.

"Boy!—a drinking nut," Pankburn called.

"It's Sydney Heads for you," Grief said. "And then what?"

"I'm coming back with you for that two hundred thousand," Pankburn answered. "In the meantime I'm going to build an island schooner. Also, I'm going to call those guardians of mine before the court to show cause why my father's money should not be turned over to me. Show cause? I'll show them cause why it should."

He swelled his biceps proudly under the thin sleeve, reached for the two black stewards, and put them above his head like a pair of dumbbells.

"Come on! Swing out on that fore-boom-tackle!" Carlsen shouted from aft, where the mainsail was being winged out.

Pankburn dropped the stewards and raced for it, beating a Rapa sailor by two jumps to the hauling part.

THREE

THE DEVILS OF FUATINO

The longest of the David Grief stories, this yarn provides, as one of its participants self-reflectingly notes, "all the romance and adventure he had read and guessed and never lived." In fact, "The Devils of Fuatino" is very like a boys' adventure story, set in a kind of Neverland—an exotic and mysterious island replete with plenty of life-threatening dangers, mountains to climb, forests to penetrate, shark attacks, kidnappings, dynamite explosions, and to top it off, a band of bloodthirsty pirates! Nowhere else is Grief so perfect. He is a model of leadership, a skilled sailor, a raconteur with a rich life's experiences, a loyal friend, a pillar of justice, a recklessly daring mountaineer, a powerful swimmer, a bold shark fighter, a champion shot, and a master of the art of the bluff. To the beleaguered people of Fuatino, Grief is not just a man, he is a kind of messiah sent by Providence to deliver them from their tormentors. It is the natural impulse of the islanders to think of David Grief in their hour of need; the people have been literally praying to their old gods to bring him to them. Grief is quick to assess the situation and immediately sets out to save the day, even though his assessment reveals that the situation is patently hopeless and he can see no clear way of accomplishing his goal. Nevertheless, Grief plunges ahead, stirring up the pot and exploiting the unpredictable results with his customary cleverness and daring. When he finally redeems Fuatino, defeats the pirates, and rescues the queen, Captain Grief requites the islanders' confidence in him and establishes his credentials as a hero.

But most readers interested in a deeper reading will immediately notice that something else is going on in this story. Fuatino is an island paradise imbued with the magic of love. "Fuatino's the island of romantic insanity," remarks Captain Glass. "Everybody's in love with somebody. They live on love. It's in the milk of the cocoanuts, or the air, or the sea. The history of the island for the last ten thousand years is nothing but love affairs. I know. I've talked with the old men." This edenic setting is disrupted by the intrusion of evil in the form of a gang of white villains who fail to see the beauty and wonder of the place, substituting a reign of murder and exploitation for the tender values espoused by the natives. To a certain extent, the tale takes on the features of a representation of the whole colonial adventure as a massive criminal project, with the pirates standing in for all the invading hordes of white men who swept into the South Pacific, destroying the people's cultural, religious, political, and economic lives and bringing with them a system built on violence, racism, disease, and greed.

In contrast to the pirates, Captain David Grief knows the spirit of the island. Though his imperviousness to romantic love makes him immune to the special appeal of the island, Grief's personal connection to the islanders is warmly demonstrated by his relationship with Mauriri, the Goat Man of Fuatino. Mauriri is not the racial Other; he is Grief's double, his alternate identity as a native of the island. As virtual blood brothers each is called by the other's name, so that there are two Davids and two Mauriris. The islander's extraordinary talents as a sure-footed climber and heroic swimmer are somehow passed on to Grief, allowing him to accomplish feats almost without knowing how he has done them. This brotherhood, characterized by identity and equality with a Pacific islander, is strikingly different from the relationships of most whites with the natives.

The mythic and messianic symbolism of the story irresistibly suggests yet another significance to the adventure. Though London provides the reader with exact information on the location of the island, there is nothing there but open sea. "The half-mythical love island of Fuatino" is, in fact, entirely mythical. This story, with its emotional and psychological complexities, its androgynous faun-man, its mountain heights and ocean dives, its double shadow-

*selves, and its erotic appeal, makes it easy to see why Jack London
became so agitated and moved when, five years later, he first read
C. G. Jung's* The Psychology of the Unconscious. *It was the shock
of the familiar: London saw that Jung had systematized the themes
and images that the author had instinctively woven into his work
for years.*

Of his many schooners, ketches and cutters that nosed about among the coral isles of the South Seas, David Grief loved most the *Rattler*—a yacht-like schooner of ninety tons with so swift a pair of heels that she had made herself famous, in the old days, opium-smuggling from San Diego to Puget Sound,[1] raiding the seal-rookeries of Bering Sea, and running arms in the Far East. A stench and an abomination to government officials, she had been the joy of all sailormen, and the pride of the shipwrights who built her. Even now, after forty years of driving, she was still the same old *Rattler,* forereaching in the same marvellous manner that compelled sailors to see in order to believe and that punctuated many an angry discussion with words and blows on the beaches of all the ports from Valparaiso to Manila Bay.

On this night, close-hauled, her big mainsail preposterously flattened down, her luffs pulsing emptily on the lift of each smooth swell, she was sliding an easy four knots through the water on the veriest whisper of a breeze. For an hour David Grief had been leaning on the rail at the lee fore-rigging, gazing overside at the steady phosphorescence of her gait. The faint back-draught from the headsails fanned his cheek and chest with a wine of coolness, and he was in an ecstasy of appreciation of the schooner's qualities.

"Eh!—She's a beauty, Taute, a beauty," he said to the Kanaka lookout, at the same time stroking the teak of the rail with an affectionate hand.

"Ay, skipper," the Kanaka answered in the rich, big-chested tones of Polynesia. "Thirty years I know ships, but never like this. On Raiatea we call her *Fanauao.*"

"The Dayborn," Grief translated the love-phrase. "Who named her so?"

"The joy of all sailormen and the pride of the shipwrights who built her. . . . " Drawing by Anton Otto Fischer.

About to answer, Taute peered ahead with sudden intensity. Grief joined him in the gaze.

"Land," said Taute.

"Yes; Fuatino," Grief agreed, his eyes still fixed on the spot where the star-luminous horizon was gouged by a blot of blackness. "It's all right. I'll tell the captain."

The *Rattler* slid along until the loom of the island could be seen as well as sensed, until the sleepy roar of breakers and the blatting of goats could be heard, until the wind, off the land, was flower-drenched with perfume.

"If it wasn't a crevice, she could run the passage a night like this," Captain Glass remarked regretfully, as he watched the wheel lashed hard down by the steersman.

The *Rattler*, run off shore a mile, had been hove to to wait until daylight ere she attempted the perilous entrance to Fuatino. It was a perfect tropic night, with no hint of rain or squall. For'ard, wherever their tasks left them, the Raiatea sailors sank down to sleep on deck. Aft, the captain and mate and Grief spread their beds with similar languid unconcern. They lay on their blankets, smoking and murmuring sleepy conjectures about Mataara, the Queen of Fuatino, and about the love affair between her daughter, Naumoo, and Motuaro.

"They're certainly a romantic lot," Brown, the mate, said. "As romantic as we whites."

"As romantic as Pilsach," Grief laughed, "and that is going some. How long ago was it, Captain, that he jumped you?"

"Eleven years," Captain Glass grunted resentfully.

"Tell me about it," Brown pleaded. "They say he's never left Fuatino since. Is that right?"

"Right O," the captain rumbled. "He's in love with his wife—the little hussy! Stole him from me, and as good a sailorman as the trade has ever seen—if he is a Dutchman."

"German," Grief corrected.

"It's all the same," was the retort. "The sea was robbed of a good man that night he went ashore and Notutu took one look at him. I reckon they looked good to each other. Before you could say skat, she'd put a wreath of some kind of white flowers on his head, and in five minutes they were off down the beach, like a couple of kids, holding hands and laughing. I hope he's blown that big coral patch out of the channel. I always start a sheet or two of copper warping past."

"Go on with the story," Brown urged.,

"That's all. He was finished right there. Got married that night. Never came on board again. I looked him up next day. Found him in a straw house in the bush, barelegged, a white savage, all mixed up with flowers and things and playing a guitar. Looked like a bally ass. Told me to send his things ashore. I told him I'd see him damned first. And that's all. You'll see her to-morrow. They've got three kiddies now—wonderful little rascals. I've a phonograph down below for him, and about a million records."

"And then you made him trader?" the mate inquired of Grief.

"What else could I do? Fuatino is a love island, and Pilsach is a lover. He knows the native, too—one of the best traders I've got, or ever had. He's responsible. You'll see him to-morrow."

"Look here, young man," Captain Glass rumbled threateningly at his mate. "Are you romantic? Because if you are, on board you stay. Fuatino's the island of romantic insanity. Everybody's in love with somebody. They live on love. It's in the milk of the cocoanuts, or the air, or the sea. The history of the island for the last ten thousand years is nothing but love affairs. I know. I've talked with the old men. And if I catch you starting down the beach hand in hand—"

His sudden cessation caused both the other men to look at him. They followed his gaze, which passed across them to the main rigging, and saw what he saw, a brown hand and arm, muscular and wet, being joined from overside by a second brown hand and arm. A head followed, thatched with long elfin locks, and then a face, with roguish black eyes, lined with the marks of wildwood's laughter.

"My God!" Brown breathed. "It's a faun—a sea-faun."

"It's the Goat Man," said Glass.

"It is Mauriri," said Grief. "He is my own blood brother by sacred plight of native custom. His name is mine, and mine is his."

Broad brown shoulders and a magnificent chest rose above the rail, and, with what seemed effortless ease, the whole grand body followed over the rail and noiselessly trod the deck. Brown, who might have been other things than the mate of an island schooner, was enchanted. All that he had ever gleaned from the books proclaimed indubitably the faun-likeness of this visitant of the deep. "But a sad faun," was the young man's judgment, as the golden-brown woods god strode forward to where David Grief sat up with outstretched hand.

"David," said David Grief.

"Mauriri, Big Brother," said Mauriri.

And thereafter, in the custom of men who have pledged blood brotherhood, each called the other, not by the other's name, but by his own. Also, they talked in the Polynesian tongue of Fuatino, and Brown could only sit and guess.

"A long swim to say *talofa,*" Grief said, as the other sat and streamed water on the deck.

"Many days and nights have I watched for your coming, Big Brother," Mauriri replied. "I have sat on the Big Rock, where the dynamite is kept, of which I have been made keeper. I saw you come up to the entrance and run back into darkness. I knew you waited till morning, and I followed. Great trouble has come upon us. Mataara has cried these many days for your coming. She is an old woman, and Motauri is dead, and she is sad."

"Did he marry Naumoo?" Grief asked, after he had shaken his head and sighed by the custom.

"Yes. In the end they ran to live with the goats, till Mataara forgave, when they returned to live with her in the Big House. But he is now dead, and Naumoo soon will die. Great is our trouble, Big Brother. Tori is dead, and Tati-Tori, and Petoo, and Nari, and Pilsach, and others."

"Pilsach, too!" Grief exclaimed. "Has there been a sickness?"

"There has been much killing. Listen, Big Brother. Three weeks ago a strange schooner came. From the Big Rock I saw her topsails above the sea. She towed in with her boats, but they did not warp by the big patch, and she pounded many times. She is now on the beach, where they are strengthening the broken timbers. There are eight white men on board. They have women from some island far to the east. The women talk a language in many ways like ours, only different. But we can understand. They say they were stolen by the men on the schooner. We do not know, but they sing and dance and are happy."

"And the men?" Grief interrupted.

"They talk French. I know, for there was a mate on your schooner who talked French long ago. There are two chief men, and they do not look like the others. They have blue eyes like you, and they are devils. One is a bigger devil than the other. The other six are also devils. They do not pay us for our yams, and taro, and breadfruit. They take everything from us, and if we complain they kill us. Thus was killed Tori, and Tati-Tori, and Petoo, and others. We cannot fight, for we have no guns—only two or three old guns.

"They ill-treat our women. Thus was killed Motuaro, who made defence of Naumoo, whom they have now taken on board their schooner. It was because of this that Pilsach was killed. Him the chief of the two chief men, the Big Devil, shot once in his whaleboat, and twice when he tried to crawl up the sand of the beach. Pilsach was a brave man, and Notutu now sits in the house and cries without end. Many of the people are afraid, and have run to live with the goats. But there is not food for all in the high mountains. And the men will not go out and fish, and they work no more in the gardens because of the devils who take all they have. And we are ready to fight.

"Big Brother, we need guns, and much ammunition. I sent word before I swam out to you, and the men are waiting. The strange white men do not know you are come. Give me a boat, and the guns, and I will go back before the sun. And when you come to-morrow we will be ready for the word from you to kill the strange white men. They must be killed. Big Brother, you have ever been of the blood with us, and the men and women have prayed to many gods for your coming. And you are come."

"I will go in the boat with you," Grief said.

"No, Big Brother," was Mauriri's reply. "You must be with the schooner. The strange white men will fear the schooner, not us. We will have the guns, and they will not know. It is only when they see your schooner come that they will be alarmed. Send the young man there with the boat."

So it was that Brown, thrilling with all the romance and adventure he had read and guessed and never lived, took his place in the sternsheets of a whaleboat, loaded with rifles and cartridges, rowed by four Raiatea sailors, steered by a golden-brown, sea-swimming faun, and directed through the warm tropic darkness toward the half-mythical love island of Fuatino, which had been invaded by twentieth century pirates.

II

If a line be drawn between Jaluit, in the Marshall Group, and Bougainville, in the Solomons, and if this line be bisected at two degrees south of the equator by a line drawn from Ukuor, in the Carolines, the high island of Fuatino will be raised in that sun-washed stretch of lonely sea.[2] Inhabited by a stock kindred to the Hawaiian, the Samoan, the Tahitian, and the Maori, Fuatino becomes the apex of the wedge driven by Polynesia far to the west and in between Melanesia and Micronesia. And it was Fuatino that David Grief raised next morning, two miles to the east and in direct line with the rising sun. The same whisper of a breeze held, and the *Rattler* slid through the smooth sea at a rate that would have been eminently proper for an island schooner had the breeze been thrice as strong.

Fuatino was nothing else than an ancient crater, thrust upward from the sea-bottom by some primordial cataclysm. The western portion, broken and crumbled to sea level, was the entrance to the crater itself, which constituted the harbour. Thus, Fuatino was like a rugged horseshoe, the heel pointing to the west. And into the opening at the heel the *Rattler* steered. Captain Glass, binoculars in hand and peering at the chart made by himself, which was spread on top the cabin, straightened up with an expression on his face that was half alarm, half resignation.

"It's coming," he said. "Fever.[3] It wasn't due till to-morrow. It always hits me hard, Mr. Grief. In five minutes I'll be off my head. You'll have to con the schooner in. Boy! Get my bunk ready! Plenty of blankets! Fill that hot-water bottle! It's so calm, Mr. Grief, that I think you can pass the big patch without warping. Take the leading wind and shoot her. She's the only craft in the South Pacific that can do it, and I know you know the trick. You can scrape the Big Rock by just watching out for the main boom."

He had talked rapidly, almost like a drunken man, as his reeling brain battled with the rising shock of the malarial stroke. When he stumbled toward the companionway, his face was purpling and mottling as if attacked by some monstrous inflammation or decay. His eyes were setting in a glassy bulge, his hands shaking, his teeth clicking in the spasms of chill.

"Two hours to get the sweat," he chattered with a ghastly grin. "And a couple more and I'll be all right. I know the damned thing to the last minute it runs its course. Y-y-you t-t-take ch-ch-ch-ch—"

His voice faded away in a weak stutter as he collapsed down into the cabin and his employer took charge. The *Rattler* was just entering the passage. The heels of the horseshoe island were two huge mountains of rock a thousand feet high, each almost broken off from the mainland and connected with it by a low and narrow peninsula. Between the heels was a half-mile stretch, all but blocked by a reef of coral extending across from the south heel. The passage, which Captain Glass had called a crevice, twisted into this reef, curved directly to the north heel, and ran along the base of the perpendicular rock. At this point, with the main-boom almost grazing the rock on the port side, Grief, peering down on the starboard side, could see bottom less than two fathoms beneath and shoaling steeply. With a whaleboat towing for steerage and as a precaution against back-draughts from the cliff, and taking advantage of a fan of breeze, he shook the *Rattler* full into it and glided by the big coral patch without warping. As it was, he just scraped, but so softly as not to start the copper.

The harbour of Fuatino opened before him. It was a circular sheet of water, five miles in diameter, rimmed with white coral beaches,

from which the verdure-clad slopes rose swiftly to the frowning crater walls. The crests of the walls were saw-toothed, volcanic peaks,
capped and halo'd with captive trade-wind clouds. Every nook and
crevice of the disintegrating lava gave foothold to creeping, climbing
vines and trees—a green foam of vegetation. Thin streams of water,
that were mere films of mist, swayed and undulated downward in
sheer descents of hundreds of feet. And to complete the magic of the
place, the warm, moist air was heavy with the perfume of the yel-
low-blossomed *cassi.*

Fanning along against light, vagrant airs, the *Rattler* worked in.
Calling the whaleboat on board, Grief searched out the shore with
his binoculars. There was no life. In the hot blaze of tropic sun the
place slept. There was no sign of welcome. Up the beach, on the
north shore, where the fringe of cocoanut palms concealed the village, he could see the black bows of the canoes in the canoe-houses.
On the beach, on even keel, rested the strange schooner. Nothing
moved on board of her or around her. Not until the beach lay fifty
yards away did Grief let go the anchor in forty fathoms.[4] Out in the
middle, long years before, he had sounded three hundred fathoms
without reaching bottom, which was to be expected of a healthy
crater-pit like Fuatino. As the chain roared and surged through the
hawse-pipe he noticed a number of native women, lusciously large
as only those of Polynesia are, in flowing *ahu's,* flower-crowned,
stream out on the deck of the schooner on the beach. Also, and what
they did not see, he saw from the galley the squat figure of a man
steal for'ard, drop to the sand, and dive into the green screen of
bush.

While the sails were furled and gasketed, awnings stretched, and
sheets and tackles coiled harbour fashion, David Grief paced the
deck and looked vainly for a flutter of life elsewhere than on the
strange schooner. Once, beyond any doubt, he heard the distant crack
of a rifle in the direction of the Big Rock. There were no further
shots, and he thought of it as some hunter shooting a wild goat.

At the end of another hour Captain Glass, under a mountain of
blankets, had ceased shivering and was in the inferno of a profound
sweat.

"I'll be all right in half an hour," he said weakly.

"Very well," Grief answered. "The place is dead, and I'm going ashore to see Mataara and find out the situation."

"It's a tough bunch; keep your eyes open," the captain warned him. "If you're not back in an hour, send word off."

Grief took the steering-sweep, and four of his Raiatea men bent to the oars. As they landed on the beach he looked curiously at the women under the schooner's awning. He waved his hand tentatively, and they, after giggling, waved back.

"*Talofa!*" he called.

They understood the greeting, but replied, "*Iorana,*" and he knew they came from the Society Group.[5]

"Huahine," one of his sailors unhesitatingly named their island. Grief asked them whence they came, and with giggles and laughter they replied, "Huahine."

"It looks like old Dupuy's schooner," Grief said, in Tahitian, speaking in a low voice. "Don't look too hard. What do you think, eh? Isn't it the *Valetta?*"

As the men climbed out and lifted the whaleboat slightly up the beach they stole careless glances at the vessel.

"It is the *Valetta,*" Taute said. "She carried her topmast away seven years ago. At Papeete they rigged a new one. It was ten feet shorter. That is the one."

"Go over and talk with the women, you boys. You can almost see Huahine from Raiatea, and you'll be sure to know some of them. Find out all you can. And if any of the white men show up, don't start a row."

An army of hermit crabs scuttled and rustled away before him as he advanced up the beach, but under the palms no pigs rooted and grunted. The cocoanuts lay where they had fallen, and at the copra-sheds there were no signs of curing. Industry and tidiness had vanished. Grass house after grass house he found deserted. Once he came upon an old man, blind, toothless, prodigiously wrinkled, who sat in the shade and babbled with fear when he spoke to him. It was as if the place had been struck with the plague, was Grief's thought, as he finally approached the Big House. All was desolation and dis-

array. There were no flower-crowned men and maidens, no brown
babies rolling in the shade of the avocado trees. In the doorway,
crouched and rocking back and forth, sat Mataara, the old queen. She
wept afresh at sight of him, divided between the tale of her woe and
regret that no follower was left to dispense to him her hospitality.

"And so they have taken Naumoo," she finished. "Motauri is
dead. My people have fled and are starving with the goats. And there
is no one to open for you even a drinking cocoanut. O Brother, your
white brothers be devils."

"They are no brothers of mine, Mataara," Grief consoled. "They
are robbers and pigs, and I shall clean the island of them—"

He broke off to whirl half around, his hand flashing to his waist
and back again, the big Colt's levelled at the figure of a man, bent
double, that rushed at him from out of the trees. He did not pull the
trigger, nor did the man pause till he had flung himself headlong at
Grief's feet and begun to pour forth a stream of uncouth and awful
noises. He recognized the creature as the one he had seen steal from
the *Valetta* and dive into the bush; but not until he raised him up and
watched the contortions of the hare-lipped mouth could he understand what he uttered.

"Save me, master, save me!" the man yammered, in English,
though he was unmistakably a South Sea native. "I know you! Save
me!"

And thereat he broke into a wild outpour of incoherence that did
not cease until Grief seized him by the shoulders and shook him into
silence.

"I know you," Grief said. "You were cook in the French Hotel at
Papeete two years ago. Everybody called you 'Hare-Lip.'"

The man nodded violently.

"I am now cook of the *Valetta*," he spat and spluttered, his mouth
writhing in a fearful struggle with its defect. "I know you. I saw you
at the hotel. I saw you at Lavina's. I saw you on the *Kittiwake*. I saw
you at the *Mariposa* wharf. You are Captain Grief, and you will save
me. Those men are devils. They killed Captain Dupuy. Me they made
kill half the crew. Two they shot from the cross-trees. The rest they
shot in the water. I knew them all. They stole the girls from Hua-

hine. They added to their strength with jail-men from Noumea. They robbed the traders in the New Hebrides. They killed the trader at Vanikori, and stole two women there.[6] They—"

But Grief no longer heard. Through the trees, from the direction of the harbour, came a rattle of rifles, and he started on the run for the beach. Pirates from Tahiti and convicts from New Caledonia![7] A pretty bunch of desperadoes that even now was attacking his schooner. Hare-Lip followed, still spluttering and spitting his tale of the white devils' doings.

The rifle-firing ceased as abruptly as it had begun, but Grief ran on, perplexed by ominous conjectures, until, in a turn of the path, he encountered Mauriri running toward him from the beach.

"Big Brother," the Goat Man panted, "I was too late. They have taken your schooner. Come! For now they will seek for you."

He started back up the path away from the beach.

"Where is Brown?" Grief demanded.

"On the Big Rock. I will tell you afterward. Come now!"

"But my men in the whaleboat?"

Mauriri was in an agony of apprehension.

"They are with the women on the strange schooner. They will not be killed. I tell you true. The devils want sailors. But you they will kill. Listen!" From the water, in a cracked tenor voice, came a French hunting song. "They are landing on the beach. They have taken your schooner—that I saw. Come!"

III

Careless of his own life and skin, nevertheless David Grief was possessed of no false hardihood. He knew when to fight and when to run, and that this was the time for running he had no doubt. Up the path, past the old men sitting in the shade, past Mataara crouched in the doorway of the Big House, he followed at the heels of Mauriri. At his own heels, dog-like, plodded Hare-Lip. From behind came the cries of the hunters, but the pace Mauriri led them was heartbreaking. The broad path narrowed, swung to the right, and pitched upward. The last grass house was left, and through high thickets of *cassi*[8] and swarms of great golden wasps the way rose steeply until it became a goat-track. Pointing upward to a bare shoulder of volcanic rock, Mauriri indicated the trail across its face.

"Past that we are safe, Big Brother," he said. "The white devils never dare it, for there are rocks we roll down on their heads, and there is no other path. Always do they stop here and shoot when we cross the rock. Come!"

A quarter of an hour later they paused where the trail went naked on the face of the rock.

"Wait, and when you come, come quickly," Mauriri cautioned.

He sprang into the blaze of sunlight, and from below several rifles pumped rapidly. Bullets smacked about him, and puffs of stone-dust flew out, but he won safely across. Grief followed, and so near did one bullet come that the dust of its impact stung his cheek. Nor was Hare-Lip struck, though he essayed the passage more slowly.

For the rest of the day, on the greater heights, they lay in a lava glen where terraced taro and *papaia* grew. And here Grief made his plans and learned the fulness of the situation.

"It was ill luck," Mauriri said. "Of all nights this one night was selected by the white devils to go fishing. It was dark as we came through the passage. They were in boats and canoes. Always do they have their rifles with them. One Raiatea man they shot. Brown was very brave. We tried to get by to the top of the bay, but they headed us off, and we were driven in between the Big Rock and the village. We saved the guns and all the ammunition, but they got the boat. Thus they learned of your coming. Brown is now on this side of the Big Rock with the guns and the ammunition."

"But why didn't he go over the top of the Big Rock and give me warning as I came in from the sea?" Grief criticised.

"They knew not the way. Only the goats and I know the way. And this I forgot, for I crept through the bush to gain the water and swim to you. But the devils were in the bush shooting at Brown and the Raiatea men; and me they hunted till daylight, and through the morning they hunted me there in the low-lying land. Then you came in your schooner, and they watched till you went ashore, and I got away through the bush, but you were already ashore."

"You fired that shot?"

"Yes; to warn you. But they were wise and would not shoot back, and it was my last cartridge."

"Now you, Hare-Lip?" Grief said to the *Valetta*'s cook.

His tale was long and painfully detailed. For a year he had been sailing out of Tahiti and through the Paumotus on the *Valetta*.[9] Old Dupuy was owner and captain. On his last cruise he had shipped two strangers in Tahiti as mate and supercargo. Also, another stranger he carried to be his agent on Fanriki. Raoul Van Asveld and Carl Lepsius were the names of the mate and supercargo.

"They are brothers, I know, for I have heard them talk in the dark, on deck, when they thought no one listened," Hare-Lip explained.

The *Valetta* cruised through the Low Islands, picking up shell and pearls at Dupuy's stations. Frans Amundson, the third stranger, relieved Pierre Gollard at Fanriki. Pierre Gollard came on board to go back to Tahiti. The natives of Fanriki said he had a quart of pearls to turn over to Dupuy. The first night out from Fanriki there was shooting in the cabin. Then the bodies of Dupuy and Pierre Gollard were thrown overboard. The Tahitian sailors fled to the forecastle. For two days, with nothing to eat and the Valetta hove to, they remained below. Then Raoul Van Asveld put poison in the meal he made Hare-Lip cook and carry for'ard. Half the sailors died.

"He had a rifle pointed at me, master; what could I do?" Hare-Lip whimpered. "Of the rest, two went up the rigging and were shot. Fanriki was ten miles away. The others went overboard to swim. They were shot as they swam. I, only, lived, and the two devils; for me they wanted to cook for them. That day, with the breeze, they went back to Fanriki and took on Frans Amundson, for he was one of them."

Then followed Hare-Lip's nightmare experiences as the schooner wandered on the long reaches to the westward. He was the one living witness and knew they would have killed him had he not been the cook. At Noumea five convicts had joined them. Hare-Lip was never permitted ashore at any of the islands, and Grief was the first outsider to whom he had spoken.

"And now they will kill me," Hare-Lip spluttered, "for they will
know I have told you. Yet am I not all a coward, and I will stay with
you, master, and die with you."

The Goat Man shook his head and stood up.

"Lie here and rest," he said to Grief. "It will be a long swim to-
night. As for this cookman, I will take him now to the higher places
where my brothers live with the goats."

IV

"It is well that you swim as a man should, Big Brother," Mauriri
whispered.

From the lava glen they had descended to the head of the bay and
taken to the water. They swam softly, without splash, Mauriri in the
lead. The black walls of the crater rose about them till it seemed they
swam on the bottom of a great bowl. Above was the sky of faintly
luminous star-dust. Ahead they could see the light which marked the
Rattler, and from her deck, softened by distance, came a gospel hymn
played on the phonograph intended for Pilsach.

The two swimmers bore to the left, away from the captured
schooner. Laughter and song followed on board after the hymn, then
the phonograph started again. Grief grinned to himself at the appo-
siteness of it as "Lead, Kindly Light," floated out over the dark water.

"We must take the passage and land on the Big Rock," Mauriri
whispered. "The devils are holding the low land. Listen!"

Half a dozen rifle shots, at irregular intervals, attested that Brown
still held the Rock and that the pirates had invested the narrow peninsula.

At the end of another hour they swam under the frowning loom
of the Big Rock. Mauriri, feeling his way, led the landing in a crevice,
up which for a hundred feet they climbed to a narrow ledge.

"Stay here," said Mauriri. "I go to Brown. In the morning I shall
return."

"I will go with you, Brother," Grief said.

Mauriri laughed in the darkness.

"Even you, Big Brother, cannot do this thing. I am the Goat Man, and I only, of all Fuatino, can go over the Big Rock in the night. Furthermore, it will be the first time that even I have done it. Put out your hand. You feel it? That is where Pilsach's dynamite is kept. Lie close beside the wall and you may sleep without falling. I go now."

And high above the sounding surf, on a narrow shelf beside a ton of dynamite, David Grief planned his campaign, then rested his cheek on his arm and slept.

In the morning, when Mauriri led him over the summit of the Big Rock, David Grief understood why he could not have done it in the night. Despite the accustomed nerve of a sailor for height and precarious clinging, he marvelled that he was able to do it in the broad light of day. There were places, always under minute direction of Mauriri, that he leaned forward, falling, across hundred-foot-deep crevices, until his outstretched hands struck a grip on the opposing wall and his legs could then be drawn across after. Once, there was a ten-foot leap, above half a thousand feet of yawning emptiness and down a fathom's length to a meagre foothold. And he, despite his cool head, lost it another time on a shelf, a scant twelve inches wide, where all hand-holds seemed to fail him. And Mauriri, seeing him sway, swung his own body far out and over the gulf and passed him, at the same time striking him sharply on the back to brace his reeling brain. Then it was, and forever after, that he fully knew why Mauriri had been named the Goat Man.

V

The defence of the Big Rock had its good points and its defects. Impregnable to assault, two men could hold it against ten thousand. Also, it guarded the passage to open sea. The two schooners, Raoul Van Asveld, and his cutthroat following were bottled up. Grief, with the ton of dynamite, which he had removed higher up the rock, was master. This he demonstrated, one morning, when the schooners attempted to put to sea. The *Valetta* led, the whaleboat towing her manned by captured Fuatino men. Grief and the Goat Man peered straight down from a safe rock-shelter, three hundred feet above.

Their rifles were beside them, also a glowing fire-stick and a big bundle of dynamite sticks with fuses and decanators attached. As the whaleboat came beneath, Mauriri shook his head.

"They are our brothers. We cannot shoot."

For'ard, on the *Valetta*, were several of Grief's own Raiatea sailors. Aft stood another at the wheel. The pirates were below, or on the other schooner, with the exception of one who stood, rifle in hand, amidships. For protection he held Naumoo, the Queen's daughter, close to him.

"That is the chief devil," Mauriri whispered, "and his eyes are blue like yours. He is a terrible man. See! He holds Naumoo that we may not shoot him."

A light air and a slight tide were making into the passage, and the schooner's progress was slow.

"Do you speak English?" Grief called down.

The man startled, half lifted his rifle to the perpendicular, and looked up. There was something quick and catlike in his movements, and in his burned blond face a fighting eagerness. It was the face of a killer.

"Yes," he answered. "What do you want?"

"Turn back, or I'll blow your schooner up," Grief warned. He blew on the fire-stick and whispered, "Tell Naumoo to break away from him and run aft."

From the *Rattler*, close astern, rifles cracked, and bullets spatted against the rock. Van Asveld laughed defiantly, and Mauriri called down in the native tongue to the woman. When directly beneath, Grief, watching, saw her jerk away from the man. On the instant Grief touched the fire-stick to the match-head in the split end of the short fuse, sprang into view on the face of the rock, and dropped the dynamite. Van Asveld had managed to catch the girl and was struggling with her. The Goat Man held a rifle on him and waited a chance. The dynamite struck the deck in a compact package, bounded, and rolled into the port scupper. Van Asveld saw it and hesitated, then he and the girl ran aft for their lives. The Goat Man fired, but splintered the corner of the galley. The spattering of bullets from the *Rattler* increased, and the two on the rock crouched low for shelter and

"Turn back, or I'll blow your schooner up!"
Drawing by Anton Otto Fischer.

waited. Mauriri tried to see what was happening below, but Grief held him back.

"The fuse was too long," he said. "I'll know better next time."

It was half a minute before the explosion came. What happened afterward, for some little time, they could not tell, for the *Rattler's* marksmen had got the range and were maintaining a steady fire. Once, fanned by a couple of bullets, Grief risked a peep. The *Valetta,* her port deck and rail torn away, was listing and sinking as she drifted back into the harbour. Climbing on board the *Rattler* were the men and the Huahine women who had been hidden in the *Valetta's* cabin and who had swum for it under the protecting fire. The Fuatino men who had been towing in the whaleboat had cast off the line, dashed back through the passage, and were rowing wildly for the south shore.

From the shore of the peninsula the discharges of four rifles announced that Brown and his men had worked through the jungle to the beach and were taking a hand. The bullets ceased coming, and Grief and Mauriri joined in with their rifles. But they could do no damage, for the men of the *Rattler* were firing from the shelter of the deck-houses, while the wind and tide carried the schooner farther in. There was no sign of the *Valetta,* which had sunk in the deep water of the crater.

Two things Raoul Van Asveld did that showed his keenness and coolness and that elicited Grief's admiration. Under the *Rattler's* rifle fire Raoul compelled the fleeing Fuatino men to come in and surrender. And at the same time, dispatching half his cutthroats in the *Rattler's* boat, he threw them ashore and across the peninsula, preventing Brown from getting away to the main part of the island. And for the rest of the morning the intermittent shooting told to Grief how Brown was being driven in to the other side of the Big Rock. The situation was unchanged, with the exception of the loss of the *Valetta.*

VI

The defects of the position on the Big Rock were vital. There was neither food nor water. For several nights, accompanied by one of the Raiatea men, Mauriri swam to the head of the bay for supplies.

Then came the night when lights flared on the water and shots were fired. After that the water-side of the Big Rock was invested as well.

"It's a funny situation," Brown remarked, who was getting all the adventure he had been led to believe resided in the South Seas. "We've got hold and can't let go, and Raoul has hold and can't let go. He can't get away, and we're liable to starve to death holding him."

"If the rain came, the rock-basins would fill," said Mauriri. It was their first twenty-four hours without water. "Big Brother, to-night you and I will get water. It is the work of strong men."

That night, with cocoanut calabashes, each of quart capacity and tightly stoppered, he led Grief down to the water from the peninsula side of the Big Rock. They swam out not more than a hundred feet. Beyond, they could hear the occasional click of an oar or the knock of a paddle against a canoe, and sometimes they saw the flare of matches as the men in the guarding boats lighted cigarettes or pipes.

"Wait here," whispered Mauriri, "and hold the calabashes."

Turning over, he swam down. Grief, face downward, watched his phosphorescent track glimmer, and dim, and vanish. A long minute afterward Mauriri broke surface noiselessly at Grief's side.

"Here! Drink!"

The calabash was full, and Grief drank sweet fresh water which had come up from the depths of the salt.

"It flows out from the land," said Mauriri.

"On the bottom?"

"No. The bottom is as far below as the mountains are above. Fifty feet down it flows. Swim down until you feel its coolness."

Several times filling and emptying his lungs in diver fashion, Grief turned over and went down through the water. Salt it was to his lips, and warm to his flesh; but at last, deep down, it perceptibly chilled and tasted brackish. Then, suddenly, his body entered the cold, sub-terranean stream. He removed the small stopper from the calabash, and, as the sweet water gurgled into it, he saw the phosphorescent glimmer of a big fish, like a sea ghost, drift sluggishly by.

Thereafter, holding the growing weight of the calabashes, he re-mained on the surface, while Mauriri took them down, one by one, and filled them.

"There are sharks," Grief said, as they swam back to shore.

"Pooh!" was the answer. "They are fish sharks. We of Fuatino are brothers to the fish sharks."

"But the tiger sharks? I have seen them here."

"When they come, Big Brother, we will have no more water to drink—unless it rains."

VII

A week later Mauriri and a Raiatea man swam back with empty calabashes. The tiger sharks had arrived in the harbour. The next day they thirsted on the Big Rock.

"We must take our chance," said Grief. "To-night I shall go after water with Mautau. To-morrow night, Brother, you will go with Tehaa."

Three quarts only did Grief get, when the tiger sharks appeared and drove them in. There were six of them on the Rock, and a pint a day, in the sweltering heat of the mid-tropics, is not sufficient moisture for a man's body. The next night Mauriri and Tehaa returned with no water. And the day following Brown learned the full connotation of thirst, when the lips crack to bleeding, the mouth is coated with granular slime, and the swollen tongue finds the mouth too small for residence.

Grief swam out in the darkness with Mautau. Turn by turn, they went down through the salt, to the cool sweet stream, drinking their fill while the calabashes were filling. It was Mautau's turn to descend with the last calabash, and Grief, peering down from the surface, saw the glimmer of sea-ghosts and all the phosphorescent display of the struggle. He swam back alone, but without relinquishing the precious burden of full calabashes.

Of food they had little. Nothing grew on the Rock, and its sides, covered with shellfish at sea level where the surf thundered in, were too precipitous for access. Here and there, where crevices permitted, a few rank shellfish and sea urchins were gleaned. Sometimes frigate birds and other sea birds were snared. Once, with a piece of frigate bird, they succeeded in hooking a shark. After that, with jealously guarded shark-meat for bait, they managed on occasion to catch more sharks.

But water remained their direst need. Mauriri prayed to the Goat God for rain. Taute prayed to the Missionary God, and his two fellow islanders, backsliding, invoked the deities of their old heathen days. Grief grinned and considered. But Brown, wild-eyed, with protruding blackened tongue, cursed. Especially he cursed the phonograph that in the cool twilights ground out gospel hymns from the deck of the *Rattler*. One hymn in particular, "Beyond the Smiling and the Weeping," drove him to madness. It seemed a favourite on board the schooner, for it was played most of all. Brown, hungry and thirsty, half out of his head from weakness and suffering, could lie among the rocks with equanimity and listen to the tinkling of ukuléles and guitars, and the hulas and himines of the Huahine women. But when the voices of the Trinity Choir floated over the water he was beside himself. One evening the cracked tenor took up the song with the machine:

> "Beyond the smiling and the weeping,
>   I shall be soon.
> Beyond the waking and the sleeping,
> Beyond the sowing and the reaping,
>   I shall be soon,
>   I shall be soon."

Then it was that Brown rose up. Again and again, blindly, he emptied his rifle at the schooner. Laughter floated up from the men and women, and from the peninsula came a splattering of return bullets; but the cracked tenor sang on, and Brown continued to fire, until the hymn was played out.

It was that night that Grief and Mauriri came back with but one calabash of water. A patch of skin six inches long was missing from Grief's shoulder in token of the scrape of the sandpaper hide of a shark whose dash he had eluded.

VIII

In the early morning of another day, before the sun-blaze had gained its full strength, came an offer of a parley from Raoul Van Asveld.

Brown brought the word in from the outpost among the rocks a hundred yards away. Grief was squatted over a small fire, broiling a strip of shark-flesh. The last twenty-four hours had been lucky. Seaweed and sea urchins had been gathered. Tehaa had caught a shark, and Mauriri had captured a fair-sized octopus at the base of the crevice where the dynamite was stored. Then, too, in the darkness they had made two successful swims for water before the tiger sharks had nosed them out.

"Said he'd like to come in and talk with you," Brown said. "But I know what the brute is after. Wants to see how near starved to death we are."

"Bring him in," Grief said.

"And then we will kill him," the Goat Man cried joyously.

Grief shook his head.

"But he is a killer of men, Big Brother, a beast and a devil," the Goat Man protested.

"He must not be killed, Brother. It is our way not to break our word."

"It is a foolish way."

"Still it is our way," Grief answered gravely, turning the strip of shark-meat over on the coals and noting the hungry sniff and look of Tehaa. "Don't do that, Tehaa, when the Big Devil comes. Look as if you and hunger were strangers. Here, cook those sea urchins, you, and you, Big Brother, cook the squid. We will have the Big Devil to feast with us. Spare nothing. Cook all."

And, still broiling meat, Grief arose as Raoul Van Asveld, followed by a large Irish terrier, strode into camp. Raoul did not make the mistake of holding out his hand.

"Hello!" he said. "I've heard of you."

"I wish I'd never heard of you," Grief answered.

"Same here," was the response. "At first, before I knew who it was, I thought I had to deal with an ordinary trading captain. That's why you've got me bottled up."

"And I am ashamed to say that I underrated you," Grief smiled. "I took you for a thieving beachcomber, and not for a really intelligent pirate and murderer. Hence, the loss of my schooner. Honours are even, I fancy, on that score."

Raoul flushed angrily under his sunburn, but he contained himself. His eyes roved over the supply of food and the full water-calabashes, though he concealed the incredulous surprise he felt. His was a tall, slender, well-knit figure, and Grief, studying him, estimated his character from his face. The eyes were keen and strong, but a bit too close together—not pinched, however, but just a trifle near to balance the broad forehead, the strong chin and jaw, and the cheekbones wide apart. Strength! His face was filled with it, and yet Grief sensed in it the intangible something the man lacked.

"We are both strong men," Raoul said, with a bow. "We might have been fighting for empires a hundred years ago."

It was Grief's turn to bow.

"As it is, we are squalidly scrapping over the enforcement of the colonial laws of those empires whose destinies we might possibly have determined a hundred years ago."

"It all comes to dust," Raoul remarked sententiously, sitting down. "Go ahead with your meal. Don't let me interrupt."

"Won't you join us?" was Grief's invitation.

The other looked at him with sharp steadiness, then accepted.

"I'm sticky with sweat," he said. "Can I wash?"

Grief nodded and ordered Mauriri to bring a calabash. Raoul looked into the Goat Man's eyes, but saw nothing save languid uninterest as the precious quart of water was wasted on the ground.

"The dog is thirsty," Raoul said.

Grief nodded, and another calabash was presented to the animal.

Again Raoul searched the eyes of the natives and learned nothing.

"Sorry we have no coffee," Grief apologized. "You'll have to drink plain water. A calabash, Tehaa. Try some of this shark. There is squid to follow, and sea urchins and a seaweed salad. I'm sorry we haven't any frigate bird. The boys were lazy yesterday, and did not try to catch any."

With an appetite that would not have stopped at wire nails dipped in lard, Grief ate perfunctorily, and tossed the scraps to the dog.

"I'm afraid I haven't got down to the primitive diet yet," he sighed, as he sat back. "The tinned goods on the *Rattler*, now I could make a hearty meal off of them, but this muck—" He took a half-pound

"We might have been fighting for empires a hundred years ago. . . ."
Drawing by Anton Otto Fischer.

strip of broiled shark and flung it to the dog. "I suppose I'll come to it if you don't surrender pretty soon."

Raoul laughed unpleasantly.

"I came to offer terms," he said pointedly.

Grief shook his head.

"There aren't any terms. I've got you where the hair is short, and I'm not going to let go."

"You think you can hold me in this hole!" Raoul cried.

"You'll never leave it alive, except in double irons." Grief surveyed his guest with an air of consideration. "I've handled your kind before. We've pretty well cleaned it out of the South Seas. But you are a—how shall I say?—a sort of an anachronism. You're a throwback, and we've got to get rid of you. Personally, I would advise you to go back to the schooner and blow your brains out. It is the only way to escape what you've got coming to you."

The parley, so far as Raoul was concerned, proved fruitless, and he went back into his own lines convinced that the men on the Big Rock could hold out for years, though he would have been swiftly unconvinced could he have observed Tehaa and the Raiateans, the moment his back was turned and he was out of sight, crawling over the rocks and sucking and crunching the scraps his dog had left uneaten.

IX

"We hunger now, Brother," Grief said, "but it is better than to hunger for many days to come. The Big Devil, after feasting and drinking good water with us in plenty, will not stay long in Fuatino. Even tomorrow may he try to leave. To-night you and I sleep over the top of the Rock, and Tehaa, who shoots well, will sleep with us if he can dare the Rock."

Tehaa, alone among the Raiateans, was cragsman enough to venture the perilous way, and dawn found him in a rock-barricaded nook, a hundred yards to the right of Grief and Mauriri.

The first warning was the firing of rifles from the peninsula, where Brown and his two Raiateans signalled the retreat and followed the besiegers through the jungle to the beach. From the eyrie on the face of the rock Grief could see nothing for another hour, when the *Rattler* appeared, making for the passage. As before, the captive Fuatino men towed in the whaleboat. Mauriri, under direction of Grief, called down instructions to them as they passed slowly beneath. By Grief's side lay several bundles of dynamite sticks, well-lashed together and with extremely short fuses.

The deck of the *Rattler* was populous. For'ard, rifle in hand, among the Raiatean sailors, stood a desperado whom Mauriri announced was Raoul's brother. Aft, by the helmsman, stood another. Attached to him, tied waist to waist, with slack, was Mataara, the old Queen. On the other side of the helmsman, his arm in a sling, was Captain Glass. Amidships, as before, was Raoul, and with him, lashed waist to waist, was Naumoo.

"Good morning, Mister David Grief," Raoul called up.

"And yet I warned you that only in double irons would you leave the island," Grief murmured down with a sad inflection.

"You can't kill all your people I have on board," was the answer.

The schooner, moving slowly, jerk by jerk, as the men pulled in the whaleboat, was almost directly beneath. The rowers, without ceasing, slacked on their oars, and were immediately threatened with the rifle of the man who stood for'ard.

"Throw, Big Brother!" Naumoo called up in the Fuatino tongue. "I am filled with sorrow and am willed to die. His knife is ready with which to cut the rope, but I shall hold him tight. Be not afraid, Big Brother. Throw, and throw straight, and good-bye."

Grief hesitated, then lowered the fire-stick which he had been blowing bright.

"Throw!" the Goat Man urged.

Still Grief hesitated.

"If they get to sea, Big Brother, Naumoo dies just the same. And there are all the others. What is her life against the many?"

"If you drop any dynamite, or fire a single shot, we'll kill all on board," Raoul cried up to them. "I've got you, David Grief. You can't kill these people, and I can. Shut up, you!"

This last was addressed to Naumoo, who was calling up in her native tongue and whom Raoul seized by the neck with one hand to choke to silence. In turn, she locked both arms about him and looked up beseechingly to Grief.

"Throw it, Mr. Grief, and be damned to them," Captain Glass rumbled in his deep voice. "They're bloody murderers, and the cabin's full of them."

The desperado who was fastened to the old Queen swung half about to menace Captain Glass with his rifle, when Tehaa, from his position farther along the Rock, pulled trigger on him. The rifle dropped from the man's hand, and on his face was an expression of intense surprise as his legs crumpled under him and he sank down on deck, dragging the Queen with him.

"Port! Hard a port!" Grief cried.

Captain Glass and the Kanaka whirled the wheel over, and the bow of the *Rattler* headed in for the Rock. Amidships Raoul still struggled with Naumoo. His brother ran from for'ard to his aid, being missed by the fusillade of quick shots from Tehaa and the Goat Man. As Raoul's brother placed the muzzle of his rifle to Naumoo's side Grief touched the fire-stick to the match-head in the split end of the fuse. Even as with both hands he tossed the big bundle of dynamite, the rifle went off, and Naumoo's fall to the deck was simultaneous with the fall of the dynamite. This time the fuse was short enough. The explosion occurred at the instant the deck was reached, and that portion of the *Rattler,* along with Raoul, his brother, and Naumoo, forever disappeared.

The schooner's side was shattered, and she began immediately to settle. For'ard, every Raiatean sailor dived overboard. Captain Glass met the first man springing up the companionway from the cabin, with a kick full in the face, but was overborne and trampled on by the rush. Following the desperadoes came the Huahine women, and as they went overboard, the *Rattler* sank on an even keel close to the base of the Rock. Her cross-trees still stuck out when she reached bottom.

Looking down, Grief could see all that occurred beneath the surface. He saw Mataara, a fathom deep, unfasten herself from the dead pirate and swim upward. As her head emerged she saw Captain Glass,

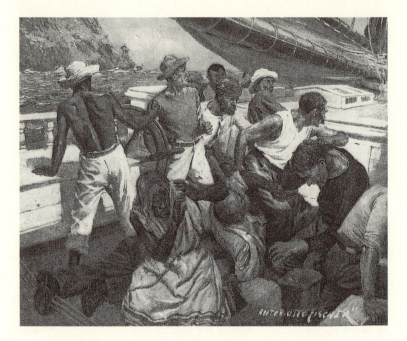

"Captain Glass was overborne and trampled on by the rush. . . . "
Drawing by Anton Otto Fischer.

who could not swim, sinking several yards away. The Queen, old woman that she was, but an islander, turned over, swam down to him, and held him up as she struck out for the unsubmerged cross-trees.

Five heads, blond and brown, were mingled with the dark heads of Polynesia that dotted the surface. Grief, rifle in hand, watched for a chance to shoot. The Goat Man, after a minute, was successful, and they saw the body of one man sink sluggishly. But to the Raiatean sailors, big and brawny, half fish, was the vengeance given. Swimming swiftly, they singled out the blond heads and the brown. Those from above watched the four surviving desperadoes, clutched and locked, dragged far down beneath and drowned like curs.

In ten minutes everything was over. The Huahine women, laughing and giggling, were holding on to the sides of the whaleboat which had done the towing. The Raiatean sailors, waiting for orders, were about the cross-tree to which Captain Glass and Mataara clung.

"The poor old *Rattler*," Captain Glass lamented.

"Nothing of the sort," Grief answered. "In a week we'll have her raised, new timbers amidships, and we'll be on our way." And to the Queen, "How is it with you, Sister?"

"Naumoo is gone, and Motauri, Brother, but Fuatino is ours again. The day is young. Word shall be sent to all my people in the high places with the goats. And to-night, once again, and as never before, we shall feast and rejoice in the Big House."

"She's been needing new timbers abaft the beam there for years," quoth Captain Glass. "But the chronometers will be out of commission for the rest of the cruise."

Front gate of the Penduffryn plantation on the island of Guadalcanal, frequently visited by the Londons. The scale of the operation is some indication of the value of copra at the time.

Solomon Islanders drying copra on the beach.

A typical island village.

South Seas adventurers, like these crew members on the *Snark*,
were a colorful lot.

FOUR

THE JOKERS OF NEW GIBBON

"The Jokers of New Gibbon" looks deeply at the complex relationship between islanders and white men as it examines the results of an acquaintance forced on one party by the other, motivated solely by the urge to exploit the resources of the Pacific.

New Gibbon, we are told, is politically divided by the sovereignties of Britain and Germany, reminding us of the colonial rivalry whose ironic legacy lingers even today, so that, for instance, one finds the island of New Britain located in the Sea of Bismarck. As the narrator comments cynically but plausibly, owing to the confused intentions of the two powers, "There was no real control at all, and never had been." In the absence of such control, a "black Napoleon, a head-hunting, man-eating Tallyrand" has emerged from the island's forest interior as the leader of the natives—the great chief Koho. In those days, such unifying monarchies were, curiously enough, not a natural cultural outgrowth of island custom; rather, they usually appeared in response to interaction with white traders and missionaries. In the early nineteenth century, the strategy of insinuation employed by both invading groups was to identify the strongest man on the island, to garner his friendship with gifts and compliments, to convert him to foreign values or vices, and finally to expand his influence (and consequently their own) into neighboring societies, ultimately proclaiming him "king." These monarchs and their heirs, confronted with apparently limitless powers, often were guilty of abominable cruelties and excesses of appetites, as was Koho on the fictional island of New Gibbon.

But for all his apparent monstrousness, London's Koho cuts a keenly tragic figure. As the story opens, the formerly mighty Koho is elderly, weak, and crippled, and his fighting spirit has been tamed. His life has fallen into the sere, the yellow leaf. Food and sex have lost their attractions. Only the sweet memory of a long-ago colossal binge reminds him of one pleasure left to him: rum—or any alcoholic variant. At one point not so many years before, however, Koho's implacable ferocity had been adequate to the task of repelling white men from New Gibbon, who had come there for all four of the big reasons that drew white men to the islands: bêche-de-mer, sandalwood, labor recruitment, and (most attractive of all) copra.

The harvest of bêche-de-mer remained for decades an economic staple. These glistening, slimy holothurian sea slugs, about the size and shape of large cucumbers, were hotly in demand in the Chinese market, where they were (and still are) sold as an aphrodisiac and an apparently tasty addition to soups.

Delicately fragrant sandalwood was used by the Chinese in the manufacture of genteel incense, soap, and small boxes. The getting of it, however, was often a life-and-death affair. The story tells us that traders had also tried and failed on New Gibbon, even though in real life their apparently insatiable greed and relentless cruelty were legendary. From boats moored offshore, heavily armed whites would trade knives, hatchets, cloth, tobacco sticks, and other items —even, with an almost suicidal lack of imagination, the ubiquitous Snider rifle, a hybrid, breech-loading weapon created by the addition of new parts to the old-fashioned muzzle-loading Enfield rifle. (It is, in fact, one of these that has wounded and crippled Koho's leg.) All that these traders wished in exchange was that the islanders would swim out to the whaleboats with sandalwood, toss it on the boat, and swim back to shore. As sandalwood grew like a weed and indeed choked and stunted other plants, the natives didn't mind getting rid of the stuff—except for the fact that on their departure, the highly competitive traders, wishing to make things difficult for any competitors following in their wake, would frequently set fire to the village and shoot several inhabitants. Thereafter, all sandalwood traders lived dangerous lives. Natives often would warmly and cheerfully lure the traders to the shore, only to *fall upon them and hatchet them to death. As sandalwooders grew more wary, they allowed only one native to swim to the whale-boat at a time; still, some islanders would swim out to the trading boat, drop off their wood, then capsize the little vessel and murder the white men.*

Because of an axiomatic (but quite untrue) assumption that white men could not do physical work in the tropical heat of the South Pacific plantations, from the middle of the nineteenth century white adventurers called "blackbirders" recruited black laborers from hundreds of little islands, offering them rewards that never materialized in exchange for a legal indenture of one to three years. Encouragements to "volunteer" for such service often included kidnapping, ransom, and threats at gunpoint.

Finally, the enormous variety of ways in which white speculators were able to use the coconut palm led to a boom of interest in copra, the dried meat of coconuts. David Grief has, as the story opens, managed to convince Koho to have his men bring coconuts from the interior to the beach.

Captain Grief has "tamed" the wild Koho, but the situation is unstable—not much would be necessary to throw this awkward balance of power into chaotic disaster. All it takes is the combined sense of humor of an Englishman and a German, who, without knowing it, decide the same prank would be funny. Some things, David Grief will learn to his horror, cannot be anticipated or kept in control.

The wealth-producer of the Pacific Islands: the coconut palm and what it gives to mankind. Drawing from the *Coconut Journal*, Manila.

I

"I'm almost afraid to take you in to New Gibbon," David Grief said.[1] "It wasn't until you and the British gave me a free hand and let the place alone that any results were accomplished."

Wallenstein, the German Resident Commissioner from Bougainville, poured himself a long Scotch and soda and smiled.[2]

"We take off our hats to you, Mr. Grief," he said in perfectly good English. "What you have done on the devil island is a miracle. And we shall continue not to interfere. It is a devil island, and old Koho is the big chief devil of them all. We never could bring him to terms. He is a liar, and he is no fool. He is a black Napoleon, a head-hunting, man-eating Talleyrand. I remember six years ago, when I landed there in the British cruiser. The niggers cleared out for the bush, of course, but we found several who couldn't get away. One was his latest wife. She had been hung up by one arm in the sun for two days and nights.[3] We cut her down, but she died just the same. And staked out in the fresh running water, up to their necks, were three more women. All their bones were broken and their joints crushed. The process is supposed to make them tender for the eating. They were still alive. Their vitality was remarkable. One woman, the oldest, lingered nearly ten days. Well, that was a sample of Koho's diet. No wonder he's a wild beast. How you ever pacified him is our everlasting puzzlement."

"I wouldn't call him exactly pacified," Grief answered. "Though he comes in once in a while and eats out of the hand."

"That's more than we accomplished with our cruisers. Neither the German nor the English ever laid eyes on him. You were the first."

"No; McTavish was the first," Grief disclaimed.

"Ah, yes, I remember him—the little, dried-up Scotchman."[4]

Wallenstein sipped his whiskey. "He's called the Trouble-mender, isn't he?"

Grief nodded.

"And they say the screw you pay him is bigger than mine or the British Resident's?"

"I'm afraid it is," Grief admitted. "You see, and no offence, he's really worth it. He spends his time wherever the trouble is. He is a wizard. He's the one who got me my lodgment on New Gibbon. He's down on Malaita now, starting a plantation for me."[5]

"The first?"

"There's not even a trading station on all Malaita. The recruiters still use covering boats and carry the old barbed wire above their rails. There's the plantation now. We'll be in in half an hour." He handed the binoculars to his guest. "Those are the boat-sheds to the left of the bungalow. Beyond are the barracks. And to the right are the copra-sheds.[6] We dry quite a bit already. Old Koho's getting civilized enough to make his people bring in the nuts. There's the mouth of the stream where you found the three women softening."

The *Wonder*, wing-and-wing, was headed directly in for the anchorage. She rose and fell lazily over a glassy swell flawed here and there by catspaws from astern. It was the tail-end of the monsoon season, and the air was heavy and sticky with tropic moisture, the sky a florid, leaden muss of formless clouds. The rugged land was swathed with cloud-banks and squall wreaths, through which headlands and interior peaks thrust darkly. On one promontory a slant of sunshine blazed torridly, on another, scarcely a mile away, a squall was bursting in furious downpour of driving rain.

This was the dank, fat, savage island of New Gibbon, lying fifty miles to leeward of Choiseul. Geographically, it belonged to the Solomon Group. Politically, the dividing line of German and British influence cut it in half, hence the joint control by the two Resident Commissioners. In the case of New Gibbon, this control existed only on paper in the colonial offices of the two countries. There was no real control at all, and never had been. The bêche de mer fishermen of the old days had passed it by. The sandalwood traders, after stern experiences, had given it up. The blackbirders had never succeed-

"There's the plantation now. We'll be in in half an hour. . . . "
Drawing by C. W. Ashley.

ed in recruiting one labourer on the island, and, after the schooner *Dorset* had been cut off with all hands, they left the place severely alone. Later, a German company had attempted a cocoanut plantation, which was abandoned after several managers and a number of contract labourers had lost their heads. German cruisers and British cruisers had failed to get the savage blacks to listen to reason. Four times the missionary societies had essayed the peaceful conquest of the island, and four times, between sickness and massacre, they had been driven away. More cruisers, more pacifications, had followed, and followed fruitlessly. The cannibals had always retreated into the bush and laughed at the screaming shells. When the warships left it was an easy matter to rebuild the burned grass houses and set up the ovens in the old-fashioned way.

New Gibbon was a large island, fully one hundred and fifty miles long and half as broad. Its windward coast was iron-bound, without anchorages or inlets, and it was inhabited by scores of warring tribes —at least it had been, until Koho had arisen, like a Kamehameha, and, by force of arms and considerable statecraft, firmly welded the greater portion of the tribes into a confederation.[7] His policy of permitting no intercourse with white men had been eminently right, so far as survival of his own people was concerned; and after the visit of the last cruiser he had had his own way until David Grief and McTavish the Trouble-mender landed on the deserted beach where once had stood the German bungalow and barracks and the various English mission-houses.

Followed wars, false peaces, and more wars. The wizened little Scotchman could make trouble as well as mend it, and, not content with holding the beach, he imported bushmen from Malaita and invaded the wild-pig runs of the interior jungle. He burned villages until Koho wearied of rebuilding them, and when he captured Koho's eldest son he compelled a conference with the old chief. It was then that McTavish laid down the rate of head-exchange. For each head of his own people he promised to take ten of Koho's. After Koho had learned that the Scotchman was a man of his word, the first true peace was made. In the meantime McTavish had built the bungalow and barracks, cleared the jungle-land along the beach, and laid out the plantation. After that he had gone on his way to mend trouble on the atoll of Tasman, where a plague of black measles had broken out and been ascribed to Grief's plantation by the devil-devil doctors. Once, a year later, he had been called back again to straighten up New Gibbon; and Koho, after paying a forced fine of two hundred thousand cocoanuts, decided it was cheaper to keep the peace and sell the nuts. Also, the fires of his youth had burned down. He was getting old and limped of one leg where a Lee-Enfield bullet had perforated the calf.

II

"I knew a chap in Hawaii," Grief said, "superintendent of a sugar plantation, who used a hammer and a ten-penny nail."[8]

They were sitting on the broad bungalow veranda, and watching Worth, the manager of New Gibbon, doctoring the sick squad. They were New Georgia boys, a dozen of them, and the one with the aching tooth had been put back to the last. Worth had just failed in his first attempt. He wiped the sweat from his forehead with one hand and waved the forceps with the other.

"And broke more than one jaw," he asserted grimly.

Grief shook his head. Wallenstein smiled and elevated his brows.

"He said not, at any rate," Grief qualified. "He assured me, furthermore, that he always succeeded on the first trial."

"I saw it done when I was second mate on a lime-juicer," Captain Ward spoke up. "The old man used a caulking mallet and a steel marlin-spike. He took the tooth out with the first stroke, too, clean as a whistle."

"Me for the forceps," Worth muttered grimly, inserting his own pair in the mouth of the black. As he pulled, the man groaned and rose in the air. "Lend a hand, somebody, and hold him down," the manager appealed.

Grief and Wallenstein, on either side, gripped the black and held him. And he, in turn, struggled against them and clenched his teeth on the forceps. The group swayed back and forth. Such exertion, in the stagnant heat, brought the sweat out on all of them. The black

"Grief and Wallenstein, on either side, gripped the black and held him. . . . " Drawing by C. W. Ashley.

sweated, too, but his was the sweat of excruciating pain. The chair on which he sat was overturned. Captain Ward paused in the act of pouring himself a drink, and called encouragement. Worth pleaded with his assistants to hang on, and hung on himself, twisting the tooth till it crackled and then attempting a straightaway pull.

Nor did any of them notice the little black man who limped up the steps and stood looking on. Koho was a conservative. His fathers before him had worn no clothes, and neither did he, not even a gee-string. The many empty perforations in nose and lips and ears told of decorative passions long since dead. The holes on both earlobes had been torn out, but their size was attested by the strips of withered flesh that hung down and swept his shoulders. He cared now only for utility, and in one of the half dozen minor holes in his right ear he carried a short clay pipe. Around his waist was buckled a cheap trade-belt, and between the imitation leather and the naked skin was thrust the naked blade of a long knife. Suspended from the belt was his bamboo betel-nut and lime box. In his hand was a short-barrelled, large-bore Snider rifle. He was indescribably filthy, and here and there marred by scars, the worst being the one left by the Lee-Enfield bullet, which had withered the calf to half the size of its mate. His shrunken mouth showed that few teeth were left to serve him. Face and body were shrunken and withered, but his black, bead-like eyes, small and close together, were very bright, withal they were restless and querulous, and more like a monkey's than a man's.

He looked on, grinning like a shrewd little ape. His joy in the torment of the patient was natural, for the world he lived in was a world of pain. He had endured his share of it, and inflicted far more than his share on others. When the tooth parted from its locked hold in the jaw and the forceps raked across the other teeth and out of the mouth with a nerve-rasping sound, old Koho's eyes fairly sparkled, and he looked with glee at the poor black, collapsed on the veranda floor and groaning terribly as he held his head in both his hands.

"I think he's going to faint," Grief said, bending over the victim. "Captain Ward, give him a drink, please. You'd better take one yourself, Worth; you're shaking like a leaf."

"And I think I'll take one," said Wallenstein, wiping the sweat from his face. His eye caught the shadow of Koho on the floor and followed it up to the old chief himself. "Hello! who's this?"

"Hello, Koho!" Grief said genially, though he knew better than to offer to shake hands.

It was one of Koho's *tambos,* given him by the devil-devil doctors when he was born, that never was his flesh to come in contact with the flesh of a white man. Worth and Captain Ward, of the *Wonder,* greeted Koho, but Worth frowned at sight of the Snider, for it was one of his *tambos* that no visiting bushman should carry a weapon on the plantation.[9] Rifles had a nasty way of going off at the hip under such circumstances. The manager clapped his hands, and a black house-boy, recruited from San Cristobal, came running. At a sign from Worth, he took the rifle from the visitor's hand and carried it inside the bungalow.

"Koho," Grief said, introducing the German Resident, "this big fella marster belong Bougainville—my word, big fella marster too much."

Koho, remembering the visits of the various German cruisers, smiled with a light of unpleasant reminiscence in his eyes.

"Don't shake hands with him, Wallenstein," Grief warned. *"Tambo,* you know." Then to Koho, "My word, you get 'm too much fat stop along you. Bime by you marry along new fella Mary, eh?"

"Too old fella me," Koho answered, with a weary shake of the head. "Me no like 'm Mary. Me no like 'm *kai-kai* (food). Close up me die along altogether." He stole a significant glance at Worth, whose head was tilted back to a long glass. "Me like 'm rum."

Grief shook his head.

"Tambo along black fella."[10]

"He black fella no *tambo,"* Koho retorted, nodding toward the groaning labourer.

"He fella sick," Grief explained.

"Me fella sick."

"You fella big liar," Grief laughed. "Rum *tambo,* all the time *tambo.* Now, Koho, we have big fella talk along this big fella marster."

And he and Wallenstein and the old chief sat down on the veranda to confer about affairs of state. Koho was complimented on the peace he had kept, and he, with many protestations of his aged decrepitude, swore peace again and everlasting. Then was discussed the matter of starting a German plantation twenty miles down the coast. The land, of course, was to be bought from Koho, and the price was arranged in terms of tobacco, knives, beads, pipes, hatchets, porpoise teeth and shell-money—in terms of everything except rum. While the talk went on, Koho, glancing through the window, could see Worth mixing medicines and placing bottles back in the medicine cupboard. Also, he saw the manager complete his labours by taking a drink of Scotch. Koho noted the bottle carefully. And, though he hung about for an hour after the conference was over, there was never a moment when some one or another was not in the room. When Grief and Worth sat down to a business talk, Koho gave it up.

"Me go along schooner," he announced, then turned and limped out.

"How are the mighty fallen," Grief laughed. "To think that used to be Koho, the fiercest red-handed murderer in the Solomons, who defied all his life two of the greatest world powers. And now he's going aboard to try and cadge Denby for a drink."

III

For the last time in his life the supercargo of the *Wonder* perpetrated a practical joke on a native. He was in the main cabin, checking off the list of goods being landed in the whaleboats, when Koho limped down the companionway and took a seat opposite him at the table.

"Close up me die along altogether," was the burden of the old chief's plaint. All the delights of the flesh had forsaken him. "Me no like 'm Mary. Me no like 'm *kai-kai*. Me too much sick fella. Me close up finish." A long, sad pause, in which his face expressed unutterable concern for his stomach, which he patted gingerly and with an assumption of pain. "Belly belong me too much sick." Another pause, which was an invitation to Denby to make suggestions. Then followed a long, weary, final sigh, and a "Me like 'm rum."

Denby laughed heartlessly. He had been cadged for drinks before by the old cannibal, and the sternest *tambo* Grief and McTavish had laid down was the one forbidding alcohol to the natives of New Gibbon.

The trouble was that Koho had acquired the taste. In his younger days he had learned the delights of drunkenness when he cut off the schooner *Dorset,* but unfortunately he had learned it along with all his tribesmen, and the supply had not held out long. Later, when he led his naked warriors down to the destruction of the German plantation, he was wiser, and he appropriated all the liquors for his sole use. The result had been a gorgeous mixed drunk, on a dozen different sorts of drink, ranging from beer doctored with quinine to absinthe and apricot brandy. The drunk had lasted for months, and it had left him with a thirst that would remain with him until he died. Predisposed toward alcohol, after the way of savages, all the chemistry of his flesh clamoured for it. This craving was to him expressed in terms of tingling and sensation, of maggots crawling warmly and deliciously in his brain, of good feeling, and well being, and high exultation. And in his barren old age, when women and feasting were a weariness, and when old hates had smouldered down, he desired more and more the revivifying fire that came liquid out of bottles—out of all sorts of bottles—for he remembered them well. He would sit in the sun for hours, occasionally drooling, in mournful contemplation of the great orgy which had been his when the German plantation was cleaned out.

Denby was sympathetic. He sought out the old chief's symptoms and offered him dyspeptic tablets from the medicine chest, pills, and a varied assortment of harmless tabloids and capsules. But Koho steadfastly declined. Once, when he cut the *Dorset* off, he had bitten through a capsule of quinine; in addition, two of his warriors had partaken of a white powder and laid down and died very violently in a very short time. No; he did not believe in drugs. But the liquids from bottles, the cool-flaming youth-givers and warm-glowing dream-makers. No wonder the white men valued them so highly and refused to dispense them.

"Rum he good fella," he repeated over and over, plaintively and with the weary patience of age.

And then Denby made his mistake and played his joke. Stepping around behind Koho, he unlocked the medicine closet and took out a four-ounce bottle labelled *essence of mustard*. As he made believe to draw the cork and drink of the contents, in the mirror on the for'ard bulkhead he glimpsed Koho, twisted half around, intently watching him. Denby smacked his lips and cleared his throat appreciatively as he replaced the bottle. Neglecting to relock the medicine closet, he returned to his chair, and, after a decent interval, went on deck. He stood beside the companionway and listened. After several moments the silence below was broken by a fearful, wheezing, propulsive, strangling cough. He smiled to himself and returned leisurely down the companionway. The bottle was back on the shelf where it belonged, and the old man sat in the same position. Denby marvelled at his iron control. Mouth and lips and tongue, and all sensitive membranes, were a blaze of fire. He gasped and nearly coughed several times, while involuntary tears brimmed in his eyes and ran down his cheeks. An ordinary man would have coughed and strangled for half an hour. But old Koho's face was grimly composed. It dawned on him that a trick had been played, and into his eyes came an expression of hatred and malignancy so primitive, so abysmal, that it sent the chills up and down Denby's spine. Koho arose proudly.

"Me go along," he said. "You sing out one fella boat stop along me."

IV

Having seen Grief and Worth start for a ride over the plantation, Wallenstein sat down in the big living-room and with gun-oil and old rags proceeded to take apart and clean his automatic pistol. On the table beside him stood the inevitable bottle of Scotch and numerous soda bottles. Another bottle, part full, chanced to stand there. It was also labelled Scotch, but its content was liniment which Worth had mixed for the horses and neglected to put away.

As Wallenstein worked, he glanced through the window and saw Koho coming up the compound path. He was limping very rapidly,

"A fearful, wheezing, propulsive, strangling cough. . . . "
Drawing by C. W. Ashley.

but when he came along the veranda and entered the room his gait
was slow and dignified. He sat down and watched the gun-cleaning.
Though mouth and lips and tongue were afire, he gave no sign. At
the end of five minutes he spoke.

"Rum he good fella. Me like 'm rum."

Wallenstein smiled and shook his head, and then it was that his
perverse imp suggested what was to be his last joke on a native. The
similarity of the two bottles was the real suggestion. He laid his pistol parts on the table and mixed himself a long drink. Standing as he

did between Koho and the table, he interchanged the two bottles, drained his glass, made as if to search for something, and left the room. From outside he heard the surprised splutter and cough; but when he returned the old chief sat as before. The liniment in the bottle, however, was lower, and it still oscillated.

Koho stood up, clapped his hands, and, when the house-boy answered, signed that he desired his rifle. The boy fetched the weapon, and according to custom preceded the visitor down the pathway. Not until outside the gate did the boy turn the rifle over to its owner. Wallenstein, chuckling to himself, watched the old chief limp along the beach in the direction of the river.

A few minutes later, as he put his pistol together, Wallenstein heard the distant report of a gun. For the instant he thought of Koho, then dismissed the conjecture from his mind. Worth and Grief had taken shotguns with them, and it was probably one of their shots at a pigeon. Wallenstein lounged back in his chair, chuckled, twisted his yellow mustache, and dozed. He was aroused by the excited voice of Worth, crying out:

"Ring the big fella bell! Ring plenty too much! Ring like hell!"

Wallenstein gained the veranda in time to see the manager jump his horse over the low fence of the compound and dash down the beach after Grief, who was riding madly ahead. A loud crackling and smoke rising through the cocoanut trees told the story. The boat-houses and the barracks were on fire. The big plantation bell was ringing wildly as the German Resident ran down the beach, and he could see whaleboats hastily putting off from the schooner.

Barracks and boat-houses, grass-thatched and like tinder, were wrapped in flames. Grief emerged from the kitchen, carrying a naked black child by the leg. Its head was missing.

"The cook's in there," he told Worth. "Her head's gone, too. She was too heavy, and I had to clear out."

"It was my fault," Wallenstein said. "Old Koho did it. But I let him take a drink of Worth's horse liniment."

"I guess he's headed for the bush," Worth said, springing astride his horse and starting. "Oliver is down there by the river. Hope he didn't get *him*."

The manager galloped away through the trees. A few minutes later, as the charred wreck of the barracks crashed in, they heard him calling and followed. On the edge of the river bank they came upon him. He still sat on his horse, very white-faced, and gazed at something on the ground. It was the body of Oliver, the young assistant manager, though it was hard to realize it, for the head was gone. The black labourers, breathless from their run in from the fields, were now crowding around, and under Grief's direction they improvised a litter for the dead man.

Wallenstein was afflicted with paroxysms of true German sorrow and contrition. The tears were frankly in his eyes by the time he ceased from lamenting and began to swear. The wrath that flared up was as truly German as the oaths, and when he tried to seize Worth's shotgun a fleck of foam had appeared on his lips.

"None of that," Grief commanded sternly. "Straighten up, Wallenstein. Don't be a fool."

"But are you going to let him escape?" the German cried wildly.

"He has escaped. The bush begins right here at the river. You can see where he waded across. He's in the wild-pig runs already. It would be like the needle in the haystack, and if we followed him some of his young men would get us. Besides, the runs are all man-trapped—you know, staked pits, poisoned thorns, and the rest. McTavish and his bushmen are the only fellows who can negotiate the runs, and three of his men were lost that way the last time. Come on back to the house. You'll hear the conches to-night, and the war-drums, and all merry hell break loose. They won't rush us, but keep all the boys close up to the house, Mr. Worth. Come on!"

As they returned along the path they came upon a black who whimpered and cried vociferously.

"Shut up mouth belong you!" Worth shouted. "What name you make 'm noise?"

"Him fella Koho finish along two fella bullamacow," the black answered, drawing a forefinger significantly across his throat.

"He's knifed the cows," Grief said. "That means no more milk for some time for you, Worth. I'll see about sending a couple up from Ugi."

Wallenstein proved inconsolable, until Denby, coming ashore, confessed to the dose of essence of mustard. Thereat the German Resident became even cheerful, though he twisted his yellow mustache up more fiercely and continued to curse the Solomons with oaths culled from four languages.

Next morning, visible from the masthead of the *Wonder,* the bush was alive with signal-smokes. From promontory to promontory, and back through the solid jungle, the smoke-pillars curled and puffed and talked. Remote villages on the higher peaks, beyond the farthest raids McTavish had ever driven, joined in the troubled conversation. From across the river persisted a bedlam of conches; while from everywhere, drifting for miles along the quiet air, came the deep, booming reverberations of the great war-drums—huge tree trunks, hollowed by fire and carved with tools of stone and shell.

"You're all right as long as you stay close," Grief told his manager. "I've got to get along to Guvutu. They won't come out in the open and attack you. Keep the work-gangs close. Stop the clearing till this blows over. They'll get any detached gangs you send out. And, whatever you do, don't be fooled into going into the bush after Koho. If you do, he'll get you. All you've got to do is wait for McTavish. I'll send him up with a bunch of his Malaita bushmen. He's the only man who can go inside. Also, until he comes, I'll leave Denby with you. You don't mind, do you, Mr. Denby? I'll send McTavish up with the *Wanda,* and you can go back on her and rejoin the *Wonder.* Captain Ward can manage without you for a trip."

"It was just what I was going to volunteer," Denby answered. "I never dreamed all this muss would be kicked up over a joke. You see, in a way I consider myself responsible for it."

"So am I responsible," Wallenstein broke in.

"But I started it," the supercargo urged.

"Maybe you did, but I carried it along."

"And Koho finished it," Grief said.

"At any rate, I, too, shall remain," said the German.

"I thought you were coming to Guvutu with me," Grief protested.

"I was. But this is my jurisdiction, partly, and I have made a fool of myself in it completely. I shall remain and help get things straight again."

V

At Guvutu, Grief sent full instructions to McTavish by a recruiting ketch which was just starting for Malaita. Captain Ward sailed in the *Wonder* for the Santa Cruz Islands; and Grief, borrowing a whaleboat and a crew of black prisoners from the British Resident, crossed the channel to Guadalcanar, to examine the grass lands back of Penduffryn.[11]

Three weeks later, with a free sheet and a lusty breeze, he threaded the coral patches and surged up the smooth water to Guvutu anchorage. The harbour was deserted, save for a small ketch which lay close in to the shore reef. Grief recognized it as the *Wanda*. She had evidently just got in by the Tulagi Passage, for her black crew was still at work furling the sails. As he rounded alongside, McTavish himself extended a hand to help him over the rail.

"What's the matter?" Grief asked. "Haven't you started yet?"

McTavish nodded. "And got back. Everything's all right on board."

"How's New Gibbon?"

"All there, the last I saw of it, barrin' a few inconsequential frills that a good eye could make out lacking from the landscape."

He was a cold flame of a man, small as Koho, and as dried up, with a mahogany complexion and small, expressionless blue eyes that were more like gimlet-points than the eyes of a Scotchman. Without fear, without enthusiasm, impervious to disease and climate and sentiment, he was lean and bitter and deadly as a snake. That his present sour look boded ill news, Grief was well aware.

"Spit it out!" he said. "What's happened?"

"'Tis a thing severely to be condemned, a damned shame, this joking with heathen niggers," was the reply. "Also, 'tis very expensive. Come below, Mr. Grief. You'll be better for the information with a long glass in your hand. After you."

"How did you settle things?" his employer demanded as soon as they were seated in the cabin.

The little Scotchman shook his head. "There was nothing to settle. It all depends how you look at it. The other way would be to say it was settled, entirely settled, mind you, before I got there."

"But the plantation, man? The plantation?"

"No plantation. All the years of our work have gone for naught. 'Tis back where we started, where the missionaries started, where the Germans started—and where they finished. Not a stone stands on another at the landing pier. The houses are black ashes. Every tree is hacked down, and the wild pigs are rooting out the yams and sweet potatoes. Those boys from New Georgia, a fine bunch they were, five score of them, and they cost you a pretty penny. Not one is left to tell the tale."

He paused and began fumbling in a large locker under the companion-steps.

"But Worth? And Denby? And Wallenstein?"

"That's what I'm telling you. Take a look."

McTavish dragged out a sack made of rice matting and emptied its contents on the floor. David Grief pulled himself together with a jerk, for he found himself gazing fascinated at the heads of the three men he had left at New Gibbon. The yellow mustache of Wallenstein had lost its fierce curl and drooped and wilted on the upper lip.

"I don't know how it happened," the Scotchman's voice went on drearily. "But I surmise they went into the bush after the old devil."

"And where is Koho?" Grief asked.

"Back in the bush and drunk as a lord. That's how I was able to recover the heads. He was too drunk to stand. They lugged him on their backs out of the village when I rushed it. And if you'll relieve me of the heads, I'll be well obliged." He paused and sighed. "I suppose they'll have regular funerals over them and put them in the ground. But in my way of thinking they'd make excellent curios.[12] Any respectable museum would pay a hundred quid apiece. Better have another drink. You're looking a bit pale—There, put that down you, and if you'll take my advice, Mr. Grief, I would say, set your face sternly against any joking with the niggers. It always makes trouble, and it is a very expensive divertissement."

FIVE

A LITTLE ACCOUNT WITH

WITH

SWITHIN HALL

On November 11, 1910, an editor from Cosmopolitan advised Jack London that "our readers enjoy best a running set of short stories in which the chief character figures in all the tales" (London, Letters, 942n). By the following spring, Jack was excited with the concept, as he planned both the Smoke Bellew and David Grief series. His practical mind could hardly have missed the ballooning magazine industry of series characters that had made several of London's contemporaries hugely successful. Could he tap into the same vein that had made, for a prime example, Sir Arthur Conan Doyle's Sherlock Holmes stories a worldwide phenomenon, several of his pet projects for Beauty Ranch might come to life. Perhaps the challenge of entering into competition with a master of the form appealed to him, as London scholar Dale L. Walker suggests in his Jack London and Conan Doyle: A Literary Kinship (1981). Several of the David Grief stories, Walker argues, indicate the author's consciousness of this narrative experiment as well as a "singular familiarity with the methods of Sherlock Holmes of Baker Street" (12). Walker points to Sherlockian elements in "A Goboto Night," when Peter Gee (a character who himself recurs in three of the stories) deduces on the basis of a series of isolated facts that David Grief's vessel has arrived at Goboto.

In "A Little Account with Swithin Hall," Grief plays Sherlock himself as he investigates yet another mysterious island as well as

*the curious behavior of the island's inhabitants. As in the Holmes
tales, an injustice has occurred, and Grief finds it entertaining to
correct it. In the process, he will employ techniques commonly associated with the Baker Street master: disguise, observation, de-
duction, cross-and-double-cross, and the revelation of guilt. And,
as Holmes so often does, Grief in the end will mete out his own
determination of justice. It is, as Walker rightly appreciates, "a
neat tale of the stinging of a con-man" (43)—but more than that,
Grief's cleverness also corrects the original crime of Swithin Hall.*

Even before the Uncle Toby *accidentally sails into Swithin Hall's
lost and legendary private island, there's adventure enough for a
separate story. Here, as Grief struggles through a Pacific hurricane,
London more than lives up to the promise he made to the editor of
the* Saturday Evening Post: *"In this series . . . I am going to give a
new South Seas, and it will be the real South Seas—the sailor's
South Seas. . . . Only two kinds of men have written up the South
Seas—artists who weren't sailors, and sailors who weren't artists"
(Letters 992). Certainly it's rare in literature for a landlocked reader to feel so vitally the impact of the gear and tackle of a ship as it
strains against the colossal fury of a Pacific hurricane.*

*As a nice touch—a kind of in-joke for himself, perhaps—Lon-
don even mentions in the story the* Sophie Sutherland, *the sealing
vessel on which, as a youth, he first got his sealegs, serving in 1893
for the first time as an able-bodied seaman. It was on the* Sophie
Sutherland *that he faced his first hurricane, and it was the adventure of saving the ship that provided the plot for his very first pub-
lished story, "Story of a Typhoon off the Coast of Japan." It was
also on the* Sophie Sutherland *that he encountered the brutal mastery of the ship's captain, Alexander McLean, whom London would
transform in 1904 to the ruthless captain of the sealer* Ghost—
calling him Wolf Larsen, the Sea-Wolf.

With a last long scrutiny at the unbroken circle of the sea, David Grief swung out of the cross-trees and slowly and dejectedly descended the ratlines to the deck.

"Leu-Leu Atoll is sunk, Mr. Snow," he said to the anxious-faced young mate.[1] "If there is anything in navigation, the atoll is surely under the sea, for we've sailed clear over it twice—or the spot where it ought to be. It's either that or the chronometer's gone wrong, or I've forgotten my navigation."

"It must be the chronometer, sir," the mate reassured his owner. "You know I made separate sights and worked them up, and that they agreed with yours."

"Yes," Grief muttered, nodding glumly, "and where your Sumner lines crossed, and mine, too, was the dead centre of Leu-Leu Atoll. It must be the chronometer—slipped a cog or something."

He made a short pace to the rail and back, and cast a troubled eye at the *Uncle Toby*'s wake. The schooner, with a fairly strong breeze on her quarter, was logging nine or ten knots.

"Better bring her up on the wind, Mr. Snow. Put her under easy sail and let her work to windward on two-hour legs. It's thickening up, and I don't imagine we can get a star observation to-night; so we'll just hold our weather position, get a latitude sight to-morrow, and run Leu-Leu down on her own latitude. That's the way all the old navigators did."

Broad of beam, heavily sparred, with high freeboard and bluff, Dutchy bow, the *Uncle Toby* was the slowest, tubbiest, safest, and most fool-proof schooner David Grief possessed. Her run was in the Banks and Santa Cruz groups and to the northwest among the several isolated atolls where his native traders collected copra, hawksbill turtle, and an occasional ton of pearl shell. Finding the skipper down with a particularly bad stroke of fever, Grief had relieved him and taken the *Uncle Toby* on her semi-annual run to the atolls. He had elected to make his first call at Leu-Leu, which lay farthest, and now found himself lost at sea with a chronometer that played tricks.

II

No stars showed that night, nor was the sun visible next day. A stuffy, sticky calm obtained, broken by big wind-squalls and heavy downpours. From fear of working too far to windward, the *Uncle Toby* was hove to, and four days and nights of cloud-hidden sky followed. Never did the sun appear, and on the several occasions that stars broke through they were too dim and fleeting for identification. By this time it was patent to the veriest tyro that the elements were preparing to break loose. Grief, coming on deck from consulting the barometer, which steadfastly remained at 29.90, encountered Jackie-Jackie, whose face was as brooding and troublous as the sky and air. Jackie-Jackie, a Tongan sailor of experience, served as a sort of bosun and semi-second mate over the mixed Kanaka crew.

"Big weather he come, I think," he said. "I see him just the same before maybe five, six times."

Grief nodded. "Hurricane weather, all right, Jackie-Jackie. Pretty soon barometer go down—bottom fall out."

"Sure," the Tongan concurred. "He goin' to blow like hell."

Ten minutes later Snow came on deck.

"She's started," he said; "29.85, going down and pumping at the same time. It's stinking hot—don't you notice it?" He brushed his forehead with his hands. "It's sickening. I could lose my breakfast without trying."

Jackie-Jackie grinned. "Just the same me. Everything inside walk about. Always this way before big blow. But *Uncle Toby* all right. He go through anything."

"Better rig that storm-trysail on the main, and a storm-jib," Grief said to the mate. "And put all the reefs into the working canvas before you furl down. No telling what we may need. Put on double gaskets while you're about it."

In another hour, the sultry oppressiveness steadily increasing and the stark calm still continuing, the barometer had fallen to 29.70. The mate, being young, lacked the patience of waiting for the portentous. He ceased his restless pacing, and waved his arms.

"If she's going to come let her come!" he cried. "There's no use shilly-shallying this way! Whatever the worst is, let us know it and have it! A pretty pickle—lost with a crazy chronometer and a hurricane that won't blow!"

The cloud-mussed sky turned to a vague copper colour, and seemed to glow as the inside of a huge heated caldron. Nobody remained below. The native sailors formed in anxious groups amidships and for'ard, where they talked in low voices and gazed apprehensively at the ominous sky and the equally ominous sea that breathed in long, low, oily undulations.

"Looks like petroleum mixed with castor oil," the mate grumbled, as he spat his disgust overside. "My mother used to dose me with messes like that when I was a kid. Lord, she's getting black!"

The lurid coppery glow had vanished, and the sky thickened and lowered until the darkness was as that of a late twilight. David Grief, who well knew the hurricane rules, nevertheless reread the "Laws of Storms," screwing his eyes in the faint light in order to see the print. There was nothing to be done save wait for the wind, so that he might know how he lay in relation to the fast-flying and deadly centre that from somewhere was approaching out of the gloom.

It was three in the afternoon, and the glass had sunk to 29.45, when the wind came. They could see it on the water, darkening the face of the sea, crisping tiny whitecaps as it rushed along. It was merely a stiff breeze, and the *Uncle Toby,* filling away under her storm canvas till the wind was abeam, sloshed along at a four-knot gait.

"No weight to that," Snow sneered. "And after such grand preparation!"

"Pickaninny wind," Jackie-Jackie agreed. "He grow big man pretty quick, you see."

Grief ordered the foresail put on, retaining the reefs, and the *Uncle Toby* mended her pace in the rising breeze. The wind quickly grew to man's size, but did not stop there. It merely blew hard, and harder, and kept on blowing harder, advertising each increase by lulls followed by fierce, freshening gusts. Ever it grew, until the *Uncle Toby*'s rail was more often pressed under than not, while her waist boiled with foaming water which the scuppers could not carry off. Grief studied the barometer, still steadily falling.

"The centre is to the south'ard," he told Snow, "and we're running across its path and into it. Now we'll turn about and run the other way. That ought to bring the glass up. Take in the foresail—it's more than she can carry already—and stand by to wear her around."

The maneuver was accomplished, and through the gloom that was almost that of the first darkness of evening the *Uncle Toby* turned and raced madly north across the face of the storm.

"It's nip and tuck," Grief confided to the mate a couple of hours later. "The storm's swinging a big curve—there's no calculating that curve—and we may win across or the centre may catch us. Thank the Lord, the glass is holding its own. It all depends on how big the curve is. The sea's too big for us to keep on. Heave her to! She'll keep working along out anyway."

"I thought I knew what wind was," Snow shouted in his owner's ear next morning. "This isn't wind. It's something unthinkable. It's impossible. It must reach ninety or a hundred miles an hour in the gusts. That don't mean anything. How could I ever tell it to anybody? I couldn't. And look at that sea! I've run my Easting down, but I never saw anything like that."[2]

Day had come, and the sun should have been up an hour, yet the best it could produce was a sombre semi-twilight. The ocean was a stately procession of moving mountains. A third of a mile across yawned the valleys between the great waves. Their long slopes, shielded somewhat from the full fury of the wind, were broken by systems of smaller whitecapping waves, but from the high crests of the big waves themselves the wind tore the whitecaps in the forming. This spume drove masthead high, and higher, horizontally, above the surface of the sea.

"We're through the worst," was Grief's judgment. "The glass is coming along all the time. The sea will get bigger as the wind eases down. I'm going to turn in. Watch for shifts in the wind. They'll be sure to come. Call me at eight bells."

By mid-afternoon, in a huge sea, with the wind after its last shift

"The ocean was a stately procession of moving mountains. . . ."
Drawing by Anton Otto Fischer.

no more than a stiff breeze, the Tongan bosun sighted a schooner bottom up. The *Uncle Toby*'s drift took them across the bow and they could not make out the name; but before night they picked up with a small, round-bottom, double-ender boat, swamped but with white lettering visible on its bow. Through the binoculars, Gray made out: *Emily L No. 3.*

"A sealing schooner," Grief said. "But what a sealer's doing in these waters is beyond me."

"Treasure-hunters, maybe?" Snow speculated. "The *Sophie Sutherland* and the *Herman* were sealers, you remember, chartered out of San Francisco by the chaps with the maps who can always go right to the spot until they get there and don't."

III

After a giddy night of grand and lofty tumbling, in which, over a big and dying sea, without a breath of wind to steady her, the *Uncle Toby* rolled every person on board sick of soul, a light breeze sprang up and the reefs were shaken out. By midday, on a smooth ocean floor, the clouds thinned and cleared and sights of the sun were obtained. Two degrees and fifteen minutes south, the observation gave them. With a broken chronometer longitude was out of the question.

"We're anywhere within five hundred and a thousand miles along that latitude line," Grief remarked, as he and the mate bent over the chart. "Leu-Leu is to the south'ard somewhere, and this section of ocean is all blank. There is neither an island nor a reef by which we can regulate the chronometer. The only thing to do—"

"Land ho, skipper!" the Tongan called down the companionway.

Grief took a quick glance at the empty blank of the chart, whistled his surprise, and sank back feebly in a chair.

"It gets me," he said. "There can't be land around here. We never drifted or ran like that. The whole voyage has been crazy. Will you kindly go up, Mr. Snow, and see what's ailing Jackie."

"It's land all right," the mate called down a minute afterward. "You can see it from the deck—tops of cocoanuts—an atoll of some sort. Maybe it's Leu-Leu after all."

Grief shook his head positively as he gazed at the fringe of palms, only the tops visible, apparently rising out of the sea.

"Haul up on the wind, Mr. Snow, close-and-by, and we'll take a look. We can just reach past to the south, and if it spreads off in that direction we'll hit the southwest corner."

Very near must palms be to be seen from the low deck of a schooner, and, slowly as the *Uncle Toby* sailed, she quickly raised the low land above the sea, while more palms increased the definition of the atoll circle.

"She's a beauty," the mate remarked. "A perfect circle. . . . Looks as if it might be eight or nine miles across. . . . Wonder if there's an entrance to the lagoon. . . . Who knows? Maybe it's a brand new find."

They coasted up the west side of the atoll, making short tacks in to the surf-pounded coral rock and out again. From the masthead, across the palm-fringe, a Kanaka announced the lagoon and a small island in the middle.

"I know what you're thinking," Grief said to his mate.

Snow, who had been muttering and shaking his head, looked up with quick and challenging incredulity.

"You're thinking the entrance will be on the northwest," Grief went on, as if reciting. "Two cable lengths wide, marked on the north by three separated cocoanuts, and on the south by pandanus trees. Eight miles in diameter, a perfect circle, with an island in the dead centre."

"I was thinking that," Snow acknowledged.

"And there's the entrance opening up just where it ought to be—"

"And the three palms," Snow almost whispered, "and the pandanus trees. If there's a windmill on the island, it's it—Swithin Hall's island. But it can't be. Everybody's been looking for it for the last ten years."

"Hall played you a dirty trick once, didn't he?" Grief queried.

Snow nodded. "That's why I'm working for you. He broke me flat. It was downright robbery. I bought the wreck of the *Cascade*, down in Sydney, out of a first instalment of a legacy from home."

"She went on Christmas Island, didn't she?"

"Yes, full tilt, high and dry, in the night. They saved the passengers and mails. Then I bought a little island schooner, which took the rest of my money, and I had to wait the final payment by the executors to fit her out. What did Swithin Hall do—he was at Honolulu at the time—but make a straightaway run for Christmas Island. Neither right nor title did he have. When I got there, the hull and engines were all that was left of the *Cascade*. She had had a fair shipment of silk on board, too. And it wasn't even damaged. I got it afterward pretty straight from his supercargo. He cleared something like sixty thousand dollars."

Snow shrugged his shoulders and gazed bleakly at the smooth surface of the lagoon, where tiny wavelets danced in the afternoon sun.

"The wreck was mine. I bought her at public auction. I'd gambled big, and I'd lost. When I got back to Sydney, the crew, and some of the tradesmen who'd extended me credit, libelled the schooner. I pawned my watch and sextant, and shovelled coal one spell, and finally got a billet in the New Hebrides on a screw of eight pounds a month. Then I tried my luck as independent trader, went broke, took a mate's billet on a recruiter down to Tanna and over to Fiji, got a job as overseer on a German plantation back of Apia, and finally settled down on the *Uncle Toby*."

"Have you ever met Swithin Hall?"

Snow shook his head.

"Well, you're likely to meet him now. There's the windmill."

In the centre of the lagoon, as they emerged from the passage, they opened a small, densely wooded island, among the trees of which a large Dutch windmill showed plainly.

"Nobody at home from the looks of it," Grief said, "or you might have a chance to collect."

The mate's face set vindictively, and his fists clenched.

"Can't touch him legally. He's got too much money now. But I can take sixty thousand dollars' worth out of his hide. I hope he is at home."

"Then I hope he is, too," Grief said, with an appreciative smile. "You got the description of his island from Bau-Oti, I suppose?"

"Yes, as pretty well everybody else has. The trouble is that Bau-

Oti can't give latitude or longitude. Says they sailed a long way from the Gilberts—that's all he knows. I wonder what became of him."

"I saw him a year ago on the beach at Tahiti. Said he was thinking about shipping for a cruise through the Paumotus. Well, here we are, getting close in. Heave the lead, Jackie-Jackie. Stand by to let go, Mr. Snow. According to Bau-Oti, anchorage three hundred yards off the west shore in nine fathoms, coral patches to the southeast. There are the patches. What do you get, Jackie?"

"Nine fadom."

"Let go, Mr. Snow."

The *Uncle Toby* swung to her chain, headsails ran down, and the Kanaka crew sprang to fore and main-halyards and sheets.

IV

The whaleboat laid alongside the small, coral-stone landing-pier, and David Grief and his mate stepped ashore.

"You'd think the place deserted," Grief said, as they walked up a sanded path to the bungalow. "But I smell a smell that I've often smelled. Something doing, or my nose is a liar. The lagoon is carpeted with shell. They're rotting the meat out not a thousand miles away. Get that whiff?"

Like no bungalow in the tropics was this bungalow of Swithin Hall. Of mission architecture, when they had entered through the unlatched screen door they found decoration and furniture of the same mission style. The floor of the big living-room was covered with the finest Samoan mats. There were couches, window seats, cozy corners, and a billiard table. A sewing table, and a sewing-basket, spilling over with sheer linen in the French embroidery of which stuck a needle, tokened a woman's presence. By screen and veranda the blinding sunshine was subdued to a cool, dim radiance. The sheen of pearl push-buttons caught Grief's eye.

"Storage batteries, by George, run by the windmill!" he exclaimed as he pressed the buttons. "And concealed lighting!"

Hidden bowls glowed, and the room was filled with diffused golden light. Many shelves of books lined the walls. Grief fell to running over their titles. A fairly well-read man himself, for a sea-adventurer, he glimpsed a wideness of range and catholicity of taste that were beyond him. Old friends he met, and others that he had heard of but never read. There were complete sets of Tolstoy, Turgenieff, and Gorky; of Cooper and Mark Twain; of Hugo, and Zola, and Sue; and of Flaubert, De Maupassant, and Paul de Koch. He glanced curiously at the pages of Metchnikoff, Weininger, and Schopenhauer, and wonderingly at those of Ellis, Lydston, Krafft-Ebbing, and Forel. Woodruff's *Expansion of Races* was in his hands when Snow returned from further exploration of the house.[3]

"Enamelled bath-tub, separate room for a shower, and a sitz-bath!" he exclaimed. "Fitted up for a king! And I reckon some of my money went to pay for it. The place must be occupied. I found fresh-opened butter and milk tins in the pantry, and fresh turtle-meat hanging up. I'm going to see what else I can find."

Grief, too, departed, through a door that led out of the opposite end of the living-room. He found himself in a self-evident woman's bedroom. Across it, he peered through a wire-mesh door into a screened and darkened sleeping porch. On a couch lay a woman asleep. In the soft light she seemed remarkably beautiful in a dark Spanish way. By her side, opened and face downward, a novel lay on a chair. From the colour in her cheeks, Grief concluded that she had not been long in the tropics. After the one glimpse he stole softly back, in time to see Snow entering the living-room through the other door. By the naked arm he was clutching an age-wrinkled black who grinned in fear and made signs of dumbness.

"I found him snoozing in a little kennel out back," the mate said. "He's the cook, I suppose. Can't get a word out of him. What did you find?"

"A sleeping princess. S-sh! There's somebody now."

"If it's Hall," Snow muttered, clenching his fist.

Grief shook his head. "No rough-house. There's a woman here. And if it is Hall, before we go I'll maneuver a chance for you to get action."

The door opened, and a large, heavily built man entered. In his belt was a heavy, long-barrelled Colt's. One quick, anxious look he

"From the color in her cheeks Grief concluded that she had not been long in the tropics. . . . " Drawing by Anton Otto Fischer.

gave them, then his face wreathed in a genial smile and his hand was extended.

"Welcome, strangers. But if you don't mind my asking, how, by all that's sacred, did you ever manage to find my island?"

"Because we were out of our course," Grief answered, shaking hands.

"My name's Hall, Swithin Hall," the other said, turning to shake Snow's hand. "And I don't mind telling you that you're the first visitors I've ever had."

"And this is your secret island that's had all the beaches talking for years?" Grief answered. "Well, I know the formula now for finding it."

"How's that?" Hall asked quickly.

"Smash your chronometer, get mixed up with a hurricane, and then keep your eyes open for cocoanuts rising out of the sea."

"And what is your name?" Hall asked, after he had laughed perfunctorily.

"Anstey—Phil Anstey," Grief answered promptly. "Bound on the *Uncle Toby* from the Gilberts to New Guinea, and trying to find my longitude. This is my mate, Mr. Gray, a better navigator than I, but who has lost his goat just the same to the chronometer."

Grief did not know his reason for lying, but he had felt the prompting and succumbed to it. He vaguely divined that something was wrong, but could not place his finger on it. Swithin Hall was a fat, round-faced man, with a laughing lip and laughter-wrinkles in the corners of his eyes. But Grief, in his early youth, had learned how deceptive this type could prove, as well as the deceptiveness of blue eyes that screened the surface with fun and hid what went on behind.

"What are you doing with my cook?—lost yours and trying to shanghai him?" Hall was saying. "You'd better let him go, if you're going to have any supper. My wife's here, and she'll be glad to meet you—dinner, she calls it, and calls me down for misnaming it, but I'm old fashioned. My folks always ate dinner in the middle of the day. Can't get over early training. Don't you want to wash up? I do.

Look at me. I've been working like a dog—out with the diving crew
—shell, you know. But of course you smelt it."

V

Snow pleaded charge of the schooner, and went on board. In addition to his repugnance at breaking salt with the man who had
robbed him, it was necessary for him to impress the inviolableness of
Grief's lies on the Kanaka crew. By eleven o'clock Grief came on
board, to find his mate waiting up for him.

"There's something doing on Swithin Hall's island," Grief said,
shaking his head. "I can't make out what it is, but I get the feel of it.
What does Swithin Hall look like?"

Snow shook his head.

"That man ashore there never bought the books on the shelves,"
Grief declared with conviction. "Nor did he ever go in for concealed
lighting. He's got a surface flow of suavity, but he's rough as a hoof-
rasp underneath. He's an oily bluff. And the bunch he's got with
him—Watson and Gorman their names are; they came in after you
left—real sea-dogs, middle-aged, marred and battered, tough as rusty
wrought-iron nails and twice as dangerous; real ugly customers, with
guns in their belts, who don't strike me as just the right sort to be on
such comradely terms with Swithin Hall. And the woman! She's a
lady. I mean it. She knows a whole lot of South America, and of
China, too. I'm sure she's Spanish, though her English is natural.
She's travelled. We talked bull-fights. She's seen them in Guyaquil, in
Mexico, in Seville. She knows a lot about sealskins.

"Now here's what bothers me. She knows music. I asked her if
she played. And he's fixed that place up like a palace. That being so,
why hasn't he a piano for her? Another thing: she's quick and lively
and he watches her whenever she talks. He's on pins and needles,
and continually breaking in and leading the conversation. Say, did
you ever hear that Swithin Hall was married?"

"Bless me, I don't know," the mate replied. "Never entered my
head to think about it."

"He introduced her as Mrs. Hall. And Watson and Gorman call him Hall. They're a precious pair, those two men. I don't understand it at all."

"What are you going to do about it?" Snow asked.

"Oh, hang around a while. There are some books ashore there I want to read. Suppose you send that topmast down in the morning and generally overhaul. We've been through a hurricane, you know. Set up the rigging while you're about it. Get things pretty well adrift, and take your time."

VI

The next day Grief's suspicions found further food. Ashore early, he strolled across the little island to the barracks occupied by the divers. They were just boarding the boats when he arrived, and it struck him that for Kanakas they behaved more like chain-gang prisoners. The three white men were there, and Grief noted that each carried a rifle. Hall greeted him jovially enough, but Gorman and Watson scowled as they grunted curt good mornings.

A moment afterward one of the Kanakas, as he bent to place his oar, favoured Grief with a slow, deliberate wink. The man's face was familiar, one of the thousands of native sailors and divers he had encountered drifting about in the island trade.

"Don't tell them who I am," Grief said, in Tahitian. "Did you ever sail for me?"

The man's head nodded and his mouth opened, but before he could speak he was suppressed by a savage "Shut up!" from Watson, who was already in the sternsheets.

"I beg pardon," Grief said. "I ought to have known better."

"That's all right," Hall interposed. "The trouble is they're too much talk and not enough work. Have to be severe with them, or they wouldn't get enough shell to pay their grub."

Grief nodded sympathetically. "I know them. Got a crew of them myself—the lazy swine. Got to drive them like niggers to get a half-day's work out of them."

"What was you sayin' to him?" Gorman blurted in bluntly.

"I was asking how the shell was, and how deep they were diving."

"Thick," Hall took over the answering. "We're working now in about ten fathom. It's right out there, not a hundred yards off. Want to come along?"

Half the day Grief spent with the boats, and had lunch in the bungalow. In the afternoon he loafed, taking a siesta in the big living-room, reading some, and talking for half an hour with Mrs. Hall. After dinner, he played billiards with her husband. It chanced that Grief had never before encountered Swithin Hall, yet the latter's fame as an expert at billiards was the talk of the beaches from Levuka to Honolulu. But the man Grief played with this night proved most indifferent at the game. His wife showed herself far cleverer with the cue.

When he went on board the *Uncle Toby* Grief routed Jackie-Jackie out of bed. He described the location of the barracks, and told the Tongan to swim softly around and have talk with the Kanakas. In two hours Jackie-Jackie was back. He shook his head as he stood dripping before Grief.

"Very funny t'ing," he reported. "One white man stop all the time. He has big rifle. He lay in water and watch. Maybe twelve o'clock, other white man come and take rifle. First white man go to bed. Other man stop now with rifle. No good. Me cannot talk with Kanakas. Me come back."

"By George!" Grief said to Snow, after the Tongan had gone back to his bunk. "I smell something more than shell. Those three men are standing watches over their Kanakas. That man's no more Swithin Hall than I am."

Snow whistled from the impact of a new idea.

"I've got it!" he cried.

"And I'll name it," Grief retorted. "It's in your mind that the *Emily L.* was their schooner?"

"Just that. They're raising and rotting the shell, while she's gone for more divers, or provisions, or both."

"And I agree with you." Grief glanced at the cabin clock and evinced signs of bed-going. "He's a sailor. The three of them are. But they're not island men. They're new in these waters."

Again Snow whistled.

"And the *Emily L.* is lost with all hands," he said. "We know that. They're marooned here till Swithin Hall comes. Then he'll catch them with all the shell."

"Or they'll take possession of his schooner."

"Hope they do!" Snow muttered vindictively. "Somebody ought to rob him. Wish I was in their boots. I'd balance off that sixty thousand."

VII

A week passed, during which time the *Uncle Toby* was ready for sea, while Grief managed to allay any suspicion of him by the shore crowd. Even Gorman and Watson accepted him at his self-description. Throughout the week Grief begged and badgered them for the longitude of the island.

"You wouldn't have me leave here lost," he finally urged. "I can't get a line on my chronometer without your longitude."

Hall laughingly refused.

"You're too good a navigator, Mr. Anstey, not to fetch New Guinea or some other high land."

"And you're too good a navigator, Mr. Hall," Grief replied, "not to know that I can fetch your island any time by running down its latitude. "

On the last evening, ashore, as usual, to dinner, Grief got his first view of the pearls they had collected. Mrs. Hall, waxing enthusiastic, had asked her husband to bring forth the "pretties," and had spent half an hour showing them to Grief. His delight in them was genuine, as well as was his surprise that they had made so rich a haul.

"The lagoon is virgin," Hall explained. "You saw yourself that most of the shell is large and old. But it's funny that we got most of the valuable pearls in one small patch in the course of a week. It was a little treasure house. Every oyster seemed filled—seed pearls by the quart, of course, but the perfect ones, most of that bunch there, came out of the small patch."

Grief ran his eye over them and knew their value ranged from one hundred to a thousand dollars each, while the several selected large ones went far beyond.

"Oh, the pretties! the pretties!" Mrs. Hall cried, bending forward suddenly and kissing them.

A few minutes later she arose to say good-night.

"It's good-bye," Grief said, as he took her hand. "We sail at day-light."

"So suddenly!" she cried, while Grief could not help seeing the quick light of satisfaction in her husband's eyes.

"Yes," Grief continued. "All the repairs are finished. I can't get the longitude of your island out of your husband, though I'm still in hopes he'll relent."

Hall laughed and shook his head, and, as his wife left the room, proposed a last farewell nightcap. They sat over it, smoking and talking.

"What do you estimate they're worth?" Grief asked, indicating the spread of pearls on the table. "I mean what the pearl-buyers would give you in open market?"

"Oh, seventy-five or eighty thousand," Hall said carelessly.

"I'm afraid you're underestimating. I know pearls a bit. Take that biggest one. It's perfect. Not a cent less than five thousand dollars. Some multimillionaire will pay double that some day, when the deal-ers have taken their whack. And never minding the seed pearls, you've got quarts of baroques there. And baroques are coming into fashion. They're picking up and doubling on themselves every year."

Hall gave the trove of pearls a closer and longer scrutiny, estimat-ing the different parcels and adding the sum aloud.

"You're right," he admitted. "They're worth a hundred thousand right now."

"And at what do you figure your working expenses?" Grief went on. "Your time, and your two men's, and the divers'?"

"Five thousand would cover it."

"Then they stand to net you ninety-five thousand?"

"Something like that. But why so curious?"

"Why, I was just trying—" Grief paused and drained his glass. "Just trying to reach some sort of an equitable arrangement. Suppose I should give you and your people a passage to Sydney and the five thousand dollars—or, better, seven thousand five hundred. You've worked hard."

Without commotion or muscular movement the other man became alert and tense. His round-faced geniality went out like the flame of a snuffed candle. No laughter clouded the surface of the eyes, and in their depths showed the hard, dangerous soul of the man. He spoke in a low, deliberate voice.

"Now just what in hell do you mean by that?"

Grief casually relighted his cigar.

"I don't know just how to begin," he said. "The situation is— er—is embarrassing—for you. You see, I'm trying to be fair. As I say, you've worked hard. I don't want to confiscate the pearls. I want to pay you for your time and trouble, and expense."

Conviction, instantaneous and absolute, froze on the other's face.

"And I thought you were in Europe," he muttered. Hope flickered for a moment. "Look here, you're joking me. How do I know you're Swithin Hall?"

Grief shrugged his shoulders. "Such a joke would be in poor taste, after your hospitality. And it is equally in poor taste to have two Swithin Halls on the island."

"Since you're Swithin Hall, then who the deuce am I? Do you know that, too?"

"No," Grief answered airily. "But I'd like to know."

"Well, it's none of your business."

"I grant it. Your identity is beside the point. Besides, I know your schooner, and I can find out who you are from that."

"What's her name?"

"The *Emily L.*"

"Correct. I'm Captain Raffy, owner and master."

"The seal-poacher? I've heard of you. What under the sun brought you down here on my preserves?"

"Needed the money. The seal herds are about finished."

"And the out-of-the-way places of the world are better policed, eh?"

"Pretty close to it. And now about this present scrape, Mr. Hall. I can put up a nasty fight. What are you going to do about it?"

"What I said. Even better. What's the *Emily L.* worth?"

"She's seen her day. Not above ten thousand, which would be robbery. Every time she's in a rough sea I'm afraid she'll jump her ballast through her planking."

"She has jumped it, Captain Raffy. I sighted her bottom-up after the blow. Suppose we say she was worth seven thousand five hundred. I'll pay over to you fifteen thousand and give you a passage. Don't move your hands from your lap." Grief stood up, went over to him, and took his revolver. "Just a necessary precaution, Captain. Now you'll go on board with me. I'll break the news to Mrs. Raffy afterward, and fetch her out to join you."

"You're behaving handsomely, Mr. Hall, I must say," Captain Raffy volunteered, as the whaleboat came alongside the *Uncle Toby*. "But watch out for Gorman and Watson. They're ugly customers. And, by the way, I don't like to mention it, but you've seen my wife. I've given her four or five pearls. Watson and Gorman were willing."

"Say no more, Captain. Say no more. They shall remain hers. Is that you, Mr. Snow? Here's a friend I want you to take charge of— Captain Raffy. I'm going ashore for his wife."

VIII

David Grief sat writing at the library table in the bungalow living-room. Outside, the first pale of dawn was showing. He had had a busy night. Mrs. Raffy had taken two hysterical hours to pack her and Captain Raffy's possessions. Gorman had been caught asleep, but Watson, standing guard over the divers, had shown fight. Matters did not reach the shooting stage, but it was only after it had been demonstrated to him that the game was up that he consented to join his companions on board. For temporary convenience, he and Gorman were shackled in the mate's room, Mrs. Raffy was confined in Grief's, and Captain Raffy made fast to the cabin table.

Grief finished the document and read over what he had written:

To Swithin Hall,
    for pearls taken from his lagoon. . . . .(estimated) $100,000

To Herbert Snow,
    paid in full for salvage from steamship *Cascade* in pearls. . .(estimated) 60,000

To Captain Raffy,
    salary and expenses for collecting pearls. 7,500

To Captain Raffy,
    reimbursement for schooner *Emily L.,* lost in hurricane. 7,500

To Mrs. Raffy,
    for good will, five fair pearls . . . .(estimated) 1,100

To passage to Sydney, four persons, at 120. 480

To white lead for painting Swithin Hall's two whaleboats. 9

To Swithin Hall,
    balance, in pearls (estimated) which are to be found
    in drawer of library table. 23,411

                                  $100,000 – $100,000

Grief signed and dated, paused, and added at the bottom:

P.S.—Still owing to Swithin Hall three books, borrowed from library:
Hudson's *Law of Psychic Phenomena,* Zola's *Paris,* and Mahan's *Problem of Asia.* These books, or full value, can be collected of said David
Grief's Sydney office.

He shut off the electric light, picked up the bundle of books, carefully latched the front door, and went down to the waiting whaleboat.

SIX

A GOBOTO NIGHT

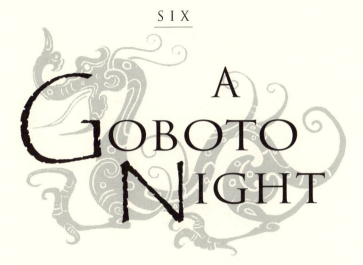

The Londons' adventure on the Snark *took them to places that even now have not yet developed into tourist stops. Interested in the practice of blackbirding, on August 8, 1908, the Londons took what they thought would be a few days' jaunt on the recruiting ketch* Minota *under the command of the colorful Captain Jansen. The eccentric wildman Jansen appears in "A Goboto Night" as Captain Jensen, but omitted is the harrowing series of events that took place during their voyage. On August 19, the* Minota, *with Jack and Charmian aboard, had just recruited three Melanesians as laborers when it ran aground on a reef just off Maluu, on the northwestern tip of Malaita, an island the Londons believed to be populated by cannibals. Every effort to free the vessel failed as the stranded party watched the tide go out. Jansen determined at once to send a boat to find the* Eugenie, *which he knew to be relatively nearby.*

Within hours, intrigued headhunters began to gather in canoes, surrounding the troubled vessel. As the day wore on and the party struggled desperately to budge the ketch, more islanders came to join their fellows; in a letter, Jack estimated that the mass of cannibals numbered a thousand. Jansen and the Londons wondered if this might indeed be their last adventure. Rescue finally came when the Eugenie *arrived on August 20, and Jack and Charmian returned to the comparative civilization of Ghavutu in the Florida*

Islands. Knowledge of mishaps and hairbreadth escapes such as these point out that the primitive and dangerous Pacific world of David Grief was not fiction, nor were the colorful characters depicted in the stories all the work of London's imagination.

The grimly comic sordidness of the company post on Goboto is an accurate, rather than romanticized, picture of the European and American colonial project at the beginning of the twentieth century. It was a rough-and-tumble batch of most unusual white men who manned such stations, and as London shows, stopovers by passing vessels were all that kept these lonely and often uncultivated men from "going native"—a very real danger most famously depicted in Conrad's Heart of Darkness. *With comic brilliance, London stresses this concern in his discussion of the urgency with which the island managers require white visitors to wear pants. Card games, with their carefully organized rules, are also seen as vital to the preservation of customs of group civility and Western logic. Finally, the wild yet highly formalized abuse of alcohol is only a distorted (and ultimately fatal) variation of "civilized" European traditions of social drinking.*

The crux of the tale, in fact, is the regulation of behavior that will secure the whites' identity as whites. Decades before Hemingway employed the idea of the "code hero," David Grief uses his own self-mastery to instruct the loutish, racist, and generally unpleasant Deacon with a creed that will provide him with new ideas and standards that will in time help him to become a man.

At Goboto[1] the traders come off their schooners and the planters drift in from far, wild coasts, and one and all they assume shoes, white duck trousers, and various other appearances of civilization. At Goboto mail is received, bills are paid, and newspapers, rarely more than five weeks old, are accessible; for the little island, belted with its coral reefs, affords safe anchorage, is the steamer port of call, and serves as the distributing point for the whole wide-scattered group.

Life at Goboto is heated, unhealthy, and lurid, and for its size it asserts the distinction of more cases of acute alcoholism than any other spot in the world. Guvutu, over in the Solomons, claims that it drinks between drinks. Goboto does not deny this. It merely states, in passing, that in the Goboton chronology no such interval of time is known. It also points out its import statistics, which show a far larger per capita consumption of spiritous liquors. Guvutu explains this on the basis that Goboto does a larger business and has more visitors. Goboto retorts that its resident population is smaller and that its visitors are thirstier. And the discussion goes on interminably, principally because of the fact that the disputants do not live long enough to settle it.

Goboto is not large. The island is only a quarter of a mile in diameter, and on it are situated an admiralty coal-shed (where a few tons of coal have lain untouched for twenty years),[2] the barracks for a handful of black labourers, a big store and warehouse with sheet-iron roofs, and a bungalow inhabited by the manager and his two clerks. They are the white population. An average of one man out of the three is always to be found down with fever. The job at Goboto is a hard one. It is the policy of the company to treat its patrons well, as invading companies have found out, and it is the task of the manager and clerks to do the treating. Throughout the year traders and recruiters arrive from far, dry cruises, and planters from equally distant and dry shores, bringing with them magnificent thirsts. Goboto is the mecca of sprees, and when they have spread they go back to their schooners and plantations to recuperate.

Some of the less hardy require as much as six months between visits. But for the manager and his assistants there are no such intervals. They are on the spot, and week by week, blown in by monsoon or southeast trade, the schooners come to anchor, cargo'd with copra, ivory nuts, pearl-shell, hawksbill turtle, and thirst.

It is a very hard job at Goboto. That is why the pay is twice that on other stations, and that is why the company selects only courageous and intrepid men for this particular station. They last no more than a year or so, when the wreckage of them is shipped back to Australia, or the remains of them are buried in the sand across on the windward side of the islet. Johnny Bassett, almost the legendary hero of Goboto, broke all records. He was a remittance man with a remarkable constitution, and he lasted seven years. His dying request was duly observed by his clerks, who pickled him in a cask of trade-rum (paid for out of their own salaries) and shipped him back to his people in England.

Nevertheless, at Goboto, they tried to be gentlemen. For that matter, though something was wrong with them, they were gentlemen, and had been gentlemen. That was why the great unwritten rule of Goboto was that visitors should put on pants and shoes. Breechclouts, lava-lavas, and bare legs were not tolerated. When Captain Jensen, the wildest of the Blackbirders though descended from old New York Knickerbocker stock, surged in, clad in loin-cloth, undershirt, two belted revolvers and a sheath-knife, he was stopped at the beach. This was in the days of Johnny Bassett, ever a stickler in matters of etiquette. Captain Jensen stood up in the sternsheets of his whaleboat and denied the existence of pants on his schooner. Also, he affirmed his intention of coming ashore. They of Goboto nursed him back to health from a bullet-hole through his shoulder, and in addition handsomely begged his pardon, for no pants had they found on his schooner. And finally, on the first day he sat up, Johnny Bassett kindly but firmly assisted his guest into a pair of pants of his

"Life at Goboto is heated, unhealthy, and lurid. . . . "
Drawing by Anton Otto Fischer.

own. This was the great precedent. In all the succeeding years it had
never been violated. White men and pants were undivorceable. Only
niggers ran naked. Pants constituted caste.

II

On this night things were, with one exception, in nowise different from any other night. Seven of them, with glimmering eyes and
steady legs, had capped a day of Scotch with swivel-sticked cocktails
and sat down to dinner. Jacketed, trousered, and shod, they were:
Jerry McMurtrey, the manager; Eddy Little and Jack Andrews, clerks;
Captain Stapler, of the recruiting ketch *Merry;* Darby Shryleton, plant-
er from Tito-Ito; Peter Gee, a half-caste Chinese pearl-buyer who
ranged from Ceylon to the Paumotus, and Alfred Deacon, a visitor
who had stopped off from the last steamer. At first wine was served
by the black servants to those that drank it, though all quickly shift-
ed back to Scotch and soda, pickling their food as they ate it, ere it
went into their calcined, pickled stomachs.

Over their coffee, they heard the rumble of an anchor-chain
through a hawse-pipe, tokening the arrival of a vessel.

"It's David Grief," Peter Gee remarked.[3]

"How do you know?" Deacon demanded truculently, and then
went on to deny the half-caste's knowledge. "You chaps put on a lot
of side over a new chum. I've done some sailing myself, and this
naming a craft when its sail is only a blur, or naming a man by the
sound of his anchor—it's—it's unadulterated poppycock."

Peter Gee was engaged in lighting a cigarette, and did not answer.

"Some of the niggers do amazing things that way," McMurtrey
interposed tactfully.

As with the others, this conduct of their visitor jarred on the manager. From the moment of Peter Gee's arrival that afternoon Deacon
had manifested a tendency to pick on him. He had disputed his statements and been generally rude.

"Maybe it's because Peter's got Chink blood in him," had been
Andrews' hypothesis. "Deacon's Australian, you know, and they're
daffy down there on colour."

"I fancy that's it," McMurtrey had agreed. "But we can't permit any bullying, especially of a man like Peter Gee, who's whiter than most white men."

In this the manager had been in nowise wrong. Peter Gee was that rare creature, a good as well as clever Eurasian. In fact, it was the stolid integrity of the Chinese blood that toned the recklessness and licentiousness of the English blood which had run in his father's veins.[4] Also, he was better educated than any man there, spoke better English as well as several other tongues, and knew and lived more of their own ideals of gentlemanness than they did themselves. And, finally, he was a gentle soul. Violence he deprecated, though he had killed men in his time. Turbulence he abhorred. He always avoided it as he would the plague.

Captain Stapler stepped in to help McMurtrey:

"I remember, when I changed schooners and came into Altman, the niggers knew right off the bat it was me. I wasn't expected, either, much less to be in another craft. They told the trader it was me. He used the glasses, and wouldn't believe them. But they did know. Told me afterward they could see it sticking out all over the schooner that I was running her."

Deacon ignored him, and returned to the attack on the pearl-buyer.

"How do you know from the sound of the anchor that it was this whatever-you-called-him man?" he challenged.

"There are so many things that go to make up such a judgment," Peter Gee answered. "It's very hard to explain. It would require almost a text book."

"I thought so," Deacon sneered. "Explanation that doesn't explain is easy."

"Who's for bridge?" Eddy Little, the second clerk, interrupted, looking up expectantly and starting to shuffle. "You'll play, won't you, Peter?"

"If he does, he's a bluffer," Deacon cut back. "I'm getting tired of all this poppycock. Mr. Gee, you will favour me and put yourself in a better light if you tell how you know who that man was that just dropped anchor. After that I'll play you piquet."

"Peter Gee, who's whiter than most white men. . . . "
Drawing by Anton Otto Fischer.

"I'd prefer bridge," Peter answered. "As for the other thing, it's something like this: By the sound it was a small craft—no square-rigger. No whistle, no siren, was blown—again a small craft. It anchored close in-still again a small craft, for steamers and big ships must drop hook outside the middle shoal. Now the entrance is tortuous. There is no recruiting nor trading captain in the group who dares to run the passage after dark. Certainly no stranger would. There *were* two exceptions. The first was Margonville. But he was executed by the High Court at Fiji. Remains the other exception, David Grief. Night or day, in any weather, he runs the passage. This is well known to all. A possible factor, in case Grief were somewhere else, would be some young dare-devil of a skipper. In this connection, in the first place, I don't know of any, nor does anybody else. In the second place, David Grief is in these waters, cruising on the *Gunga,* which is shortly scheduled to leave here for Karo-Karo. I spoke to Grief, on the *Gunga,* in Sandfly Passage, day before yesterday.[5] He was putting a trader ashore on a new station. He said he was going to call in at Babo, and then come on to Goboto. He has had ample time to get here. I have heard an anchor drop. Who else than David Grief can it be? Captain Donovan is skipper of the *Gunga,* and him I know too well to believe that he'd run in to Goboto after dark unless his owner were in charge. In a few minutes David Grief will enter through that door and say, 'In Guvutu they merely drink between drinks.' I'll wager fifty pounds he's the man that enters and that his words will be, 'In Guvutu they merely drink between drinks.'"

Deacon was for the moment crushed. The sullen blood rose darkly in his face.

"Well, he's answered you," McMurtrey laughed genially. "And I'll back his bet myself for a couple of sovereigns."

"Bridge! Who's going to take a hand?" Eddy Little cried impatiently. "Come on, Peter!"

"The rest of you play," Deacon said. "He and I are going to play piquet. "

"I'd prefer bridge," Peter Gee said mildly.

"Don't you play piquet?"

The pearl-buyer nodded.

"Then come on. Maybe I can show I know more about that than I do about anchors."

"Oh, I say—" McMurtrey began.

"You can play bridge," Deacon shut him off. "We prefer piquet."

Reluctantly, Peter Gee was bullied into a game that he knew would be unhappy.

"Only a rubber," he said, as he cut for deal.

"For how much?" Deacon asked.

Peter Gee shrugged his shoulders. "As you please."

"Hundred up—five pounds a game?"

Peter Gee agreed.

"With the lurch double, of course, ten pounds?"

"All right," said Peter Gee.

At another table four of the others sat in at bridge. Captain Stapler, who was no cardplayer, looked on and replenished the long glasses of Scotch that stood at each man's right hand. McMurtrey, with poorly concealed apprehension, followed as well as he could what went on at the piquet table. His fellow Englishmen as well were shocked by the behaviour of the Australian, and all were troubled by fear of some untoward act on his part. That he was working up his animosity against the half-caste, and that the explosion might come any time, was apparent to all.

"I hope Peter loses," McMurtrey said in an undertone.

"Not if he has any luck," Andrews answered. "He's a wizard at piquet. I know by experience."

That Peter Gee was lucky was patent from the continual badgering of Deacon, who filled his glass frequently. He had lost the first game, and, from his remarks, was losing the second, when the door opened and David Grief entered.

"In Guvutu they merely drink between drinks," he remarked casually to the assembled company, ere he gripped the manager's hand. "Hello, Mac! Say, my skipper's down in the whaleboat. He's got a silk shirt, a tie, and tennis shoes, all complete, but he wants you to send a pair of pants down. Mine are too small, but yours will fit him. Hello, Eddy! How's that *ngari-ngari*? You up, Jock? The miracle has happened. No one down with fever, and no one remarkably drunk." He sighed, "I suppose the night is young yet. Hello, Peter! Did you catch that big squall an hour after you left us? We had to let go the second anchor."

While he was being introduced to Deacon, McMurtrey dispatched a house-boy with the pants, and when Captain Donovan came in it was as a white man should—at least in Goboto.

Deacon lost the second game, and an outburst heralded the fact. Peter Gee devoted himself to lighting a cigarette and keeping quiet.

"What?—are you quitting because you're ahead?" Deacon demanded.

Grief raised his eyebrows questioningly to McMurtrey, who frowned back his own disgust.

"It's the rubber," Peter Gee answered.

"It takes three games to make a rubber. It's my deal. Come on!"

Peter Gee acquiesced, and the third game was on.

"Young whelp—he needs a lacing," McMurtrey muttered to Grief. "Come on, let us quit, you chaps. I want to keep an eye on him. If he goes too far I'll throw him out on the beach, company instructions or no."

"Who is he?" Grief queried.

"A left-over from last steamer. Company's orders to treat him nice. He's looking to invest in a plantation. Has a ten-thousand-pound letter of credit with the company. He's got 'all-white Australia' on the brain. Thinks because his skin is white and because his father was once Attorney-General of the Commonwealth that he can be a cur. That's why he's picking on Peter, and you know Peter's the last man in the world to make trouble or incur trouble. Damn the company. I didn't engage to wet-nurse its infants with bank accounts. Come on, fill your glass, Grief. The man's a blighter, a blithering blighter."

"Maybe he's only young," Grief suggested.

"He can't contain his drink—that's clear." The manager glared his disgust and wrath. "If he raises a hand to Peter, so help me, I'll give him a licking myself, the little overgrown cad!"

The pearl-buyer pulled the pegs out of the cribbage board on which he was scoring and sat back. He had won the third game. He glanced across to Eddy Little, saying:

"I'm ready for the bridge, now."

"I wouldn't be a quitter," Deacon snarled.

"Oh, really, I'm tired of the game," Peter Gee assured him with his habitual quietness.

"Come on and be game," Deacon bullied. "One more. You can't take my money that way. I'm out fifteen pounds. Double or quits."

McMurtrey was about to interpose, but Grief restrained him with his eyes.

"If it positively is the last, all right," said Peter Gee, gathering up the cards. "It's my deal, I believe. As I understand it, this final is for fifteen pounds. Either you owe me thirty or we quit even?"

"That's it, chappie. Either we break even or I pay you thirty."

"Getting blooded, eh?" Grief remarked, drawing up a chair.

The other men stood or sat around the table, and Deacon played again in bad luck. That he was a good player was clear. The cards were merely running against him. That he could not take his ill luck with equanimity was equally clear. He was guilty of sharp, ugly curses, and he snapped and growled at the imperturbable half-caste. In the end Peter Gee counted out, while Deacon had not even made his fifty points. He glowered speechlessly at his opponent.

"Looks like a lurch," said Grief.

"Which is double," said Peter Gee.

"There's no need your telling me," Deacon snarled. "I've studied arithmetic. I owe you forty-five pounds. There, take it!"

The way in which he flung the nine five-pound notes on the table was an insult in itself. Peter Gee was even quieter, and flew no signals of resentment.

"You've got fool's luck, but you can't play cards, I can tell you that much," Deacon went on. "I could teach you cards."

The half-caste smiled and nodded acquiescence as he folded up the money.

"There's a little game called casino—I wonder if you ever heard of it?—a child's game."

"I've seen it played," the half-caste murmured gently.

"What's that?" snapped Deacon. "Maybe you think you can play it?"

"Oh, no, not for a moment. I'm afraid I haven't head enough for it."

"It's a bully game, casino," Grief broke in pleasantly. "I like it very much."

Deacon ignored him.

"I'll play you ten quid a game—thirty-one points out," was the challenge to Peter Gee. "And I'll show you how little you know about cards. Come on! Where's a full deck?"

"No, thanks," the half-caste answered. "They are waiting for me in order to make up a bridge set."

"Yes, come on," Eddy Little begged eagerly. "Come on, Peter, let's get started."

"Afraid of a little game like casino," Deacon girded. "Maybe the stakes are too high. I'll play you for pennies—or farthings, if you say so."

The man's conduct was a hurt and an affront to all of them. McMurtrey could stand it no longer.

"Now hold on, Deacon. He says he doesn't want to play. Let him alone."

Deacon turned raging upon his host; but before he could blurt out his abuse, Grief had stepped into the breach.

"I'd like to play casino with you," he said.

"What do you know about it?"

"Not much, but I'm willing to learn."

"Well, I'm not teaching for pennies to-night."

"Oh, that's all right," Grief answered. "I'll play for almost any sum—within reason, of course."

Deacon proceeded to dispose of this intruder with one stroke.

"I'll play you a hundred pounds a game, if that will do you any good."

Grief beamed his delight. "That will be all right, very right. Let us begin. Do you count sweeps?"

Deacon was taken aback. He had not expected a Goboton trader to be anything but crushed by such a proposition.

"Do you count sweeps?" Grief repeated.

Andrews had brought him a new deck, and he was throwing out the joker.

"Certainly not," Deacon answered. "That's a sissy game."

"I'm glad," Grief coincided. "I don't like sissy games either."

"You don't, eh? Well, then, I'll tell you what we'll do. We'll play for five hundred pounds a game."

Again Deacon was taken aback.

"I'm agreeable," Grief said, beginning to shuffle. "Cards and spades go out first, of course, and then big and little casino, and the aces in the bridge order of value. Is that right?"

"You're a lot of jokers down here," Deacon laughed, but his laughter was strained. "How do I know you've got the money?"

"By the same token I know you've got it. Mac, how's my credit with the company?"

"For all you want," the manager answered.

"You personally guarantee that?" Deacon demanded.

"I certainly do," McMurtrey said. "Depend upon it, the company will honour his paper up and past your letter of credit."

"Low deals," Grief said, placing the deck before Deacon on the table.

The latter hesitated in the midst of the cut and looked around with querulous misgiving at the faces of the others. The clerks and captains nodded.

"You're all strangers to me," Deacon complained. "How am I to know? Money on paper isn't always the real thing."

Then it was that Peter Gee, drawing a wallet from his pocket and borrowing a fountain pen from McMurtrey, went into action.

"I haven't gone to buying yet," the half-caste explained, "so the account is intact. I'll just indorse it over to you, Grief. It's for fifteen thousand. There, look at it."

Deacon intercepted the letter of credit as it was being passed across the table. He read it slowly, then glanced up at McMurtrey.

"Is that right?"

"Yes. It's just the same as your own, and just as good. The company's paper is always good."

Deacon cut the cards, won the deal, and gave them a thorough shuffle. But his luck was still against him, and he lost the game.

"Another game," he said. "We didn't say how many, and you can't quit with me a loser. I want action."

Grief shuffled and passed the cards for the cut.

"Let's play for a thousand," Deacon said, when he had lost the second game. And when the thousand had gone the way of the two five hundred bets he proposed to play for two thousand.

"That's progression," McMurtrey warned, and was rewarded by a glare from Deacon. But the manager was insistent. "You don't have to play progression, Grief, unless you're foolish."

"Who's playing this game?" Deacon flamed at his host; and then, to Grief: "I've lost two thousand to you. Will you play for two thousand?"

Grief nodded, the fourth game began, and Deacon won. The manifest unfairness of such betting was known to all of them. Though he had lost three games out of four, Deacon had lost no money. By the child's device of doubling his wager with each loss, he was bound, with the first game he won, no matter how long delayed, to be even again.

He now evinced an unspoken desire to stop, but Grief passed the deck to be cut.

"What?" Deacon cried. "You want more?"

"Haven't got anything yet," Grief murmured whimsically, as he began the deal. "For the usual five hundred, I suppose?"

The shame of what he had done must have tingled in Deacon, for he answered, "No, we'll play for a thousand. And say! Thirty-one points is too long. Why not twenty-one points out—if it isn't too rapid for you?"

"That will make it a nice, quick, little game," Grief agreed.

The former method of play was repeated. Deacon lost two games, doubled the stake, and was again even. But Grief was patient, though the thing occurred several times in the next hour's play. Then happened what he was waiting for—a lengthening in the series of losing games for Deacon. The latter doubled to four thousand and lost, doubled to eight thousand and lost, and then proposed to double to sixteen thousand.

Grief shook his head. "You can't do that, you know. You're only ten thousand credit with the company."

"You mean you won't give me action?" Deacon asked hoarsely. "You mean that with eight thousand of my money you're going to quit?"

Grief smiled and shook his head.

"It's robbery, plain robbery," Deacon went on. "You take my money and won't give me action."

"No, you're wrong. I'm perfectly willing to give you what action you've got coming to you. You've got two thousand pounds of action yet.

"Well, we'll play it," Deacon took him up. "You cut."

The game was played in silence, save for irritable remarks and curses from Deacon. Silently the onlookers filled and sipped their

"You mean that with eight thousand of my money you're going to quit?"
Drawing by Anton Otto Fischer.

long Scotch glasses. Grief took no notice of his opponent's outbursts, but concentrated on the game. He was really playing cards, and there were fifty-two in the deck to be kept track of, and of which he did keep track. Two thirds of the way through the last deal he threw down his hand.

"Cards put me out," he said. "I have twenty-seven."

"If you've made a mistake," Deacon threatened, his face white and drawn.

"Then I shall have lost. Count them."

Grief passed over his stack of takings, and Deacon, with trembling fingers, verified the count. He half shoved his chair back from the table and emptied his glass. He looked about him at unsympathetic faces.

"I fancy I'll be catching the next steamer for Sydney," he said, and for the first time his speech was quiet and without bluster.

As Grief told them afterward: "Had he whined or raised a roar I wouldn't have given him that last chance. As it was, he took his medicine like a man, and I had to do it."

Deacon glanced at his watch, simulated a weary yawn, and started to rise.

"Wait," Grief said. "Do you want further action?"

The other sank down in his chair, strove to speak, but could not, licked his dry lips, and nodded his head.

"Captain Donovan here sails at daylight in the *Gunga* for Karo-Karo," Grief began with seeming irrelevance. "Karo-Karo is a ring of sand in the sea, with a few thousand cocoanut trees. Pandanus grows there, but they can't grow sweet potatoes nor taro. There are about eight hundred natives, a king and two prime ministers, and the last three named are the only ones who wear any clothes. It's a sort of Godforsaken little hole, and once a year I send a schooner up from Goboto. The drinking water is brackish, but old Tom Butler has survived on it for a dozen years. He's the only white man there, and he has a boat's crew of five Santa Cruz boys who would run away or kill him if they could. That is why they were sent there. They can't run away. He is always supplied with the hard cases from the plantations. There are no missionaries. Two native Samoan teachers were clubbed to death on the beach when they landed several years ago.

"Naturally, you are wondering what it is all about. But have patience. As I have said, Captain Donovan sails on the annual trip to Karo-Karo at daylight to-morrow. Tom Butler is old, and getting quite helpless. I've tried to retire him to Australia, but he says he wants to remain and die on Karo-Karo, and he will in the next year or so. He's a queer old codger. Now the time is due for me to send some white man up to take the work off his hands. I wonder how you'd like the job. You'd have to stay two years.

"Hold on! I've not finished. You've talked frequently of action this evening. There's no action in betting away what you've never sweated for. The money you've lost to me was left you by your father or some other relative who did the sweating. But two years of work as trader on Karo-Karo would mean something. I'll bet the ten thousand I've won from you against two years of your time. If you win, the money's yours. If you lose, you take the job at Karo-Karo and sail at daylight. Now that's what might be called real action. Will you play?"

Deacon could not speak. His throat lumped and he nodded his head as he reached for the cards.

"One thing more," Grief said. "I can do even better. If you lose, two years of your time are mine—naturally without wages. Nevertheless, I'll pay you wages. If your work is satisfactory, if you observe all instructions and rules, I'll pay you five thousand pounds a year for two years. The money will be deposited with the company, to be paid to you, with interest, when the time expires. Is that all right?"

"Too much so," Deacon stammered. "You are unfair to yourself. A trader only gets ten or fifteen pounds a month."

"Put it down to action, then," Grief said, with an air of dismissal. "And before we begin, I'll jot down several of the rules. These you will repeat aloud every morning during the two years-if you lose. They are for the good of your soul. When you have repeated them aloud seven hundred and thirty Karo-Karo mornings I am confident they will be in your memory to stay. Lend me your pen, Mac. Now, let's see-"

He wrote steadily and rapidly for some minutes, then proceeded to read the matter aloud:

> "*I must always remember that one man is as good as another, save and except when he thinks he is better.*
>
> "*No matter how drunk I am I must not fail to be a gentleman. A gentleman is a man who is gentle. Note: It would be better not to get drunk.*
>
> "*When I play a man's game with men I must play like a man.*
>
> "*A good curse, rightly used and rarely, is an efficient thing. Too many curses spoil the cursing. Note: A curse cannot change a card sequence nor cause the wind to blow.*
>
> "*There is no license for a man to be less than a man. Ten thousand pounds cannot purchase such a license.*"

At the beginning of the reading Deacon's face had gone white with anger. Then had arisen, from neck to forehead, a slow and terrible flush that deepened to the end of the reading.

"There, that will be all," Grief said, as he folded the paper and tossed it to the centre of the table. "Are you still ready to play the game?"

"I deserve it," Deacon muttered brokenly. "I've been an ass. Mr. Gee, before I know whether I win or lose, I want to apologize. Maybe it was the whiskey, I don't know, but I'm an ass, a cad, a bounder—everything that's rotten."

He held out his hand, and the half-caste took it beamingly.

"I say, Grief," he blurted out, "the boy's all right. Call the whole thing off, and let's forget it in a final nightcap."

Grief showed signs of debating, but Deacon cried:

"No; I won't permit it. I'm not a quitter. If it's Karo-Karo, it's Karo-Karo. There's nothing more to it."

"Right," said Grief, as he began the shuffle. "If he's the right stuff to go to Karo-Karo, Karo-Karo won't do him any harm."

The game was close and hard. Three times they divided the deck between them and "cards" was not scored. At the beginning of the fifth and last deal, Deacon needed three points to go out, and Grief needed four. "Cards" alone would put Deacon out, and he played for "cards." He no longer muttered or cursed, and played his best game of the evening. Incidentally he gathered in the two black aces and the ace of hearts.

"I suppose you can name the four cards I hold," he challenged, as the last of the deal was exhausted and he picked up his hand.

Grief nodded.

"Then name them."

"The knave of spades, the deuce of spades, the tray of hearts, and the ace of diamonds," Grief answered.

Those behind Deacon and looking at his hand made no sign. Yet the naming had been correct.

"I fancy you play casino better than I," Deacon acknowledged. "I can name only three of yours, a knave, an ace, and big casino."

"Wrong. There aren't five aces in the deck. You've taken in three and you hold the fourth in your hand now."

"By Jove, you're right," Deacon admitted. "I did scoop in three. Anyway, I'll make 'cards' on you. That's all I need."

"I'll let you save little casino—" Grief paused to calculate. "Yes, and the ace as well, and still I'll make 'cards' and go out with big casino. Play."

"No 'cards,' and I win!" Deacon exulted as the last of the hand was played. "I go out on little casino and the four aces. 'Big casino' and 'spades' only bring you to twenty."

Grief shook his head. "Some mistake, I'm afraid."

"No," Deacon declared positively. "I counted every card I took in. That's the one thing I was correct on. I've twenty-six, and you've twenty-six."

"Count again," Grief said.

Carefully and slowly, with trembling fingers, Deacon counted the cards he had taken. There were twenty-five. He reached over to the corner of the table, took up the rules Grief had written, folded them, and put them in his pocket. Then he emptied his glass, and stood up. Captain Donovan looked at his watch, yawned, and also arose.

"Going aboard, Captain?" Deacon asked.

"Yes," was the answer. "What time shall I send the whaleboat for you?"

"I'll go with you now. We'll pick up my luggage from the *Billy* as we go by. I was sailing on her for Babo in the morning."

Deacon shook hands all around, after receiving a final pledge of good luck on Karo-Karo.

"Does Tom Butler play cards?" he asked Grief.

"Solitaire," was the answer.

"Then I'll teach him double solitaire." Deacon turned toward the door, where Captain Donovan waited, and added with a sigh, "And I fancy he'll skin me, too, if he plays like the rest of you island men."

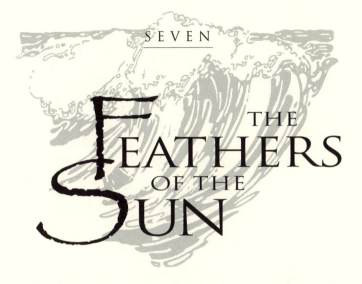

SEVEN

THE FEATHERS OF THE SUN

As he indicated in a letter to his editor at the Saturday Evening Post, *even at the first planning stages, Jack London wanted to try experimenting with humor in the David Grief adventures: "I hope to make several of them really funny"* (Letters, 992). *However, as the stories were appearing in the magazine during the last half of 1911, the author was not confident that he had hit his mark: "I know that I am rotten at humor"* (Letters, 1035). *Today, our judgment is likely to be less harsh. In 1992, in fact,* Thalia, *a journal devoted to the study of literary humor, came out with a special edition on Jack London, alerting readers to many aspects of London's work hitherto neglected. Though many of the Grief stories are fraught with physical danger, wild struggles against the elements, and conflict with criminals, there is an undeniable vein of humor running through them.*

Recall the splendid opening of "A Goboto Night," for example, with its fine joke about the comparative drinking habits of Gavutu and Goboto, or the fanatic insistence on the importance of white people wearing pants, and the singular affair of Captain Jensen:

> *When Captain Jensen, the wildest of the Blackbirders though descended from old New York Knickerbocker stock, surged in, clad in loin-cloth, undershirt, two belted revolvers and a sheath-knife, he was stopped at the beach. This was in the days of Johnny*

Bassett, ever a stickler in matters of etiquette. Captain Jensen stood up in the sternsheets of his whaleboat and denied the existence of pants on his schooner. Also, he affirmed his intention of coming ashore. They of Goboto nursed him back to health from a bullet-hole through his shoulder, and in addition handsomely begged his pardon, for no pants had they found on his schooner.

Here, the real action of the story—the quarrel (couched in the theological categories of affirmation and denial), the drawing of guns, the showdown, and the shooting itself—are all indirectly implied for the reader's imagination. No doubt, London discovered much that was funny in the activities of these rag-tailed adventurers who sailed the South Seas.

But nowhere else in these stories is the author's sense of humor displayed to such rollicking effect as in "The Feathers of the Sun," the hilarious story of an ambitious con man, a rogue European with a plot to float a paper money scam on the island of Fitu Iva. By now, the reader can anticipate that this rascal will meet his Waterloo when he tries his game on Captain David Grief, and seeing the way he ultimately gets his comeuppance provides most of the fun.

Underlying London's humor, however, is a typically dark reality, once again joining the threads of exploitation and dependency that also run through the whole series. Fitu Iva (actually spelled Fatu Hiva) is an island in the Marquesas in Polynesia discovered by Europeans in the sixteenth century and annexed by the French in the 1840s. In practical fact, however, Fatu Hiva's remoteness resulted in an absence of colonial government; even today, no French administrator resides on the island.

It is this situation that the colorful Irish scamp Cornelius Deasy seeks to exploit in his takeover bid. Though the Olympian drinking feats of the alcoholic monarch Tulifau are played somewhat for laughs, the historic fact is that the first three things brought to the Pacific islands by white invaders were religion, alcohol, and tobacco. Some missionaries were Catholic, while others represented a wide variety of Protestant opinions, all of them equally certain that they possessed the Truth. The confusion of all these claims resulted in a marked parochialism among the islanders, who even *today take serious note of their visitors' religious affiliations; religion became a divisive force throughout the region, rather than a unifying one. But on one principle most of the missionary groups were agreed: islanders ought not to be given spirits, because of their inherent propensity to addiction. Missionaries fought bitterly against the trade in liquor. Tulifau represents the typical result of the white rumrunners' unscrupulous use of alcohol as a tool to dominate an island population.*

Deasy also exploits concern about infectious diseases in his attempt to quarantine Grief's vessel. Although he is utterly insincere, the concern itself was a valid one. When the French annexed the Marquesas in the 1840s, their initial census indicated a native population of 20,000. After a century under French possession, the population of the Marquesas in the 1942 census had dwindled to 2,699, while today the people of Fatu Hiva number around 500. The powers and authority usurped by Deasy, and thwarted by the high-handed confidence of David Grief, are really yet another of Jack London's microcosmic representations of the casual piracy and thoughtless genocide that constituted the colonial impulse in the South Seas.

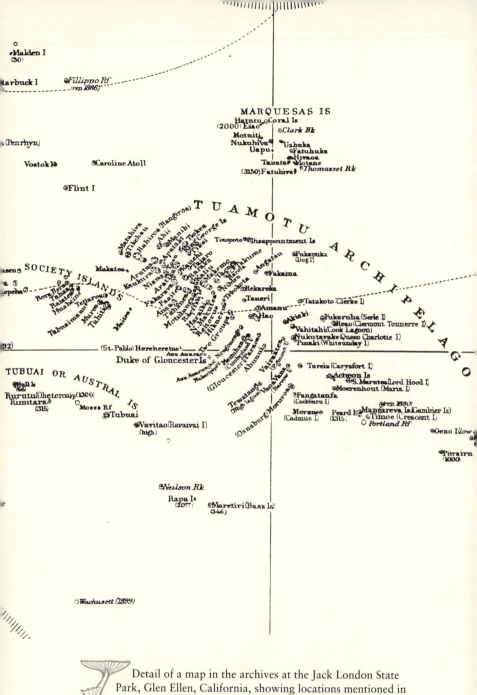

Detail of a map in the archives at the Jack London State
Park, Glen Ellen, California, showing locations mentioned in
"Feathers of the Sun" and "The Pearls of Parlay."

It was the island of Fitu-Iva—the last independent Polynesian stronghold in the South Seas.[1] Three factors conduced to Fitu-Iva's independence. The first and second were its isolation and the war-likeness of its population. But these would not have saved it in the end had it not been for the fact that Japan, France, Great Britain, Germany, and the United States discovered its desirableness simultaneously. It was like gamins scrambling for a penny. They got in one another's way. The war vessels of the five Powers cluttered Fitu-Iva's one small harbour. There were rumours of war and threats of war. Over its morning toast all the world read columns about Fitu-Iva. As a Yankee blue jacket epitomized it at the time, they all got their feet in the trough at once.

So it was that Fitu-Iva escaped even a joint protectorate, and King Tulifau, otherwise Tui Tulifau, continued to dispense the high justice and the low in the frame-house palace built for him by a Sydney trader out of California redwood. Not only was Tui Tulifau every inch a king, but he was every second a king. When he had ruled fifty-eight years and five months, he was only fifty-eight years and three months old. That is to say, he had ruled over five million seconds more than he had breathed, having been crowned two months before he was born.

He was a kingly king, a royal figure of a man, standing six feet and a half, and, without being excessively fat, weighing three hundred and twenty pounds. But this was not unusual for Polynesian "chief stock." Sepeli, his queen, was six feet three inches and weighed two hundred and sixty, while her brother, Uiliami, who commanded the army in the intervals of resignation from the premiership, topped her by an inch and notched her an even half-hundred-weight. Tui Tulifau was a merry soul, a great feaster and drinker. So were all his people merry souls, save in anger, when, on occasion, they could be guilty even of throwing dead pigs at those who made them wroth. Nevertheless, on occasion, they could fight like Maoris,[2] as piratical sandalwood traders and Blackbirders in the old days learned to their cost.

II

Grief's schooner, the *Cantani,* had passed the Pillar Rocks at the entrance two hours before and crept up the harbour to the whispering flutters of a breeze that could not make up its mind to blow.[3] It was a cool, starlight evening, and they lolled about the poop waiting till their snail's pace would bring them to the anchorage. Willie Smee, the supercargo, emerged from the cabin, conspicuous in his shore clothes.[4] The mate glanced at his shirt, of the finest and whitest silk, and giggled significantly.

"Dance, to-night, I suppose?" Grief observed.

"No," said the mate. "It's Taitua. Willie's stuck on her."

"Catch me," the supercargo disclaimed.

"Then she's stuck on you, and it's all the same," the mate went on. "You won't be ashore half an hour before you'll have a flower behind your ear, a wreath on your head, and your arm around Taitua."

"Simple jealousy," Willie Smee sniffed. "You'd like to have her yourself, only you can't."

"I can't find shirts like that, that's why. I'll bet you half a crown you won't sail from Fitu-Iva with that shirt."

"And if Taitua doesn't get it, it's an even break Tui Tulifau does," Grief warned. "Better not let him spot that shirt, or it's all day with it."

"That's right," Captain Boig agreed, turning his head from watching the house lights on the shore. "Last voyage he fined one of my Kanakas out of a fancy belt and sheath-knife." He turned to the mate. "You can let go any time, Mr. Marsh. Don't give too much slack. There's no sign of wind, and in the morning we may shift opposite the copra-sheds."

A minute later the anchor rumbled down. The whaleboat, already hoisted out, lay alongside, and the shore-going party dropped into it. Save for the Kanakas, who were all bent for shore, only Grief and the supercargo were in the boat. At the head of the little coral-stone pier Willie Smee, with an apologetic gurgle, separated from his employer and disappeared down an avenue of palms. Grief turned in the opposite direction past the front of the old mission church. Here, among the graves on the beach, lightly clad in *ahu's* and *lava-lavas*,[5] flower-crowned and garlanded, with great phosphorescent hibiscus blossoms in their hair, youths and maidens were dancing. Farther on, Grief passed the long, grass-built *himine* house, where a few score of the elders sat in long rows chanting the old hymns taught them by forgotten missionaries.[6] He passed also the palace of Tui Tulifau, where, by the lights and sounds, he knew the customary revelry was going on. For of the happy South Sea isles, Fitu-Iva was the happiest. They feasted and frolicked at births and deaths, and the dead and the unborn were likewise feasted.

Grief held steadily along the Broom Road, which curved and twisted through a lush growth of flowers and fern-like algarobas. The warm air was rich with perfume, and overhead, outlined against the stars, were fruit-burdened mangoes, stately avocado trees, and slender-tufted palms. Every here and there were grass houses. Voices and laughter rippled through the darkness. Out on the water flickering lights and soft-voiced choruses marked the fishers returning from the reef.

At last Grief stepped aside from the road, stumbling over a pig that grunted indignantly. Looking through an open door, he saw a stout and elderly native sitting on a heap of mats a dozen deep. From time to time, automatically, he brushed his naked legs with a cocoa-nut-fibre fly-flicker. He wore glasses, and was reading methodically in what Grief knew to be an English Bible. For this was Ieremia, his trader, so named from the prophet Jeremiah.[7]

Ieremia was lighter-skinned than the Fitu-Ivans, as was natural in a full-blooded Samoan. Educated by the missionaries, as lay teacher he had served their cause well over in the cannibal atolls to the westward. As a reward, he had been sent to the paradise of Fitu-Iva, where all were or had been good converts, to gather in the backslid-

ers. Unfortunately, Ieremia had become too well educated. A stray
volume of Darwin, a nagging wife, and a pretty Fitu-Ivan widow
had driven him into the ranks of the backsliders. It was not a case of
apostasy. The effect of Darwin had been one of intellectual fatigue.
What was the use of trying to understand this vastly complicated
and enigmatical world, especially when one was married to a nagging woman? As Ieremia slackened in his labours, the mission board
threatened louder and louder to send him back to the atolls, while
his wife's tongue grew correspondingly sharper. Tui Tulifau was a
sympathetic monarch, whose queen, on occasions when he was particularly drunk, was known to beat him. For political reasons—the
queen belonging to as royal stock as himself and her brother com-
manding the army—Tui Tulifau could not divorce her, but he could
and did divorce Ieremia, who promptly took up with commercial
life and the lady of his choice. As an independent trader he had
failed, chiefly because of the disastrous patronage of Tui Tulifau. To
refuse credit to that merry monarch was to invite confiscation; to
grant him credit was certain bankruptcy. After a year's idleness on
the beach, Ieremia had become David Grief's trader, and for a dozen
years his service had been honourable and efficient, for Grief had
proven the first man who successfully refused credit to the king or
who collected when it had been accorded.

Ieremia looked gravely over the rims of his glasses when his employer entered, gravely marked the place in the Bible and set it aside,
and gravely shook hands.

"I am glad you came in person," he said.

"How else could I come?" Grief laughed.

But Ieremia had no sense of humour, and he ignored the remark.

"The commercial situation on the island is damn bad," he said
with great solemnity and an unctuous mouthing of the many-syl-
labled words. "My ledger account is shocking."

"Trade bad?"

"On the contrary. It has been excellent. The shelves are empty,
exceedingly empty. But—" His eyes glistened proudly. "But there are
many goods remaining in the storehouse; I have kept it carefully
locked."

"Been allowing Tui Tulifau too much credit?"

"On the contrary. There has been no credit at all. And every old account has been settled up."

"I don't follow you, Ieremia," Grief confessed. "What's the joke? —shelves empty, no credit, old accounts all square, storehouse carefully locked—what's the answer?"

Ieremia did not reply immediately. Reaching under the rear corner of the mats, he drew forth a large cash-box. Grief noted and wondered that it was not locked. The Samoan had always been fastidiously cautious in guarding cash. The box seemed filled with paper money. He skinned off the top note and passed it over.

"There is the answer."

Grief glanced at a fairly well executed banknote. *"The First Royal Bank of Fitu-Iva will pay to bearer on demand one pound sterling,"* he read. In the centre was the smudged likeness of a native face. At the bottom was the signature of Tui Tulifau, and the signature of Fulualea, with the printed information appended, *"Chancellor of the Exchequer."*

"Who the deuce is Fulualea?" Grief demanded. "It's Fijian, isn't it?—meaning the feathers of the sun?"

"Just so. It means the feathers of the sun. Thus does this base interloper caption himself. He has come up from Fiji to turn Fitu-Iva upside down—that is, commercially."

"Some one of those smart Levuka boys, I suppose?"[8]

Ieremia shook his head sadly. "No, this low fellow is a white man and a scoundrel. He has taken a noble and high-sounding Fijian name and dragged it in the dirt to suit his nefarious purposes. He has made Tui Tulifau drunk. He has made him very drunk. He has kept him very drunk all the time. In return, he has been made Chancellor of the Exchequer and other things. He has issued this false paper and compelled the people to receive it. He has levied a store tax, a copra tax, and a tobacco tax. There are harbour dues and regulations, and other taxes. But the people are not taxed—only the traders. When the copra tax was levied, I lowered the purchasing price accordingly. Then the people began to grumble, and Feathers of the Sun passed a new law, setting the old price back and forbidding any man to lower it. Me he fined two pounds and five pigs, it being well known that I possessed five pigs. You will find them entered in the ledger. Hawkins, who is trader for the Fulcrum Company, was fined first pigs, then gin, and, because he continued to make loud conversation, the army came and burned his store. When I declined to sell, this Feathers of the Sun fined me once more and promised to burn the store if again I offended. So I sold all that was on the shelves, and there is the box full of worthless paper. I shall be chagrined if you pay me my salary in paper, but it would be just, no more than just. Now, what is to be done?"

Grief shrugged his shoulders. "I must first see this Feathers of the Sun and size up the situation."

"Then you must see him soon," Ieremia advised. "Else he will have an accumulation of many fines against you. Thus does he absorb all the coin of the realm. He has it all now, save what has been buried in the ground."

III

On his way back along the Broom Road, under the lighted lamps that marked the entrance to the palace grounds, Grief encountered a short, rotund gentleman, in unstarched ducks, smooth-shaven and of florid complexion, who was just emerging. Something about his tentative, saturated gait was familiar. Grief knew it on the instant. On the beaches of a dozen South Sea ports had he seen it before.

"Of all men, Cornelius Deasy!" he cried.

"If it ain't Grief himself, the old devil," was the return greeting, as they shook hands.

"If you'll come on board I've some choice smoky Irish," Grief invited.

Cornelius threw back his shoulders and stiffened.

"Nothing doin', Mr. Grief. 'Tis Fulualea I am now. No blarneyin' of old times for me. Also, and by the leave of his gracious Majesty King Tulifau, 'tis Chancellor of the Exchequer I am, an' Chief Justice I am, save in moments of royal sport when the king himself chooses to toy with the wheels of justice."

Grief whistled his amazement. "So you're Feathers of the Sun!"

"Me he fined two pounds and five pigs. . . . "
Drawing by Anton Otto Fischer.

"I prefer the native idiom," was the correction. "Fulualea, an' it please you. Not forgettin' old times, Mr. Grief, it sorrows the heart of me to break you the news. You'll have to pay your legitimate import duties same as any other trader with mind intent on robbin' the gentle Polynesian savage on coral isles implanted.—Where was I? Ah! I remember. You've violated the regulations. With malice intent have you entered the port of Fitu-Iva after sunset without sidelights burnin'. Don't interrupt. With my own eyes did I see you. For which offence are you fined the sum of five pounds. Have you any gin? 'Tis a serious offence. Not lightly are the lives of the mariners of our commodious port to be risked for the savin' of a penny'orth of oil. Did I ask: have you any gin? 'Tis the harbour master that asks."

"You've taken a lot on your shoulders," Grief grinned.

"'Tis the white man's burden. These rapscallion traders have been puttin' it all over poor Tui Tulifau, the best-hearted old monarch that ever sat a South Sea throne an' mopped grog-root from the imperial calabash. 'Tis I, Cornelius—Fulualea, rather—that am here to see justice done. Much as I dislike the doin' of it, as harbour master 'tis my duty to find you guilty of breach of quarantine."

"Quarantine?"

"'Tis the rulin' of the port doctor. No intercourse with the shore till the ship is passed. What dire calamity to the confidin' native if chicken pox or whoopin' cough was aboard of you! Who is there to protect the gentle, confidin' Polynesian? I, Fulualea, the Feathers of the Sun, on my high mission."

"Who in hell is the port doctor?" Grief queried.

"'Tis me, Fulualea. Your offence is serious. Consider yourself fined five cases of first-quality Holland gin."

Grief laughed heartily. "We'll compromise, Cornelius. Come aboard and have a drink."

The Feathers of the Sun waved the proffer aside grandly. "'Tis bribery. I'll have none of it—me faithful to my salt. And wherefore did you not present your ship's papers? As chief of the custom house you are fined five pounds and two more cases of gin."

"Look here, Cornelius. A joke's a joke, but this one has gone far enough. This is not Levuka. I've half a mind to pull your nose for you. You can't buck me."

The Feathers of the Sun retreated unsteadily and in alarm.

"Lay no violence on me," he threatened. "You're right. This is not Levuka. And by the same token, with Tui Tulifau and the royal army behind me, buck you is just the thing I can and will. You'll pay them fines promptly, or I'll confiscate your vessel. You're not the first. What does that Chink pearl-buyer, Peter Gee, do but slip into harbour, violatin' all regulations an' makin' rough house for the matter of a few paltry fines. No; he wouldn't pay 'em, and he's on the beach now thinkin' it over."

"You don't mean to say—"

"Sure an' I do. In the high exercise of office I seized his schooner. A fifth of the loyal army is now in charge on board of her. She'll be sold this day week. Some ten tons of shell in the hold, and I'm wonderin' if I can trade it to you for gin. I can promise you a rare bargain. How much gin did you say you had?"

"Still more gin, eh?"

"An' why not? 'Tis a royal souse is Tui Tulifau. Sure it keeps my wits workin' overtime to supply him, he's that amazin' liberal with it. The whole gang of hanger-on chiefs is perpetually loaded to the guards. It's disgraceful. Are you goin' to pay them fines, Mr. Grief, or is it to harsher measures I'll be forced?"

Grief turned impatiently on his heel.

"Cornelius, you're drunk. Think it over and come to your senses. The old rollicking South Sea days are gone. You can't play tricks like that now."

"If you think you're goin' on board, Mr. Grief, I'll save you the trouble. I know your kind. I foresaw your stiff-necked stubbornness. An' it's forestalled you are. 'Tis on the beach you'll find your crew. The vessel's seized."

Grief turned back on him in the half-belief still that he was joking. Fulualea again retreated in alarm. The form of a large man loomed beside him in the darkness.

"Is it you, Uiliami?" Fulualea crooned. "Here is another sea pirate. Stand by me with the strength of thy arm, O Herculean brother."

"Greeting, Uiliami," Grief said. "Since when has Fitu-Iva come to be run by a Levuka beachcomber? He says my schooner has been seized. Is it true?"

"It is true," Uiliami boomed from his deep chest. "Have you any more silk shirts like Willie Smee's? Tui Tulifau would like such a shirt. He has heard of it."

"'Tis all the same," Fulualea interrupted. "Shirts or schooners, the king shall have them."

"Rather high-handed, Cornelius," Grief murmured. "It's rank piracy. You seized my vessel without giving me a chance."

"A chance is it? As we stood here, not five minutes gone, didn't you refuse to pay your fines?"

"But she was already seized."

"Sure, an' why not? Didn't I know you'd refuse? 'Tis all fair, an' no injustice done—Justice, the bright, particular star at whose shining altar Cornelius Deasy—or Fulualea, 'tis the same thing—ever worships. Get thee gone, Mr. Trader, or I'll set the palace guards on you. Uiliami, 'tis a desperate character, this trader man. Call the guards."

Uiliami blew the whistle suspended on his broad bare chest by a cord of cocoanut sennit. Grief reached out an angry hand for Cornelius, who titubated into safety behind Uiliami's massive bulk. A dozen strapping Polynesians, not one under six feet, ran down the palace walk and ranged behind their commander.

"Get thee gone, Mr. Trader," Cornelius ordered. "The interview is terminated. We'll try your several cases in the mornin'. Appear promptly at the palace at ten o'clock to answer to the followin' charges, to wit: breach of the peace; seditious and treasonable utterance; violent assault on the chief magistrate with intent to cut, wound, maim, an' bruise; breach of quarantine; violation of harbour regulations; and gross breakage of custom house rules. In the mornin', fellow, in the mornin', justice shall be done while the breadfruit falls. And the Lord have mercy on your soul."

IV

Before the hour set for the trial Grief, accompanied by Peter Gee, won access to Tui Tulifau. The king, surrounded by half a dozen chiefs, lay on mats under the shade of the avocados in the palace compound. Early as was the hour, palace maids were industriously

"Grief reached out an angry hand for Cornelius. . . . "
Drawing by Anton Otto Fischer.

serving square-faces of gin.⁹ The king was glad to see his old friend
Davida, and regretful that he had run foul of the new regulations.
Beyond that he steadfastly avoided discussion of the matter in hand.
All protests of the expropriated traders were washed away in prof-
fers of gin. "Have a drink," was his invariable reply, though once he
unbosomed himself enough to say that Feathers of the Sun was a
wonderful man. Never had palace affairs been so prosperous. Never
had there been so much money in the treasury, nor so much gin in
circulation. "Well pleased am I with Fulualea," he concluded. "Have
a drink."

"We've got to get out of this *pronto,*" Grief whispered to Peter
Gee a few minutes later, "or we'll be a pair of boiled owls. Also, I am
to be tried for arson, or heresy, or leprosy, or something, in a few
minutes, and I must control my wits."

As they withdrew from the royal presence, Grief caught a glimpse
of Sepeli, the queen. She was peering out at her royal spouse and his
fellow tipplers, and the frown on her face gave Grief his cue. Whatever was to be accomplished must be through her.

In another shady corner of the big compound Cornelius was holding court. He had been at it early, for when Grief arrived the case of
Willie Smee was being settled. The entire royal army, save that portion in charge of the seized vessels, was in attendance.

"Let the defendant stand up," said Cornelius, "and receive the
just and merciful sentence of the Court for licentious and disgraceful
conduct unbecomin' a supercargo. The defendant says he has no
money. Very well. The Court regrets it has no calaboose. In lieu there-
of, and in view of the impoverished condition of the defendant, the
Court fines said defendant one white silk shirt of the same kind,
make and quality at present worn by defendant."

Cornelius nodded to several of the soldiers, who led the supercargo away behind an avocado tree. A minute later he emerged, mi-
nus the garment in question, and sat down beside Grief.

"What have you been up to?" Grief asked.

"Blessed if I know. What crimes have you committed?"

"Next case," said Cornelius in his most extra-legal tones. "David
Grief, defendant, stand up. The Court has considered the evidence in

the case, or cases, and renders the following judgment, to wit:—Shut up!" he thundered at Grief, who had attempted to interrupt. "I tell you the evidence has been considered, deeply considered. It is no wish of the Court to lay additional hardship on the defendant, and the Court takes this opportunity to warn the defendant that he is liable for contempt. For open and wanton violation of harbour rules and regulations, breach of quarantine, and disregard of shipping laws, his schooner, the *Cantani*, is hereby declared confiscated to the Government of Fitu-Iva, to be sold at public auction, ten days from date, with all appurtenances, fittings, and cargo thereunto pertaining. For the personal crimes of the defendant, consisting of violent and turbulent conduct and notorious disregard of the laws of the realm, he is fined in the sum of one hundred pounds sterling and fifteen cases of gin. I will not ask you if you have anything to say. But will you pay? That is the question."

Grief shook his head.

"In the meantime," Cornelius went on, "consider yourself a prisoner at large. There is no calaboose in which to confine you. And finally, it has come to the knowledge of the Court, that at an early hour of this morning, the defendant did wilfully and deliberately send Kanakas in his employ out on the reef to catch fish for breakfast. This is distinctly an infringement of the rights of the fisherfolk of Fitu-Iva. Home industries must be protected. This conduct of the defendant is severely reprehended by the Court, and on any repetition of the offence the offender and offenders, all and sundry, shall be immediately put to hard labour on the improvement of the Broom Road. The court is dismissed."

As they left the compound, Peter Gee nudged Grief to look where Tui Tulifau reclined on the mats. The supercargo's shirt, stretched and bulged, already encased the royal fat.

V

"The thing is clear," said Peter Gee, at a conference in Ieremia's house. "Deasy has about gathered in all the coin. In the meantime he keeps the king going on the gin he's captured on our vessels. As soon as he can maneuver it he'll take the cash and skin out on your craft or mine."

"He is a low fellow," Ieremia declared, pausing in the polishing of his spectacles. "He is a scoundrel and a blackguard. He should be struck by a dead pig, by a particularly dead pig."

"The very thing," said Grief. "He shall be struck by a dead pig. Ieremia, I should not be surprised if you were the man to strike him with the dead pig. Be sure and select a particularly dead one. Tui Tulifau is down at the boat house broaching a case of my Scotch. I'm going up to the palace to work kitchen politics with the queen. In the meantime you get a few things on your shelves from the store-room. I'll lend you some, Hawkins. And you, Peter, see the German store. Start in all of you, selling for paper. Remember, I'll back the losses. If I'm not mistaken, in three days we'll have a national council or a revolution. You, Ieremia, start messengers around the island to the fishers and farmers, everywhere, even to the mountain goat-hunters. Tell them to assemble at the palace three days from now."

"But the soldiers," Ieremia objected.

"I'll take care of them. They haven't been paid for two months. Besides, Uiliami is the queen's brother. Don't have too much on your shelves at a time. As soon as the soldiers show up with paper, stop selling."

"Then will they burn the stores," said Ieremia.

"Let them. King Tulifau will pay for it if they do."

"Will he pay for my shirt?" Willie Smee demanded.

"That is purely a personal and private matter between you and Tui Tulifau," Grief answered.

"It's beginning to split up the back," the supercargo lamented. "I noticed that much this morning when he hadn't had it on ten minutes. It cost me thirty shillings and I only wore it once."

"Where shall I get a dead pig?" Ieremia asked.

"Kill one, of course," said Grief. "Kill a small one."

"A small one is worth ten shillings."

"Then enter it in your ledger under operating expenses." Grief paused a moment. "If you want it particularly dead, it would be well to kill it at once."

VI

"You have spoken well, Davida," said Queen Sepeli. "This Fulualea has brought a madness with him, and Tui Tulifau is drowned in gin. If he does not grant the big council, I shall give him a beating. He is easy to beat when he is in drink."

She doubled up her fist, and such were her Amazonian proportions and the determination in her face that Grief knew the council would be called. So akin was the Fitu-Ivan tongue to the Samoan that he spoke it like a native.

"And you, Uiliami," he said, "have pointed out that the soldiers have demanded coin and refused the paper Fulualea has offered them. Tell them to take the paper and see that they be paid to-morrow."

"Why trouble?" Uiliami objected. "The king remains happily drunk. There is much money in the treasury. And I am content. In my house are two cases of gin and much goods from Hawkins's store."

"Excellent pig, O my brother!" Sepeli erupted. "Has not Davida spoken? Have you no ears? When the gin and the goods in your house are gone, and no more traders come with gin and goods, and Feathers of the Sun has run away to Levuka with all the cash money of Fitu-Iva, what then will you do? Cash money is silver and gold, but paper is only paper. I tell you the people are grumbling. There is no fish in the palace. Yams and sweet potatoes seem to have fled from the soil, for they come not. The mountain dwellers have sent no wild goat in a week. Though Feathers of the Sun compels the traders to buy copra at the old price, the people sell not, for they will have none of the paper money. Only to-day have I sent messengers to twenty houses. There are no eggs. Has Feathers of the Sun put a blight upon the hens? I do not know. All I know is that there are no eggs. Well it is that those who drink much eat little, else would there be a palace famine. Tell your soldiers to receive their pay. Let it be in his paper money."

"And remember," Grief warned, "though there be selling in the stores, when the soldiers come with their paper it will be refused. And in three days will be the council, and Feathers of the Sun will be as dead as a dead pig."

VII

The day of the council found the population of the island crowded into the capital. By canoe and whaleboat, on foot and donkey-back, the five thousand inhabitants of Fitu-Iva had trooped in. The three intervening days had had their share of excitement. At first there had been much selling from the sparse shelves of the traders. But when the soldiers appeared, their patronage was declined and they were told to go to Fulualea for coin. "Says it not so on the face of the paper," the traders demanded, "that for the asking the coin will be given in exchange?"

Only the strong authority of Uiliami had prevented the burning of the traders' houses. As it was, one of Grief's copra-sheds went up in smoke and was duly charged by Ieremia to the king's account. Ieremia himself had been abused and mocked, and his spectacles broken. The skin was off Willie Smee's knuckles. This had been caused by three boisterous soldiers who violently struck their jaws thereon in quick succession. Captain Boig was similarly injured. Peter Gee had come off undamaged, because it chanced that it was bread-baskets and not jaws that struck him on the fists.

Tui Tulifau, with Sepeli at his side and surrounded by his convivial chiefs, sat at the head of the council in the big compound. His right eye and jaw were swollen as if he too had engaged in assaulting somebody's fist. It was palace gossip that morning that Sepeli had administered a conjugal beating. At any rate, her spouse was sober, and his fat bulged spiritlessly through the rips in Willie Smee's silk shirt. His thirst was prodigious, and he was continually served with young drinking nuts. Outside the compound, held back by the army, was the mass of the common people. Only the lesser chiefs, village maids, village beaux, and talking men with their staffs of office were permitted inside. Cornelius Deasy, as befitted a high and favoured official, sat near to the right hand of the king. On the left of the queen, opposite Cornelius and surrounded by the white traders he was to represent, sat Ieremia. Bereft of his spectacles, he peered short-sightedly across at the Chancellor of the Exchequer.

In turn, the talking man of the windward coast, the talking man

"Five thousand inhabitants had trooped in. . . ."
Drawing by Anton Otto Fischer.

of the leeward coast, and the talking man of the mountain villages, each backed by his group of lesser talking men and chiefs, arose and made oration. What they said was much the same. They grumbled about the paper money. Affairs were not prosperous. No more copra was being smoked. The people were suspicious. To such a pass had things come that all people wanted to pay their debts and no one wanted to be paid. Creditors made a practice of running away from debtors. The money was cheap. Prices were going up and commodities were getting scarce. It cost three times the ordinary price to buy a fowl, and then it was tough and like to die of old age if not immediately sold. The outlook was gloomy. There were signs and omens. There was a plague of rats in some districts. The crops were bad. The custard apples were small. The best-bearing avocado on the windward coast had mysteriously shed all its leaves. The taste had gone from the mangoes. The plantains were eaten by a worm. The fish had forsaken the ocean and vast numbers of tiger-sharks appeared. The wild goats had fled to inaccessible summits. The poi in the poi-pits had turned bitter. There were rumblings in the mountains, night-walking of spirits; a woman of Punta-Puna had been struck speechless, and a five-legged she-goat had been born in the village of Eiho. And that all was due to the strange money of Fulualea was the firm conviction of the elders in the village councils assembled.

Uiliami spoke for the army. His men were discontented and mutinous. Though by royal decree the traders were bidden accept the money, yet did they refuse it. He would not say, but it looked as if the strange money of Fulualea had something to do with it.

Ieremia, as talking man of the traders, next spoke. When he arose, it was noticeable that he stood with legs spraddled over a large grass basket. He dwelt upon the cloth of the traders, its variety and beauty and durability, which so exceeded the Fitu-Ivan wet-pounded tapa, fragile and coarse. No one wore tapa any more. Yet all had worn tapa, and nothing but tapa, before the traders came. There was the mosquito-netting, sold for a song, that the cleverest Fitu-Ivan net-weaver could not duplicate in a thousand years. He enlarged on the incomparable virtues of rifles, axes, and steel fish-hooks, down through needles, thread and cotton fish-lines to white flour and kerosene oil.

He expounded at length, with firstlies and secondlies and all minor subdivisions of argument, on organization, and order, and civilization. He contended that the trader was the bearer of civilization, and that the trader must be protected in his trade else he would not come. Over to the westward were islands which would not protect the traders. What was the result? The traders would not come, and the people were like wild animals. They wore no clothes, no silk shirts (here he peered and blinked significantly at the king), and they ate one another.

The queer paper of the Feathers of the Sun was not money. The traders knew what money was, and they would not receive it. If Fitu-Iva persisted in trying to make them receive it they would go away and never come back. And then the Fitu-Ivans, who had forgotten how to make tapa, would run around naked and eat one another.

Much more he said, talking a solid hour, and always coming back to what their dire condition would be when the traders came no more. "And in that day," he perorated, "how will the Fitu-lvan be known in the great world? *Kai-kanak* will men call him. '*Kai-kanak! Kai-kanak!*'"[10]

Tui Tulifau spoke briefly. The case had been presented, he said, for the people, the army, and the traders. It was now time for Feathers of the Sun to present his side. It could not be denied that he had wrought wonders with his financial system. "Many times has he explained to me the working of his system," Tui Tulifau concluded. "It is very simple. And now he will explain it to you."

It was a conspiracy of the white traders, Cornelius contended. Ieremia was right so far as concerned the manifold blessings of white flour and kerosene oil. Fitu-Iva did not want to become *kai-kanak*. Fitu-Iva wanted civilization; it wanted more and more civilization. Now that was the very point, and they must follow him closely. Paper money was an ear-mark of higher civilization. That was why he, the Feathers of the Sun, had introduced it. And that was why the traders opposed it. They did not want to see Fitu-Iva civilized. Why did they come across the far ocean stretches with their goods to Fitu-Iva? He, the Feathers of the Sun, would tell them why, to their faces, in grand council assembled. In their own countries men were too civilized to let the traders make the immense profits that they made out of the Fitu-Ivans. If the Fitu-Ivans became properly civilized, the trade of the traders would be gone. In that day every Fitu-Ivan could become a trader if he pleased.

That was why the white traders fought the system of paper money, that he, the Feathers of the Sun, had brought. Why was he called the Feathers of the Sun? Because he was the Light-Bringer from the World Beyond the Sky. The paper money was the light. The robbing white traders could not flourish in the light. Therefore they fought the light.

He would prove it to the good people of Fitu-Iva, and he would prove it out of the mouths of his enemies. It was a well-known fact that all highly civilized countries had paper-money systems. He would ask Ieremia if this was not so.

Ieremia did not answer.

"You see," Cornelius went on, "he makes no answer. He cannot deny what is true. England, France, Germany, America, all the great *Papalangi* countries, have the paper-money system. It works. From century to century it works. I challenge you, Ieremia, as an honest man, as one who was once a zealous worker in the Lord's vineyard, I challenge you to deny that in the great *Papalangi* countries the system works."

Ieremia could not deny, and his fingers played nervously with the fastening of the basket on his knees.

"You see, it is as I have said," Cornelius continued. "Ieremia agrees that it is so. Therefore, I ask you, all good people of Fitu-Iva, if a system is good for the *Papalangi* countries, why is it not good for Fitu-Iva?"

"It is not the same!" Ieremia cried. "The paper of the Feathers of the Sun is different from the paper of the great countries."

That Cornelius had been prepared for this was evident. He held up a Fitu-Ivan note that was recognized by all.

"What is that?" he demanded.

"Paper, mere paper," was Ieremia's reply.

"And that?"

This time Cornelius held up a Bank of England note.

"It is the paper money of the English," he explained to the Council, at the same time extending it for Ieremia to examine. "Is it not true, Ieremia, that it is paper money of the English?"

Ieremia nodded reluctantly.

"You have said that the paper money of Fitu-Iva was paper, now how about this of the English? What is it? . . . You must answer like a true man. . . . All wait for your answer, Ieremia."

"It is—it is—" the puzzled Ieremia began, then spluttered helplessly, the fallacy beyond his penetration.

"Paper, mere paper," Cornelius concluded for him, imitating his halting utterance.

Conviction sat on the faces of all. The king clapped his hands admiringly and murmured, "It is most clear, very clear."

"You see, he himself acknowledges it." Assured triumph was in Deasy's voice and bearing. "He knows of no difference. There is no difference. 'Tis the very image of money. 'Tis money itself."

In the meantime Grief was whispering in Ieremia's ear, who nodded and began to speak.

"But it is well known to all the *Papalangi* that the English Government will pay coin money for the paper."

Deasy's victory was now absolute. He held aloft a Fitu-Ivan note.

"Is it not so written on this paper as well?"

Again Grief whispered.

"That Fitu-Iva will pay coin money?" asked Ieremia.

"It is so written."

A third time Grief prompted.

"On demand?" asked Ieremia.

"On demand," Cornelius assured him.

"Then I demand coin money now," said Ieremia, drawing a small package of notes from the pouch at his girdle.

Cornelius scanned the package with a quick, estimating eye.

"Very well," he agreed. "I shall give you the coin money now. How much?"

"And we will see the system work," the king proclaimed, partaking in his Chancellor's triumph.

"You have heard!—He will give coin money now!" Ieremia cried in a loud voice to the assemblage.

At the same time he plunged both hands in the basket and drew forth many packages of Fitu-Ivan notes. It was noticed that a peculiar odour was adrift about the council.

"I have here," Ieremia announced, "one thousand and twenty-eight pounds twelve shillings and sixpence. Here is a sack to put the coin money in."

Cornelius recoiled. He had not expected such a sum, and everywhere about the council his uneasy eyes showed him chiefs and talking men drawing out bundles of notes. The army, its two months' pay in its hands, pressed forward to the edge of the council, while behind it the populace, with more money, invaded the compound.

"'Tis a run on the bank you've precipitated," he said reproachfully to Grief.

"Here is the sack to put the coin money in," Ieremia urged.

"It must be postponed," Cornelius said desperately. "'Tis not in banking hours."

Ieremia flourished a package of money. "Nothing of banking hours is written here. It says on demand, and I now demand."

"Let them come to-morrow, O Tui Tulifau," Cornelius appealed to the king. "They shall be paid to-morrow."

Tui Tulifau hesitated, but his spouse glared at him, her brawny arm tensing as the fist doubled into a redoubtable knot. Tui Tulifau tried to look away, but failed. He cleared his throat nervously.

"We will see the system work," he decreed. "The people have come far."

"'Tis good money you're asking me to pay out," Deasy muttered in a low voice to the king.

Sepeli caught what he said, and grunted so savagely as to startle the king, who involuntarily shrank away from her.

"Forget not the pig," Grief whispered to Ieremia, who immediately stood up.

With a sweeping gesture he stilled the babel of voices that was beginning to rise.

"It was an ancient and honourable custom of Fitu-Iva," he said, "that when a man was proved a notorious evildoer his joints were broken with a club and he was staked out at low water to be fed upon alive by the sharks. Unfortunately, that day is past. Nevertheless another ancient and honourable custom remains with us. You all know what it is. When a man is a proven thief and liar he shall be struck with a dead pig."

His right hand went into the basket, and, despite the lack of his spectacles, the dead pig that came into view landed accurately on Deasy's neck. With such force was it thrown that the Chancellor, in his sitting position, toppled over sidewise. Before he could recover, Sepeli, with an agility unexpected of a woman who weighed two hundred and sixty pounds, had sprung across to him. One hand clutched his shirt collar, the other hand brandished the pig, and amid the vast uproar of a delighted kingdom she royally swatted him.

There remained nothing for Tui Tulifau but to put a good face on his favourite's disgrace, and his mountainous fat lay back on the mats and shook in a gale of Gargantuan laughter.

When Sepeli dropped both pig and Chancellor, a talking man from the windward coast picked up the carcass. Cornelius was on his feet and running, when the pig caught him on the legs and tripped him. The people and the army, with shouts and laughter, joined in the sport. Twist and dodge as he would, everywhere the ex-Chancellor of the Exchequer was met or overtaken by the flying pig. He scuttled like a frightened rabbit in and out among the avocados and the palms. No hand was laid upon him, and his tormentors made way before him, but ever they pursued, and ever the pig flew as fast as hands could pick it up.

As the chase died away down the Broom Road, Grief led the traders to the royal treasury, and the day was well over ere the last Fitu-Ivan bank note had been redeemed with coin.

VIII

Through the mellow cool of twilight a man paddled out from a clump of jungle to the *Cantani*. It was a leaky and abandoned dug-out, and he paddled slowly, desisting from time to time in order to

"It was a leaky and abandoned dugout, and he paddled slowly. . . . "
Drawing by Anton Otto Fischer.

bale. The Kanaka sailors giggled gleefully as he came alongside and painfully drew himself over the rail. He was bedraggled and filthy, and seemed half-dazed.

"Could I speak a word with you, Mr. Grief?" he asked sadly and humbly.

"Sit to leeward and farther away," Grief answered. "A little farther away. That's better."

Cornelius sat down on the rail and held his head in both his hands.

"'Tis right," he said. "I'm as fragrant as a recent battlefield. My head aches to burstin'. My neck is fair broken. The teeth are loose in my jaws. There's nests of hornets buzzin' in my ears. My medulla oblongata is dislocated. I've been through earthquake and pestilence, and the heavens have rained pigs." He paused with a sigh that ended in a groan. "'Tis a vision of terrible death. One that the poets never dreamed. To be eaten by rats, or boiled in oil, or pulled apart by wild horses—that would be unpleasant. But to be beaten to death with a dead pig!" He shuddered at the awfulness of it. "Sure it transcends the human imagination."

Captain Boig sniffed audibly, moved his canvas chair farther to windward, and sat down again.

"I hear you're runnin' over to Yap, Mr. Grief," Cornelius went on.[11] "An' two things I'm wantin' to beg of you: a passage an' the nip of the old smoky I refused the night you landed."

Grief clapped his hands for the black steward and ordered soap and towels.

"Go for'ard, Cornelius, and take a scrub first," he said. "The boy will bring you a pair of dungarees and a shirt. And by the way, before you go, how was it we found more coin in the treasury than paper you had issued?"

"'Twas the stake of my own I'd brought with me for the adventure."

"We've decided to charge the demurrage and other expenses and loss to Tui Tulifau," Grief said.[12] "So the balance we found will be turned over to you. But ten shillings must be deducted."

"For what?"

"Do you think dead pigs grow on trees? The sum of ten shillings for that pig is entered in the accounts."

Cornelius bowed his assent with a shudder.

"Sure it's grateful I am it wasn't a fifteen-shilling pig or a twenty-shilling one."

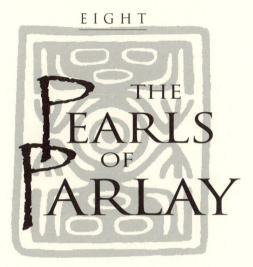

EIGHT

THE PEARLS OF PARLAY

The last of the David Grief stories deals with the darkest themes: racism, infidelity, death, greed, madness, and revenge. Enough action happens offstage to serve the needs of a novel, and enough passion and tragedy occurs to swell a grand opera. All this is framed against a backdrop of a slowly building typhoon that may have been awakened by a supernatural power, for the natives believe that the fabulously wealthy Parlay, like a latter-day Prospero, can control the winds. "The Pearls of Parlay" takes our hero, along with several other seafarers, to the isolated atolls of Tuamoto to participate in the pearl auction of a lifetime.

Parlay himself is one of those white monarchs of the islands so common in South Seas fiction. Over the years, with relentless passion, Parlay has gathered a fortune in pearls; now he has determined to sell them to the highest bidder, promising that this will be their very last opportunity to acquire the riches he has accumulated. Drawn to this irresistible invitation are traders, adventurers, scalawags, and businessmen from all of the white nations that have engaged in the commercial exploitation of the Pacific. This international throng constitutes a portrait of commercial exploitation itself, and it is soon clear that they have been trapped by their own greed into an insane plot engineered by Parlay to take revenge on these individuals as representatives of the entire colonial macrocosm. "You'll be doing your buying in hell," cackles the maniacal Parlay as he sees "his" storm begin to swell.

Not surprisingly, David Grief knows the backstory. As Grief explains, Parlay's madness has been caused by the death of his beloved daughter, his own and "real" pearl of great price, who had been subjected to social rejection and sexual exploitation by the insensitive and racist community of South Seas white people. The story of Armande's pitiable decline and fall recalls the tragedy of Puccini's Madama Butterfly, which had debuted seven years before London wrote this story. London, however, explores the issue of racial bigotry further than the mere evocation of pity. Not only does the story feelingly condemn the pointless and inhuman restrictions imposed on people by the conventions of a racist society, but it goes on to suggest that nature itself recoils at the enormities committed in the cause of white supremacy. Nonetheless, at the same time that the characters implicitly condemn the racism that leads to Armande's death, they willingly participate in anti-Jewish bigotry directed at the half-breed pearl merchant, Narii Herring. The last line of dialogue, in fact, is an invective hurled in Narii's direction by Captain Warfield, who is disappointed that Narii Herring has not been killed by the storm.

Much of the text is taken up with the detailed depiction of the typhoon that sweeps the island clear of its riches, its greed, and its madness. But something more than nature appears to be at work. The brilliance of this tale may lie in the ambiguity of its form—is it, like some of the other Grief yarns, an adventure story grounded in realistic characters and action, or does it exhibit the telltale marks of Victorian gothic narrative? Is Parlay merely an ordinary individual driven to seek revenge, his madness logically portrayed? Or is his power to call up storms more than the stuff of native legend and instead evidence of supernatural power? After all, he has made plans for the pearl auction far in advance and so could not forecast the storm that he requires to serve as his agent of destruction. In the end, after all this sound and fury, the storm subsides, leaving behind in a tattered basket only one blind kitten "that feebly mewed and staggered on awkward legs."

The Kanaka[1] helmsman put the wheel down, and the *Malahini* slipped into the eye of the wind and righted to an even keel. Her head-sails emptied, there was a rat-tat of reef-points and quick shifting of boom-tackles, and she was heeled over and filled away on the other tack. Though it was early morning and the wind brisk, the five white men who lounged on the poop-deck were scantily clad. David Grief, and his guest, Gregory Mulhall, an Englishman, were still in pajamas, their naked feet thrust into Chinese slippers. The captain and mate were in thin undershirts and unstarched duck pants, while the supercargo still held in his hands the undershirt he was reluctant to put on. The sweat stood out on his forehead, and he seemed to thrust his bare chest thirstily into the wind that did not cool.

"Pretty muggy, for a breeze like this," he complained.

"And what's it doing around in the west? That's what I want to know," was Grief's contribution to the general plaint.

"It won't last, and it ain't been there long," said Hermann, the Holland mate. "She is been chop around all night—five minutes here, ten minutes there, one hour somewhere other quarter."

"Something makin', something makin'," Captain Warfield croaked, spreading his bushy beard with the fingers of both hands and shoving the thatch of his chin into the breeze in a vain search for coolness. "Weather's been crazy for a fortnight. Haven't had the proper trades in three weeks. Everything's mixed up. Barometer was pumping at sunset last night, and it's pumping now, though the weather sharps say it don't mean anything. All the same, I've got a prejudice against seeing it pump. Gets on my nerves, sort of, you know. She was pumping that way the time we lost the *Lancaster*. I was only an apprentice, but I can remember that well enough. Brand new, four-masted steel ship; first voyage; broke the old man's heart. He'd been forty years in the company. Just faded way and died the next year."

Despite the wind and the early hour, the heat was suffocating. The wind whispered coolness, but did not deliver coolness. It might have blown off the Sahara, save for the extreme humidity with which it was laden. There was no fog nor mist, nor hint of fog or mist, yet the dimness of distance produced the impression. There were no defined clouds, yet so thickly were the heavens covered by a messy cloud-pall that the sun failed to shine through.

"Ready about!" Captain Warfield ordered with slow sharpness.

The brown, breech-clouted Kanaka sailors moved languidly but quickly to head-sheets and boom-tackles.

"Hard a-lee!"

The helmsman ran the spokes over with no hint of gentling, and the *Malahini* darted prettily into the wind and about.

"Jove! she's a witch!" was Mulhall's appreciation. "I didn't know you South Sea traders sailed yachts."

"She was a Gloucester fisherman originally," Grief explained, "and the Gloucester boats are all yachts when it comes to build, rig, and sailing."

"But you're heading right in—why don't you make it?" came the Englishman's criticism.

"Try it, Captain Warfield," Grief suggested. "Show him what a lagoon entrance is on a strong ebb."

"Close-and-by!" the captain ordered.

"Close-and-by," the Kanaka repeated, easing half a spoke.

The *Malahini* laid squarely into the narrow passage which was the lagoon entrance of a large, long, and narrow oval of an atoll. The atoll was shaped as if three atolls, in the course of building, had collided and coalesced and failed to rear the partition walls. Cocoa-nut palms grew in spots on the circle of sand, and there were many gaps where the sand was too low to the sea for cocoanuts, and through which could be seen the protected lagoon where the water lay flat like the ruffled surface of a mirror. Many square miles of water were in the irregular lagoon, all of which surged out on the ebb through the one narrow channel. So narrow was the channel, so large the outflow of water, that the passage was more like the rapids of a river than the mere tidal entrance to an atoll. The water boiled and whirled and swirled and drove outward in a white foam of stiff, serrated waves. Each heave and blow on her bows of the upstanding waves of the current swung the *Malahini* off the straight lead and wedged her as with wedges of steel toward the side of the passage. Part way in she was, when her closeness to the coral edge compelled her to go about. On the opposite tack, broadside to the current, she swept seaward with the current's speed.

"Now's the time for that new and expensive engine of yours," Grief jeered good-naturedly.

That the engine was a sore point with Captain Warfield was patent. He had begged and badgered for it, until in the end Grief had given his consent.

"It will pay for itself yet," the captain retorted. "You wait and see. It beats insurance and you know the underwriters won't stand for insurance in the Paumotus."[2]

Grief pointed to a small cutter beating up astern of them on the same course.

"I'll wager a five-franc piece the little *Nuhiva* beats us in."

"Sure," Captain Warfield agreed. "She's overpowered. We're like a liner alongside of her, and we've only got forty horsepower. She's got ten horse, and she's a little skimming dish. She could skate across the froth of hell, but just the same she can't buck this current. It's running ten knots right now."

And at the rate of ten knots, buffeted and jerkily rolled, the *Malahini* went out to sea with the tide.

"She'll slacken in half an hour—then we'll make headway," Captain Warfield said, with an irritation explained by his next words. "He has no right to call it Parlay. It's down on the admiralty charts, and the French charts, too, as Hikihoho. Bougainville discovered it and named it from the natives."

"What's the name matter?" the supercargo demanded, taking advantage of speech to pause with arms shoved into the sleeves of the undershirt. "There it is, right under our nose, and old Parlay is there with the pearls."[3]

"Who see them pearl?" Hermann queried, looking from one to another.

"It's well known," was the supercargo's reply. He turned to the steersman: "Tai-Hotauri, what about old Parlay's pearls?"

The Kanaka, pleased and self-conscious, took and gave a spoke.

"My brother dive for Parlay three, four month, and he make much talk about pearl. Hikihoho very good place for pearl."

"And the pearl-buyers have never got him to part with a pearl," the captain broke in.

"And they say he had a hatful for Armande when he sailed for Tahiti," the supercargo carried on the tale. "That's fifteen years ago, and he's been adding to it ever since—stored the shell as well. Everybody's seen that—hundreds of tons of it. They say the lagoon's fished clean now. Maybe that's why he's announced the auction."

"If he really sells, this will be the biggest year's output of pearls in the Paumotus," Grief said.

"I say, now, look here!" Mulhall burst forth, harried by the humid heat as much as the rest of them. "What's it all about? Who's the old beachcomber anyway? What are all these pearls? Why so secretious about it?"

"Hikihoho belongs to old Parlay," the supercargo answered. "He's got a fortune in pearls, saved up for years and years, and he sent the word out weeks ago that he'd auction them off to the buyers tomorrow. See those schooners' masts sticking up inside the lagoon?"

"Eight, so I see," said Hermann.

"What are they doing in a dinky atoll like this?" the supercargo went on. "There isn't a schooner-load of copra a year in the place. They've come for the auction. That's why we're here. That's why the little *Nuhiva's* bumping along astern there, though what she can buy is beyond me. Narii Herring—he's an English Jew half-caste—owns and runs her, and his only assets are his nerve, his debts, and his whiskey bills.[4] He's a genius in such things. He owes so much that there isn't a merchant in Papeete who isn't interested in his welfare. They go out of their way to throw work in his way. They've got to, and a dandy stunt it is for Narii. Now I owe nobody. What's the result? If I fell down in a fit on the beach they'd let me lie there and die. They wouldn't lose anything. But Narii Herring?—what wouldn't they do if he fell in a fit? Their best wouldn't be too good for him. They've got too much money tied up in him to let him lie. They'd

take him into their homes and hand-nurse him like a brother. Let me
tell you, honesty in paying bills ain't what it's cracked up to be."

"What's this Narii chap got to do with it?" was the Englishman's
short-tempered demand. And, turning to Grief, he said, "What's all
this pearl nonsense? Begin at the beginning."

"You'll have to help me out," Grief warned the others, as he began. "Old Parlay is a character. From what I've seen of him I believe
he's partly and mildly insane. Anyway, here's the story: Parlay's a
full-blooded Frenchman. He told me once that he came from Paris.
His accent is the true Parisian. He arrived down here in the old days.
Went to trading and all the rest. That's how he got in on Hikihoho.
Came in trading when trading was the real thing. About a hundred
miserable Paumotans lived on the island. He married the queen—
native fashion. When she died, everything was his. Measles came
through, and there weren't more than a dozen survivors. He fed
them, and worked them, and was king. Now before the queen died
she gave birth to a girl. That's Armande. When she was three he sent
her to the convent at Papeete. When she was seven or eight he sent
her to France. You begin to glimpse the situation. The best and most
aristocratic convent in France was none too good for the only daughter of a Paumotan island king and capitalist, and you know the old
country French draw no colour line. She was educated like a princess, and she accepted herself in much the same way. Also, she thought
she was all-white, and never dreamed of a bar sinister.

"Now comes the tragedy. The old man had always been cranky
and erratic, and he'd played the despot on Hikihoho so long that
he'd got the idea in his head that there was nothing wrong with the
king—or the princess either. When Armande was eighteen he sent
for her. He had slews and slathers of money, as Yankee Bill would
say. He'd built the big house on Hikihoho, and a whacking fine bungalow in Papeete. She was to arrive on the mail boat from New
Zealand, and he sailed in his schooner to meet her at Papeete. And
he might have carried the situation off, despite the hens and bull-
beasts of Papeete, if it hadn't been for the hurricane. That was the
year, wasn't it, when Manu-Huhi was swept and eleven hundred
drowned?"

The others nodded, and Captain Warfield said: "I was in the *Mag-*

pie that blow, and we went ashore, all hands and the cook, *Magpie* and all, a quarter of a mile into the cocoanuts at the head of Taiohae Bay—and it a supposedly hurricane-proof harbour."

"Well," Grief continued, "old Parlay got caught in the same blow, and arrived in Papeete with his hatful of pearls three weeks too late. He'd had to jack up his schooner and build half a mile of ways before he could get her back into the sea.

"And in the meantime there was Armande at Papeete. Nobody called on her. She did, French fashion, make the initial calls on the Governor and the port doctor. They saw her, but neither of their hen-wives was at home to her nor returned the call. She was out of caste, without caste, though she had never dreamed it, and that was the gentle way they broke the information to her. There was a gay young lieutenant on the French cruiser. He lost his heart to her, but not his head. You can imagine the shock to this young woman, refined, beautiful, raised like an aristocrat, pampered with the best of old France that money could buy. And you can guess the end." He shrugged his shoulders. "There was a Japanese servant in the bungalow. He saw it. Said she did it with the proper spirit of the Samurai. Took a stiletto—no thrust, no drive, no wild rush for annihilation—took the stiletto, placed the point carefully against her heart, and with both hands, slowly and steadily, pressed home.

"Old Parlay arrived after that with his pearls. There was one single one of them, they say, worth sixty thousand francs. Peter Gee saw it, and has told me he offered that much for it. The old man went clean off for a while. They had him strait-jacketed in the Colonial Club two days—"

"His wife's uncle, an old Paumotan, cut him out of the jacket and turned him loose," the supercargo corroborated.

"And then old Parlay proceeded to eat things up," Grief went on. "Pumped three bullets into the scalawag of a lieutenant—"

"Who lay in sick bay for three months," Captain Warfield contributed.

"Flung a glass of wine in the Governor's face; fought a duel with the port doctor; beat up his native servants; wrecked the hospital; broke two ribs and the collarbone of a man nurse, and escaped; and went down to his schooner, a gun in each hand, daring the chief of police and all the gendarmes to arrest him, and sailed for Hikihoho. And they say he's never left the island since."

The supercargo nodded. "That was fifteen years ago, and he's never budged."

"And added to his pearls," said the captain. "He's a blithering old lunatic. Makes my flesh creep. He's a regular Finn."

"What's that?" Mulhall inquired.

"Bosses the weather—that's what the natives believe, at any rate. Ask Tai-Hotauri there. Hey, Tai-Hotauri! what you think old Parlay do along weather?"

"Just the same one big weather devil," came the Kanaka's answer. "I know. He want big blow, he make big blow. He want no wind, no wind come."

"A regular old Warlock," said Mulhall.

"No good luck them pearl," Tai-Hotauri blurted out, rolling his head ominously. "He say he sell. Plenty schooner come. Then he make big hurricane, everybody finish, you see. All native men say so."

"It's hurricane season now," Captain Warfield laughed morosely. "They're not far wrong. It's making for something right now, and I'd feel better if the *Malahini* was a thousand miles away from here."

"He is a bit mad," Grief concluded. "I've tried to get his point of view. It's—well, it's mixed. For eighteen years he'd centred everything on Armande. Half the time he believes she's still alive, not yet come back from France. That's one of the reasons he held on to the pearls. And all the time he hates white men. He never forgets they killed her, though a great deal of the time he forgets she's dead. Hello! Where's your wind?"

The sails bellied emptily overhead, and Captain Warfield grunted his disgust. Intolerable as the heat had been, in the absence of wind it was almost overpowering. The sweat oozed out on all their faces, and now one, and again another, drew deep breaths, involuntarily questing for more air.

"Here she comes again—an eight point haul! Boom-tackles across! Jump!"

The Kanakas sprang to the captain's orders, and for five minutes the schooner laid directly into the passage and even gained on the current. Again the breeze fell flat, then puffed from the old quarter, compelling a shift back of sheets and tackles.

"Here comes the *Nuhiva*," Grief said. "She's got her engine on. Look at her skim."

"All ready?" the captain asked the engineer, a Portuguese half-caste, whose head and shoulders protruded from the small hatch just for'ard of the cabin, and who wiped the sweat from his face with a bunch of greasy waste.

"Sure," he replied.

"Then let her go."

The engineer disappeared into his den, and a moment later the exhaust muffler coughed and spluttered overside. But the schooner could not hold her lead. The little cutter made three feet to her two and was quickly alongside and forging ahead. Only natives were on her deck, and the man steering waved his hand in derisive greeting and farewell.

"That's Narii Herring," Grief told Mulhall. "The big fellow at the wheel—the nerviest and most conscienceless scoundrel in the Paumotus."

Five minutes later a cry of joy from their own Kanakas centred all eyes on the *Nuhiva*. Her engine had broken down and they were overtaking her. The *Malahini*'s sailors sprang into the rigging and jeered as they went by; the little cutter heeled over by the wind with a bone in her teeth, going backward on the tide.

"Some engine that of ours," Grief approved, as the lagoon opened before them and the course was changed across it to the anchorage.

Captain Warfield was visibly cheered, though he merely grunted, "It'll pay for itself, never fear."

The *Malahini* ran well into the centre of the little fleet ere she found swinging room to anchor.

"There's Isaacs on the *Dolly*," Grief observed, with a hand wave of greeting. "And Peter Gee's on the *Roberta*. Couldn't keep him away from a pearl sale like this. And there's Francini on the *Cactus*. They're all here, all the buyers. Old Parlay will surely get a price."

"That's Narii Herring, the nerviest and most conscienceless scoundrel in the Paumotos. . . . " Drawing by Anton Otto Fischer.

"They haven't repaired the engine yet," Captain Warfield grumbled gleefully.

He was looking across the lagoon to where the *Nuhiva*'s sails showed through the sparse cocoanuts.

II

The house of Parlay was a big two-story frame affair, built of California lumber, with a galvanized iron roof. So disproportionate was it to the slender ring of the atoll that it showed out upon the sand-strip and above it like some monstrous excrescence. They of the *Malahini* paid the courtesy visit ashore immediately after anchoring. Other captains and buyers were in the big room examining the pearls that were to be auctioned next day. Paumotan servants, natives of Hikihoho, and relatives of the owner, moved about dispensing whiskey and absinthe. And through the curious company moved Parlay himself, cackling and sneering, the withered wreck of what had once been a tall and powerful man. His eyes were deep sunken and feverish, his cheeks fallen in and cavernous. The hair of his head seemed to have come out in patches, and his mustache and imperial had shed in the same lopsided way.

"Jove!" Mulhall muttered under his breath. "A long-legged Napoleon the Third, but burnt out, baked, and fire-crackled. And mangy! No wonder he crooks his head to one side. He's got to keep the balance."

"Goin' to have a blow," was the old man's greeting to Grief. "You must think a lot of pearls to come a day like this."

"They're worth going to inferno for," Grief laughed genially back, running his eyes over the surface of the table covered by the display.

"Other men have already made that journey for them," old Parlay cackled. "See this one!" He pointed to a large, perfect pearl the size of a small walnut that lay apart on a piece of chamois. "They offered me sixty thousand francs for it in Tahiti. They'll bid as much and more for it to-morrow, if they aren't blown away. Well, that pearl, it was found by my cousin, my cousin by marriage. He was a native, you see. Also, he was a thief. He hid it. It was mine. His cousin, who was also my cousin—we're all related here—killed him for it and fled away in a cutter to Noo-Nau. I pursued, but the chief of Noo-Nau had killed him for it before I got there. Oh, yes, there are many dead men represented on the table there. Have a drink, Captain. Your face is not familiar. You are new in the islands?"

"It's Captain Robinson of the *Roberta*," Grief said, introducing them.

In the meantime Mulhall had shaken hands with Peter Gee.

"I never fancied there were so many pearls in the world," Mulhall said.

"Nor have I ever seen so many together at one time," Peter Gee admitted.

"What ought they to be worth?"

"Fifty or sixty thousand pounds—and that's to us buyers. In Paris—" He shrugged his shoulders and lifted his eyebrows at the incommunicableness of the sun.

Mulhall wiped the sweat from his eyes. All were sweating profusely and breathing hard. There was no ice in the drink that was served, and whiskey and absinthe went down lukewarm.

"Yes, yes," Parlay was cackling. "Many dead men lie on the table there. I know those pearls, all of them. You see those three! Perfectly matched, aren't they? A diver from Easter Island got them for me inside a week. Next week a shark got him; took his arm off and blood poison did the business. And that big baroque there—nothing much—if I'm offered twenty francs for it to-morrow I'll be in luck; it came out of twenty-two fathoms of water. The man was from Raratonga. He broke all diving records. He got it out of twenty-two fathoms. I saw him. And he burst his lungs at the same time, or got the 'bends,' for he died in two hours. He died screaming. They could hear him for miles. He was the most powerful native I ever saw. Half a dozen of my divers have died of the bends. And more men will die, more men will die."

"Oh, hush your croaking, Parlay," chided one of the captains. "It ain't going to blow."

"If I was a strong man, I couldn't get up hook and get out fast enough," the old man retorted in the falsetto of age. "Not if I was a strong man with the taste for wine yet in my mouth. But not you. You'll all stay. I wouldn't advise you if I thought you'd go. You can't drive buzzards away from the carrion. Have another drink, my brave sailormen. Well, well, what men will dare for a few little oyster drops! There they are, the beauties! Auction to-morrow, at ten sharp. Old Parlay's selling out, and the buzzards are gathering—old Parlay who was a stronger man in his day than any of them and who will see most of them dead yet."

"If he isn't a vile old beast!" the supercargo of the *Malahini* whispered to Peter Gee.

"What if she does blow?" said the captain of the *Dolly*. "Hiki-hoho's never been swept."

"The more reason she will be, then," Captain Warfield answered back. "I wouldn't trust her."

"Who's croaking now?" Grief reproved.

"I'd hate to lose that new engine before it paid for itself," Captain Warfield replied gloomily.

Parlay skipped with astonishing nimbleness across the crowded room to the barometer on the wall.

"Take a look, my brave sailormen!" he cried exultantly.

The man nearest read the glass. The sobering effect showed plainly on his face.

"It's dropped ten," was all he said, yet every face went anxious, and there was a look as if every man desired immediately to start for the door.

"Listen!" Parlay commanded.

In the silence the outer surf seemed to have become unusually loud. There was a great rumbling roar.

"A big sea is beginning to set," some one said; and there was a movement to the windows, where all gathered.

Through the sparse cocoanuts they gazed seaward. An orderly succession of huge smooth seas was rolling down upon the coral shore. For some minutes they gazed on the strange sight and talked in low voices, and in those few minutes it was manifest to all that the waves were increasing in size. It was uncanny, this rising sea in a dead calm, and their voices unconsciously sank lower. Old Parlay shocked them with his abrupt cackle.

"There is yet time to get away to sea, brave gentlemen. You can tow across the lagoon with your whaleboats."

"It's all right, old man," said Darling, the mate of the *Cactus*, a stalwart youngster of twenty-five. "The blow's to the south'ard and passing on. We'll not get a whiff of it."

An air of relief went through the room. Conversations were started, and the voices became louder. Several of the buyers even went back to the table to continue the examination of the pearls.

Parlay's shrill cackle rose higher.

"That's right," he encouraged. "If the world was coming to an end you'd go on buying."

"We'll buy these to-morrow just the same," Isaacs assured him.

"Then you'll be doing your buying in hell."

The chorus of incredulous laughter incensed the old man. He turned fiercely on Darling.

"Since when have children like you come to the knowledge of storms? And who is the man who has plotted the hurricane-courses of the Paumotus? What books will you find it in? I sailed the Paumotus before the oldest of you drew breath. I know. To the eastward the paths of the hurricanes are on so wide a circle they make a straight line. To the westward here they make a sharp curve. Remember your chart. How did it happen the hurricane of '91 swept Auri and Hiolau? The curve, my brave boy, the curve! In an hour, or two or three at most, will come the wind. Listen to that!"

A vast rumbling crash shook the coral foundations of the atoll. The house quivered to it. The native servants, with bottles of whiskey and absinthe in their hands, shrank together as if for protection and stared with fear through the windows at the mighty wash of the wave lapping far up the beach to the corner of a copra-shed.

Parlay looked at the barometer, giggled, and leered around at his guests. Captain Warfield strode across to see.

"29.75," he read. "She's gone down five more. By God! the old devil's right. She's a-coming, and it's me, for one, for aboard."

"It's growing dark," Isaacs half whispered.

"Jove! it's like a stage," Mulhall said to Grief, looking at his watch. "Ten o'clock in the morning, and it's like twilight. Down go the lights for the tragedy. Where's the slow music!"

In answer, another rumbling crash shook the atoll and the house. Almost in a panic the company started for the door. In the dim light their sweaty faces appeared ghastly. Isaacs panted asthmatically in the suffocating heat.

"What's your haste?" Parlay chuckled and girded at his departing guests. "A last drink, brave gentlemen." No one noticed him. As they took the shell-bordered path to the beach he stuck his head out the door and called, "Don't forget, gentlemen, at ten to-morrow old Parlay sells his pearls."

III

On the beach a curious scene took place. Whaleboat after whaleboat was being hurriedly manned and shoved off. It had grown still darker. The stagnant calm continued, and the sand shook under their feet with each buffet of the sea on the outer shore. Narii Herring walked leisurely along the sand. He grinned at the very evident haste of the captains and buyers. With him were three of his Kanakas, and also Tai-Hotauri.

"Get into the boat and take an oar," Captain Warfield ordered the latter.

Tai-Hotauri came over jauntily, while Narii Herring and his three Kanakas paused and looked on from forty feet away.

"I work no more for you, skipper," Tai-Hotauri said insolently and loudly. But his face belied his words, for he was guilty of a prodigious wink. "Fire me, skipper," he huskily whispered, with a second significant wink.

Captain Warfield took the cue and proceeded to do some acting himself. He raised his fist and his voice.

"Get into that boat," he thundered, "or I'll knock seven bells out of you!"

The Kanaka drew back truculently, and Grief stepped between to placate his captain.

"I go to work on the *Nuhiva*," Tai-Hotauri said, rejoining the other group.

"Come back here!" the captain threatened.

"Don't forget, gentlemen, at ten tomorrow old Parlay
sells his pearls. . . . " Drawing by Anton Otto Fischer.

"He's a free man, skipper," Narii Herring spoke up. "He's sailed with me in the past, and he's sailing again, that's all."

"Come on, we must get on board," Grief urged. "Look how dark it's getting."

Captain Warfield gave in, but as the boat shoved off he stood up in the sternsheets and shook his fist ashore.

"I'll settle with you yet, Narii," he cried. "You're the only skipper in the group that steals other men's sailors." He sat down, and in lowered voice queried: "Now what's Tai-Hotauri up to? He's on to something, but what is it?"

IV

As the boat came alongside the *Malahini*, Hermann's anxious face greeted them over the rail.

"Bottom out fall from barometer," he announced. "She's goin' to blow. I got starboard anchor overhaul."

"Overhaul the big one, too," Captain Warfield ordered, taking charge. "And here, some of you, hoist in this boat. Lower her down to the deck and lash her bottom up."

Men were busy at work on the decks of all the schooners. There was a great clanking of chains being overhauled, and now one craft, and now another, hove in, veered, and dropped a second anchor. Like the *Malahini*, those that had third anchors were preparing to drop them when the wind showed what quarter it was to blow from.

The roar of the big surf continually grew, though the lagoon lay in the mirror-like calm. There was no sign of life where Parlay's big house perched on the sand. Boat and copra-sheds and the sheds where the shell was stored were deserted.

"For two cents I'd up anchors and get out," Grief said. "I'd do it anyway if it were open sea. But those chains of atolls to the north and east have us pocketed. We've a better chance right here. What do you think, Captain Warfield?"

"I agree with you, though a lagoon is no millpond for riding it out. I wonder where she's going to start from? Hello! There goes one of Parlay's copra-sheds."

"The sand shook under their feet with each buffet of the sea on the outer shore. . . ." Drawing by Anton Otto Fischer.

They could see the grass-thatched shed lift and collapse, while a froth of foam cleared the crest of the sand and ran down to the lagoon.

"Breached across!" Mulhall exclaimed. "That's something for a starter. There she comes again!"

The wreck of the shed was now flung up and left on the sand-crest. A third wave buffeted it into fragments which washed down the slope toward the lagoon.

"If she blow I would as be cooler yet," Hermann grunted. "No longer can I breathe. It is damn hot. I am dry like a stove."

He chopped open a drinking cocoanut with his heavy sheath-knife and drained the contents. The rest of them followed his example, pausing once to watch one of Parlay's shell sheds go down in ruin. The barometer now registered 29.50.

"Must be pretty close to the centre of the area of low pressure," Grief remarked cheerfully. "I was never through the eye of a hurricane before. It will be an experience for you, too, Mulhall. From the speed the barometer's dropped, it's going to be a big one."

Captain Warfield groaned, and all eyes drew to him. He was looking through the glasses down the length of the lagoon to the southeast.

"There she comes," he said quietly.

They did not need glasses to see. A flying film, strangely marked, seemed drawing over the surface of the lagoon. Abreast of it, along the atoll, travelling with equal speed, was a stiff bending of the cocoanut palms and a blur of flying leaves. The front of the wind on the water was a solid, sharply defined strip of dark-coloured, wind-vexed water. In advance of this strip, like skirmishers, were flashes of wind-flaws. Behind this strip, a quarter of a mile in width, was a strip of what seemed glassy calm. Next came another dark strip of wind, and behind that the lagoon was all crisping, boiling whiteness.

"What is that calm streak?" Mulhall asked.

"Calm," Warfield answered.

"But it travels as fast as the wind," was the other's objection.

"It has to, or it would be overtaken and it wouldn't be any calm. It's a double-header. I saw a big squall like that off Savaii once. A regular double-header. Smash! it hit us, then it lulled to nothing, and smashed us a second time. Stand by and hold on! Here she is on top of us. Look at the *Roberta*!"

The *Roberta*, lying nearest to the wind at slack chains, was swept off broadside like a straw. Then her chains brought her up, bow on to the wind, with an astonishing jerk. Schooner after schooner, the *Malahini* with them, was now sweeping away with the first gust and fetching up on taut chains. Mulhall and several of the Kanakas were taken off their feet when the *Malahini* jerked to her anchors.

And then there was no wind. The flying calm streak had reached them. Grief lighted a match, and the unshielded flame burned without flickering in the still air. A very dim twilight prevailed. The cloud-sky, lowering as it had been for hours, seemed now to have descended quite down upon the sea.

The *Roberta* tightened to her chains when the second head of the hurricane hit, as did schooner after schooner in swift succession. The sea, white with fury, boiled in tiny, spitting wavelets. The deck of the *Malahini* vibrated under the men's feet. The taut-stretched halyards beat a tattoo against the masts, and all the rigging, as if smote by some mighty hand, set up a wild thrumming. It was impossible to face the wind and breathe. Mulhall, crouching with the others behind the shelter of the cabin, discovered this, and his lungs were filled in an instant with so great a volume of driven air which he could not expel that he nearly strangled ere he could turn his head away.

"It's incredible," he gasped, but no one heard him.

Hermann and several Kanakas were crawling for'ard on hands and knees to let go the third anchor. Grief touched Captain Warfield and pointed to the *Roberta*. She was dragging down upon them. Warfield put his mouth to Grief's ear and shouted:

"We're dragging, too!"

Grief sprang to the wheel and put it hard over, veering the *Malahini* to port. The third anchor took hold, and the *Roberta* went by, stern-first, a dozen yards away. They waved their hands to Peter Gee and Captain Robinson, who, with a number of sailors, were at work on the bow.

"He's knocking out the shackles!" Grief shouted. "Going to chance the passage! Got to! Anchors skating!"

"We're holding now!" came the answering shout. "There goes the *Cactus* down on the *Misi*. That settles them!"

The *Misi* had been holding, but the added windage of the *Cactus* was too much, and the entangled schooners slid away across the boiling white. Their men could be seen chopping and fighting to get them apart. The *Roberta,* cleared of her anchors, with a patch of tarpaulin set for'ard, was heading for the passage at the northwestern end of the lagoon. They saw her make it and drive out to sea. But the *Misi* and *Cactus,* unable to get clear of each other, went ashore on the atoll half a mile from the passage.

The wind merely increased on itself and continued to increase. To face the full blast of it required all one's strength, and several minutes of crawling on deck against it tired a man to exhaustion. Hermann, with his Kanakas, plodded steadily, lashing and making secure, putting ever more gaskets on the sails. The wind ripped and tore their thin undershirts from their backs. They moved slowly, as if their bodies weighed tons, never releasing a hand-hold until another had been secured. Loose ends of rope stood out stiffly horizontal, and, when a whipping gave, the loose end frazzled and blew away.

Mulhall touched one and then another and pointed to the shore. The grass-sheds had disappeared, and Parlay's house rocked drunkenly. Because the wind blew lengthwise along the atoll, the house had been sheltered by the miles of cocoanut trees. But the big seas, breaking across from outside, were undermining it and hammering it to pieces. Already tilted down the slope of sand, its end was imminent. Here and there in the cocoanut trees people had lashed themselves. The trees did not sway or thresh about. Bent over rigidly from the wind, they remained in that position and vibrated monstrously. Underneath, across the sand, surged the white spume of the breakers.

A big sea was likewise making down the length of the lagoon. It had plenty of room to kick up in the ten-mile stretch from the windward rim of the atoll, and all the schooners were bucking and plunging into it. The *Malahini* had begun shoving her bow and fo'c'sle head under the bigger ones, and at times her waist was filled rail-high with water.

"Now's the time for your engine!" Grief bellowed; and Captain Warfield, crawling over to where the engineer lay, shouted emphatic commands.

Under the engine, going full speed ahead, the *Malahini* behaved better. While she continued to ship seas over her bow, she was not jerked down so fiercely by her anchors. On the other hand, she was unable to get any slack in the chains. The best her forty horsepower could do was to ease the strain.

Still the wind increased. The little *Nuhiva*, lying abreast of the *Malahini* and closer in to the beach, her engine still unrepaired and her captain ashore, was having a bad time of it. She buried herself so frequently and so deeply that they wondered each time if she could clear herself of the water. At three in the afternoon, buried by a second sea before she could free herself of the preceding one, she did not come up.

Mulhall looked at Grief.

"Burst in her hatches," was the bellowed answer.

Captain Warfield pointed to the *Winifred*, a little schooner plunging and burying outside of them, and shouted in Grief's ear. His voice came in patches of dim words, with intervals of silence when whisked away by the roaring wind.

"Rotten little tub . . . Anchors hold . . . But how she holds together . . . Old as the ark—"

An hour later Hermann pointed to her. Her for'ard bits, foremast, and most of her bow were gone, having been jerked out of her by her anchors. She swung broadside, rolling in the trough and settling by the head, and in this plight was swept away to leeward.

Five vessels now remained, and of them the *Malahini* was the only one with an engine. Fearing either the *Nuhiva*'s or the *Winifred*'s fate, two of them followed the *Roberta*'s example, knocking out the chain-shackles and running for the passage. The *Dolly* was the first, but her tarpaulin was carried away, and she went to destruction on the lee-rim of the atoll near the *Misi* and the *Cactus*. Undeterred by this, the *Moana* let go and followed with the same result.

"Pretty good engine that, eh?" Captain Warfield yelled to his owner.

Grief put out his hand and shook. "She's paying for herself!" he yelled back. "The wind's shifting around to the south'ard, and we ought to lie easier!"

Slowly and steadily, but with ever-increasing velocity, the wind veered around to the south and the southwest, till the three schooners that were left pointed directly in toward the beach. The wreck of Parlay's house was picked up, hurled into the lagoon, and blown out upon them. Passing the *Malahini,* it crashed into the *Papara,* lying a quarter of a mile astern. There was wild work for'ard on her, and in a quarter of an hour the house went clear, but it had taken the *Papara*'s foremast and bowsprit with it.

Inshore, on their port bow, lay the *Tahaa,* slim and yacht-like, but excessively oversparred. Her anchors still held, but her captain, finding no abatement in the wind, proceeded to reduce windage by chopping down his masts.

"Pretty good engine that," Grief congratulated his skipper. "It will save our sticks for us yet."

Captain Warfield shook his head dubiously.

The sea on the lagoon went swiftly down with the change of wind, but they were beginning to feel the heave and lift of the outer sea breaking across the atoll. There were not so many trees remaining. Some had been broken short off, others uprooted. One tree they saw snap off halfway up, three persons clinging to it, and whirl away by the wind into the lagoon. Two detached themselves from it and swam to the *Tahaa.* Not long after, just before darkness, they saw one jump overboard from that schooner's stern and strike out strongly for the *Malahini* through the white, spitting wavelets.

"It's Tai-Hotauri," was Grief's judgment. "Now we'll have the news."

The Kanaka caught the bobstay, climbed over the bow, and crawled aft. Time was given him to breathe, and then, behind the part shelter of the cabin, in broken snatches and largely by signs, he told his story.

"Narii . . . damn robber . . . He want steal . . . pearls . . . Kill Parlay . . . One man kill Parlay . . . No man know what man . . . Three Kanakas, Narii, me . . . Five beans . . . hat . . . Narii say one bean black . . . Nobody know . . . Kill Parlay . . . Narii damn liar . . . All beans black . . . Five black . . . Copra-shed dark . . . Every man get black bean . . . Big wind come . . . No chance . . . Everybody get up tree . . . No good luck them pearls, I tell you before . . . No good luck."

"Where's Parlay?" Grief shouted.

"Up tree . . . Three of his Kanakas same tree. Narii and one Kanaka 'nother tree . . . My tree blow to hell, then I come on board."

"Where's the pearls?"

"Up tree along Parlay. Mebbe Narii get them pearl yet."

In the ear of one after another Grief passed on Tai-Hotauri's story. Captain Warfield was particularly incensed, and they could see him grinding his teeth.

Hermann went below and returned with a riding light, but the moment it was lifted above the level of the cabin wall the wind blew it out. He had better success with the binnacle lamp, which was lighted only after many collective attempts.

"A fine night of wind!" Grief yelled in Mulhall's ear. "And blowing harder all the time."

"How hard?"

"A hundred miles an hour . . . two hundred . . . I don't know . . . Harder than I've ever seen it."

The lagoon grew more and more troubled by the sea that swept across the atoll. Hundreds of leagues of ocean was being backed up by the hurricane, which more than overcame the lowering effect of the ebb tide. Immediately the tide began to rise the increase in the size of the seas was noticeable. Moon and wind were heaping the South Pacific on Hikihoho atoll.

Captain Warfield returned from one of his periodical trips to the engine room with the word that the engineer lay in a faint.

"Can't let that engine stop!" he concluded helplessly.

"All right!" Grief said. "Bring him on deck. I'll spell him."

The hatch to the engine room was battened down, access being gained through a narrow passage from the cabin. The heat and gas fumes were stifling. Grief took one hasty, comprehensive examination of the engine and the fittings of the tiny room, then blew out the

oil-lamp. After that he worked in darkness, save for the glow from
endless cigars which he went into the cabin to light. Even-tempered
as he was, he soon began to give evidences of the strain of being pent
in with a mechanical monster that toiled, and sobbed, and slubbered
in the shouting dark. Naked to the waist, covered with grease and
oil, bruised and skinned from being knocked about by the plunging,
jumping vessel, his head swimming from the mixture of gas and air
he was compelled to breathe, he laboured on hour after hour, in
turns petting, blessing, nursing, and cursing the engine and all its
parts. The ignition began to go bad. The feed grew worse. And worst
of all, the cylinders began to heat. In a consultation held in the cabin the half-caste engineer begged and pleaded to stop the engine for
half an hour in order to cool it and to attend to the water circulation.
Captain Warfield was against any stopping. The half-caste swore that
the engine would ruin itself and stop anyway and for good. Grief,
with glaring eyes, greasy and battered, yelled and cursed them both
down and issued commands. Mulhall, the supercargo, and Hermann
were set to work in the cabin at double-straining and triple-straining
the gasoline. A hole was chopped through the engine room floor,
and a Kanaka heaved bilge-water over the cylinders, while Grief continued to souse running parts in oil.

"Didn't know you were a gasoline expert," Captain Warfield ad-
mired when Grief came into the cabin to catch a breath of little less
impure air.

"I bathe in gasoline," he grated savagely through his teeth. "I eat
it."

What other uses he might have found for it were never given, for
at that moment all the men in the cabin, as well as the gasoline being
strained, were smashed for'ard against the bulkhead as the *Malahini*
took an abrupt, deep dive. For the space of several minutes, unable
to gain their feet, they rolled back and forth and pounded and ham-
mered from wall to wall. The schooner, swept by three big seas,
creaked and groaned and quivered, and from the weight of water on
her decks behaved logily. Grief crept to the engine, while Captain
Warfield waited his chance to get through the companionway and
out on deck.

It was half an hour before he came back.

"Whaleboat's gone!" he reported. "Galley's gone! Everything gone except the deck and hatches! And if that engine hadn't been going we'd be gone! Keep up the good work!"

By midnight the engineer's lungs and head had been sufficiently cleared of gas fumes to let him relieve Grief, who went on deck to get his own head and lungs clear. He joined the others, who crouched behind the cabin, holding on with their hands and made doubly secure by rope-lashings. It was a complicated huddle, for it was the only place of refuge for the Kanakas. Some of them had accepted the skipper's invitation into the cabin but had been driven out by the fumes. The *Malahini* was being plunged down and swept frequently, and what they breathed was air and spray and water commingled.

"Making heavy weather of it, Mulhall!" Grief shouted to his guest between immersions.

Mulhall, strangling and choking, could only nod. The scuppers could not carry off the burden of water on the schooner's deck. She rolled it out and took it in over one rail and the other; and at times, nose thrown skyward, sitting down on her heel, she avalanched it aft. It surged along the poop gangways, poured over the top of the cabin, submerging and bruising those that clung on, and went out over the stern-rail.

Mulhall saw him first, and drew Grief's attention. It was Narii Herring, crouching and holding on where the dim binnacle light shone upon him. He was quite naked, save for a belt and a bare-bladed knife thrust between it and the skin.

Captain Warfield untied his lashings and made his way over the bodies of the others. When his face became visible in the light from the binnacle it was working with anger. They could see him speak, but the wind tore the sound away. He would not put his lips to Narii's ear. Instead, he pointed over the side. Narii Herring understood. His white teeth showed in an amused and sneering smile, and he stood up, a magnificent figure of a man.

"It's murder!" Mulhall yelled to Grief.

"He'd have murdered Old Parlay!" Grief yelled back.

For the moment the poop was clear of water and the *Malahini* on

"He stood up—a magnificent figure of a man. . . . "
Drawing by Anton Otto Fischer.

an even keel. Narii made a bravado attempt to walk to the rail, but was flung down by the wind. Thereafter he crawled, disappearing in the darkness, though there was certitude in all of them that he had gone over the side. The *Malahini* dived deep, and when they emerged from the flood that swept aft, Grief got Mulhall's ear.

"Can't lose him! He's the Fish Man of Tahiti! He'll cross the lagoon and land on the other rim of the atoll if there's any atoll left!"

Five minutes afterward, in another submergence, a mess of bodies poured down on them over the top of the cabin. These they seized and held till the water cleared, when they carried them below and learned their identity. Old Parlay lay on his back on the floor, with closed eyes and without movement. The other two were his Kanaka cousins. All three were naked and bloody. The arm of one Kanaka hung helpless and broken at his side. The other man bled freely from a hideous scalp wound.

"Narii did that?" Mulhall demanded.

Grief shook his head. "No; it's from being smashed along the deck and over the house!"

Something suddenly ceased, leaving them in dizzying uncertainty. For the moment it was hard to realize there was no wind. With the absolute abruptness of a sword slash, the wind had been chopped off. The schooner rolled and plunged, fetching up on her anchors with a crash which for the first time they could hear. Also, for the first time they could hear the water washing about on deck. The engineer threw off the propeller and eased the engine down.

"We're in the dead centre," Grief said. "Now for the shift. It will come as hard as ever." He looked at the barometer. "29.32," he read.

Not in a moment could he tone down the voice which for hours had battled against the wind, and so loudly did he speak that in the quiet it hurt the others' ears.

"All his ribs are smashed," the supercargo said, feeling along Parlay's side. "He's still breathing, but he's a goner."

Old Parlay groaned, moved one arm impotently, and opened his eyes. In them was the light of recognition.

"My brave gentlemen," he whispered haltingly. "Don't forget . . . the auction . . . at ten o'clock . . . in hell."

His eyes dropped shut and the lower jaw threatened to drop, but he mastered the qualms of dissolution long enough to omit one final, loud, derisive cackle.

Above and below pandemonium broke out. The old familiar roar of the wind was with them. The *Malahini,* caught broadside, was pressed down almost on her beam ends as she swung the arc compelled by her anchors. They rounded her into the wind, where she jerked to an even keel. The propeller was thrown on, and the engine took up its work again.

"Northwest!" Captain Warfield shouted to Grief when he came on deck. "Hauled eight points like a shot!"

"Narii'll never get across the lagoon now!" Grief observed.

"Then he'll blow back to our side, worse luck!"

V

After the passing of the centre the barometer began to rise. Equally rapid was the fall of the wind. When it was no more than a howling gale, the engine lifted up in the air, parted its bed-plates with a last convulsive effort of its forty horsepower, and lay down on its side. A wash of water from the bilge sizzled over it and the steam arose in clouds. The engineer wailed his dismay, but Grief glanced over the wreck affectionately and went into the cabin to swab the grease off his chest and arms with bunches of cotton waste.

The sun was up and the gentlest of summer breezes blowing when he came on deck, after sewing up the scalp of one Kanaka and setting the other's arm. The *Malahini* lay close in to the beach. For'ard, Hermann and the crew were heaving in and straightening out the tangle of anchors. The *Papara* and the *Tahaa* were gone, and Captain Warfield, through the glasses, was searching the opposite rim of the atoll.

"Not a stick left of them," he said. "That's what comes of not having engines. They must have dragged across before the big shift came."

Ashore, where Parlay's house had been, was no vestige of any house. For the space of three hundred yards, where the sea had breached, no tree or even stump was left. Here and there, farther along, stood an occasional palm, and there were numbers which had been snapped off above the ground. In the crown of one surviving palm Tai-Hotauri asserted he saw something move. There were no boats left to the *Malahini,* and they watched him swim ashore and climb the tree.

When he came back, they helped over the rail a young native girl of Parley's household. But first she passed up to them a battered basket. In it was a litter of blind kittens—all dead save one, that feebly mewed and staggered on awkward legs.

"Hello!" said Mulhall. "Who's that?"

Along the beach they saw a man walking. He moved casually, as if out for a morning stroll. Captain Warfield gritted his teeth. It was Narii Herring.

"Hello, skipper!" Narii called, when he was abreast of them. "Can I come aboard and get some breakfast?"

Captain Warfield's face and neck began to swell and turn purple. He tried to speak, but choked.

"For two cents—for two cents—" was all he could manage to articulate.

NOTES

"A SON OF THE SUN"

1. **"they looked very much like monkeys"**: Evolutionary scientists and paleontologists by the early twentieth century had established and popularized an evolutionary connection between humans and apes. Explorers of the South Seas often noted what to them seemed to be an unmistakable resemblance between the people of Melanesia and the remains of ancient ape-man progenitors. The stereotype of the natives' laziness and lack of work ethic was proverbial, no doubt growing from the white men's conviction that a man is defined by the zeal with which he throws himself into his work. The islanders' apparent reluctance to adopt a middle-class lust for wholesome and character-building work was something London had observed firsthand. It is important to stress, however, with regard to this particular story, that the reason these natives have been recruited for service on the *Willi-Waw* is that they are better workers than could be gathered from the white population (see Oliver, *The Pacific Islands*, 87–93). The characterization of these boat workers is without question racist in its intent, and the use of the word "nigger" runs through most of the stories, often being used by the narrator as well as by David Grief himself. Joseph Bristow, a senior lecturer in English at the University of York and a scholar specializing in the adventure story, comments on this problem in his introduction to *The Oxford Book of Adventure Stories*: "The gradual decline of empire, together with increasing sensitivity to the ruthless authority that was often the result of imperialist domination on each and every continent, has made it difficult for certain kinds of adventure writing not to cause offense. The issue of racism is unquestionably the one that shocks many right-minded modern readers encountering such stories for the first time. It is abhorrent, and it is also instructive, that the foundation on which the effortless assumption of superiority was based became ultimately as fragile as the empire itself" (ix–xx).

2. **"Each was clad in a six-penny undershirt . . . strip of cloth"**: Contemporary photographs bear out the accuracy of London's depiction of the dress—or lack of it. White men wore wraparound skirts called *lava-lavas*, while the Solomoners often went quite naked, unless imposed upon by missionaries. Body piercing was ubiquitous, and as interaction with whites increased, islanders took to decorating themselves with civilized gewgaws, such as doorknobs and coffee cup handles, which were to them exotically dashing and ornamental when depending from the ear or nostril.

3. **"Shylocking me for what he wouldn't light his pipe with"**: Prejudicial beliefs about Jews, of course, were common in America at the turn of the century. It is troublesome that London (as did many thinkers and writers) subscribed to the "truth" of these ideas. Moreover, it so happens that at the time London was writing these stories, he was having personal difficulty with two people he guessed were Jews. A Judge George Samuels, who decided against London in a suit over a barroom brawl, earned the author's ire when it transpired that the judge himself owned the bar in question (*Letters*, 916–18). In England, London was suspicious about the treatment he had received from Sydney S. Pawling over arrangements with his English publisher, Heinemann. London ascribed these problems to Pawling's and Heineman's being Jews, referring disparagingly to Pawling's "cleverness" and comparing Pawling to a "Jew pawnbroker" (*Letters*, 974–75). The language of his letters seems to indicate that he was conscious of the impropriety of anti-Semitism and that he was concerned only to hint at Jewish stereotypes instead of coming straight out with them. On the other hand, he seems also to have been unaware that he held any group prejudices whatever. For example, London wrote to the editor of the *American Hebrew and Jewish Messenger* in 1911: "I have made villains, scoundrels, weaklings, and degenerates, of Cockneys, Scotchmen, Englishmen, Americans, Frenchmen and Irish, and I don't know what other nationalities. I have no recollection of having made a Jew serve a mean fictional function. But I see no reason why I should not, if the need and setting of my story demanded it. I cannot reconcile myself to the attitude that in humor and fiction the Jew should be a favored race . . . used only for his exalted qualities. . . . I have consorted more with Jews than with any other nationality; I have among the Jews some of my finest and noblest friends; and, being a Socialist, I subscribe to the Brotherhood of Man" (*Letters*, 1024).

4. **"over in the Santa Cruz. . . . in the bight at Gooma"**: Grief has been in the island group just to the southeast of Guadalcanal. Santa Cruz, by the way, was the setting for the first full-scale attempt on the part of Europeans to effect a settlement. In 1595 the Spanish explorer Mendana, in a failed attempt to find the Solomon Islands more than three decades after he had originally discovered them, landed on an island he christened Santa Cruz. He had a fleet of ships and some three hundred men, women, and children intent on creating a new civilization in the wild. Less than a year later, the ambitious project was abandoned in disorder, Mendana had died, and bloody conflicts between the Spanish soldiers and the islanders had reduced the place to a shambles. "Gooma" is a village located near the center of Guadalcanal's southern coastline, more accurately rendered as "Kuma."

5. **"the New Hebrides"**: This island group, known today as Vanuatu, lies to the south of the Solomon Islands.

6. **"Tulagi is a hundred and fifty miles away"**: Located in the Florida Islands, also known as the Ngele Islands, between Guadalcanal and Malaita, Tulagi was the government center of the Solomons until its destruction in World War II. Griffiths is suggesting that he may commit crimes with impunity this far from any legal powers.

7. **"Ontong Java Atoll"**: Also known as Lord Howe Atoll, this circle of tiny islands is just north of the Solomons and is populated largely by light-skinned Polynesians, though it is geographically located in Melanesia.

8. Though Hikihu has yet to be identified, phosphates were in demand for use in fertilizers, and the search for them sent prospectors all over the world. In Oceania, American and British companies harvested the phosphate deposits of such islands as Ocean, Nauru, Makatea, and Angaur. Phosphate mining proved to be disastrous to the native populations, which soon abandoned their traditional ways, becoming completely dependent upon the companies. When the mining companies departed the islands, having taken everything they needed, very often a generation of natives had lost the ability to live independently.

9. **"Other white men were pervious"**: Though David Grief's heroic status is upheld by his imperviousness to the tropical sun, London is careful to add, "one in ten thousand was he." The author himself was not so lucky, and during the voyage of the *Snark* London picked up a panoply of exotic, grotesque, and painful ailments while cruising the South Pacific. Many of the characters in the South Seas stories of Jack London will blame the climate for their faults of character.

10. **"Guadalcanar"**: This is the earlier spelling of the island's name, which in turn reflects the Arab origins of Gallego, one of the officers accompanying the Spanish explorer Mendana, who first saw the place in 1568. The voyager was moved to call the unknown island "Wadi-al-canar," after his home village. Sometime during the nineteenth century the term was finally anglicized as Guadalcanal.

11. **"the days of Bully Hayes all over again"**: Hayes was a swashbuckling scoundrel, thief, and pirate of the 1860s, operating most notoriously in the Caroline Islands.

12. **"Griffiths lay at Savo"**: Savo is a small island off the northern tip of Guadalcanal.

13. **"they were coming down . . . to Gabera"**: We have been unable to identify Gabera, though its proximity to Savo and the intervening reefs mentioned in the text suggest that Grief's trick is played out somewhere on the northeast coastline of Guadalcanal, between Tassafaronga Point and Point Cruz, near modern-day Honiara, the capital of the Solomons. Near Mendana Reef, Point Cruz is still the port from which to catch a motor canoe to Savo.

"THE PROUD GOAT OF ALOYSIUS PANKBURN"

1. **"The short run from Raiatea to Papeete"**: Raiatea—pronounced "Ry-eh-TAY-eh"—is a nearby island in Polynesia, located just to the west of Tahiti. Papeete—pronounced "Pah-pay-EH-tay"—is the capital city of Tahiti. Jack and Charmian London visited the area in early April 1908.

2. **"I pay him a good screw"**: British slang for a more-than-fair salary.

3. **"I've offered them fifty thousand"**: A working man or valuable servant might expect to earn $350 to $500 a year at the turn of the twentieth century.

4. **"the *Folies Bergeres*"**: A key process associated with the colonialist movement involved the transformation of the cultural Other into the familiar. Beginning with the formation of the French Protectorate in 1847, the French found the urge to reshape the beauties of the Society Islands irresistible. So successful were their efforts that Paul Gauguin, arriving in 1891, was shocked to find that Papeete "was Europe—the Europe which I had thought to shake off." What he saw, he said, "filled me with horror."

5. **"the *Mariposa*"**: This was the actual name of the ship on which Jack and Charmian London sailed on January 13, 1908, from Tahiti to San Francisco, temporarily breaking off the voyage of the *Snark* to straighten out some business affairs at the ranch. On February 2 they started the return voyage on the same ship. It is also the vessel that plays a key part in the last chapter of *Martin Eden*. (How different might have been Martin's end, had he only bumped into David Grief on the *Mariposa!*)

6. **"Rapa"**: Rapa Island is the southernmost island in Polynesia, located below the Tuamotos.

7. **"I didn't have a sou-markee"**: A continental expression for being completely without resources, based on the issuance of a practically worthless French coin in the eighteenth century, the *sou marqué*. Pankburn may be speaking literally, however, since the coin was primarily circulated in the French colonies.

8. **"I learned the crawl-stroke from the first of the Cavilles"**: Pankburn claims to have studied swimming with Frederick Caville, an English-born Australian who began teaching the sport in 1878. Apparently based on a swimming stroke invented by South Seas natives, the crawl—often the "Australian crawl"—became instantly successful in competitions and has been in wide use since 1896. Caville's sons, Syd and Charles, brought the stroke to England and the United States by 1903.

9. **"the revolutionists were marching on Guayaquil"**: In 1875 the conservative dictator of Ecuador, Garcia Moreno, was assassinated on the steps of his administrative palace by a machete-wielding critic. This event

began a period of governmental instability marked by frequent takeovers and tensions as the nation moved gradually toward liberalism. Guayaquil's roads had been a pet project of Moreno, as he hoped to make commercial access to Quito, in the interior, more convenient. Ironically, they probably facilitated the revolt against his government, as well as several subsequent ones.

10. **"Between the Banks Group and the New Hebrides":** The Banks Islands lie to the north of the New Hebrides, both located in the island group today known as Vanuatu, in the eastern part of the Coral Sea.

11. **"Wrote him from Levuka. . . . out of Thursday Island":** Levuka is a town on the east coast of the island of Ovalau, lying just to the east of the island of Viti Levu in the Fiji group. Thursday Island lies in the channel between Papua New Guinea and Cape York in northernmost Queensland, Australia.

12. **"Francis Island. . . . Bougainville named it Barbour Island. . . . Lies between New Ireland and New Guinea":** The earliest evidence of French interest in the region came with the 1766 expeditions of Louis-Antoine de Bougainville, for whom the northernmost portion of the Solomon group is named. The region between New Ireland and New Guinea is dotted with islands—principally New Britain—but we have found no chart or reference to either Francis or Barbour. It may be that these names have been superseded, or London may have made them up.

13. **"recruiting labour for the Upolu plantations":** Upolu is the eastern island in Western Samoa. The South Pacific colonial ambitions of Germany had been the last to develop of the major European powers, but as early as the middle of the nineteenth century German commercial enterprises became established, which later led to the basis for a political claim to the region. Like the other Europeans, German businessmen planted coconut palms and harvested copra using blackbirded "recruits" from Melanesia as well as indentured laborers from China. In 1894 Robert Louis Stevenson died on Upolu, and on May 9, 1908, Jack and Charmian made the pilgrimage up the mountain to the grave, a few miles south of Apia. The act was uncharacteristic for the materialistic London. He admitted to his wife, "I wouldn't have gone out of my way to visit the grave of any other man in the world" (Kingman, *Pictorial Life*, 199–200).

14. **"He stopped to take a look-in at uninhabited Rose Island. . . . Next, he paid his respects to Tui Manua":** Rose Island is in the Samoan group, east of Pago Pago. Tui Manua was the leader of the people of Manua Island, the last to sign an agreement presenting several islands as a gift to President Roosevelt in 1905. In 1930 Congress finally accepted, and American Samoa was born.

15. **"Trade goods to the Gilberts. . . . Ontong Java Atoll . . . Ysabel. . . . Malaita":** Grief is sailing northwest from Samoa to the Gilbert Islands, located in Micronesia. He then turns to the southwest, heading down to the

Solomon Islands via Ontong Java (Lord Howe) Atoll. London set many of
his *South Sea Tales* in this area, which he knew well.

16. **"the Tivoli, out of which he had been disorderly thrown by Charley Roberts"**: In fact, Charley Roberts, the owner and bartender of this
Apia pub, was one of Jack's friends, whom he met during the *Snark* voyage, and he appears as well in "The Inevitable White Man" (1910). A
colorful turf character, the real Roberts had had his brushes with the law.
Kicked off the race tracks of England, America, Australia, and even New
Zealand, Roberts had withdrawn to the comparative peace of Apia, hop-
ing to continue horse racing without the intrusive oversight of the authori-
ties.

"THE DEVILS OF FUATINO"

1. **"opium-smuggling from San Diego to Puget Sound"**: By the middle of the nineteenth century, one in ten California residents was a male
Chinese immigrant. All along the Pacific coastline, thousands of Chinese
laborers, moved by the promise of higher wages and fortified by a habit
of spartan living that made it possible to save nearly all of their income,
flooded into the American workforce. It was to be expected that white
American workers would soon mount an attack on the disturbing avail-
ability of cheap labor, and they did. By 1882 public anti-Chinese sentiment was sufficient to pass the Chinese Exclusion Act, effectively stopping
Chinese immigration to the United States. One of the strategies employed
by anti-Chinese activists was to denigrate the Asians' lifestyles and expos-
tulate on their vices. The Chinese government first expressed concern early
in the seventeenth century, as opium smoking began to increase in popularity. Early in the nineteenth century, British entrepreneurs, finding that
the opium poppy grew successfully in northern India, began efforts to create a market for the refined opium in China. The government of China
outlawed opium use in the 1830s, but the British had succeeded in creating a nation of increasing addiction. The two Opium Wars of the mid-
nineteenth century failed to help, and many Chinese laborers coming to
America brought their problem with them. Opium dens opened first in the
Chinatowns of the big cities, then spread out into the white communities,
until the issue reached the proportion that local governments felt it necessary to intervene and ban opium use outside of Chinatown. Opium impor-
tation to America was not illegal but only taxable until 1909, so that the
smuggling mentioned in the "old days" was apparently merely an effort to
escape import duties.

2. **"If a line be drawn . . . the high island of Fuatino will be raised"**:
Though the directions to Fuatino offered in the text are detailed, they are
actually fictitious. There is no evidence of any island at these coordinates,
nor can we find any reference to any island of this name. There is an island
named Futuna in the Hoorn Islands, just west of Samoa, and this location

is more likely to be populated by the specified groups: "a stock kindred to the Hawaiian, the Samoan, the Tahitian, and the Maori." the narrator insists, however, on its location "between Melanesia and Micronesia." It is certainly true that Ontong Java Atoll and Tasman Island (today called Nukumanu), which are nearby the specified location, are populated by Polynesians, in contrast to the other Solomon Islands. There is also another island named Futuna, east of Tanna in the New Hebrides (present-day Vanuatu), but this is wrong both in terms of geography and racial population.

   3. "'It's coming,' he said. 'Fever'": The World Health Organization in the early 1990s cited the Solomon Islands as one of the world's most dangerous environments for malarial infection. Recently, insecticide spraying has brought the danger down, but in London's time, anybody who spent time on Guadalcanal was likely to catch the mosquito-carried fever. The very serious form of the illness, falciparum, or cerebral malaria, accounts for two out of three cases in the Solomons.

   4. "Grief let go the anchor in forty fathoms": The water is 240 feet deep.

   5. "he knew they came from the Society Group": The women turn out to be the near neighbors of Grief's Raiatea men. They come from Huahine, just to the immediate east of Raiatea; both are west of Tahiti.

   6. "They killed the trader at Vanikori": Vanikoru (more commonly Vanikolo) Island lies southeast of the Solomons in the southernmost end of the Santa Cruz Group.

   7. "convicts from New Caledonia": A large, long island to the northeast of Brisbane, Australia. Between 1860 and 1894 more than forty thousand imported white convicts provided the French masters of New Caledonia with the workforce necessary to mine cobalt, nickel, and chromium. In 1883 Chinese indentured laborers were introduced. Before 1905 New Caledonia was the world's largest source for these metals. For Jack London's take on the New Caledonian justice system, see his fine short story "The Chinago," as well as the editors' essay, "Misinterpreting the Unreadable," in *Studies in Short Fiction* 34 (1997):507–18.

   8. "thickets of *cassi*": Cassia is a tropical shrub with feathery leaves and cuplike flowers.

   9. "For a year he had been sailing out of Tahiti and through the Paumotos": More commonly referred to as the Tuamotu Archipelago, and sometimes the Dangerous Archipelago, this massive chain of seventy-eight coral atolls lies due east of Tahiti.

"THE JOKERS OF NEW GIBBON"

   1. "New Gibbon": The political divisions London depicts on New Gibbon are not uncommon features of the active international commercial rivalry during the colonialist period. Shortland Island, south of Bou-

gainville, is geographically part of the Solomons, yet it lies close enough to the range of German influence that it may be a possible candidate for New Gibbon. London may also have been thinking of Fauro Island, or even Treasury Island as well, since they also lie within fifty miles of Choiseul. Until 1899 Germany had controlled the Shortlands as well as other nearby islands, but thereafter, as part of an arrangement with the British over their contending claims in Samoa, Germany ceded its interests in the area to Britain. None of these islands, however, is large enough to match London's description of one hundred miles long by fifty miles wide.

2. **"German Resident Commissioner from Bougainville"**: The German presence in Papua New Guinea began when Germany annexed the area in 1884. Two years later, Germans had expanded their control to the northern Solomons, including Bougainville and the island of Buka, just to the north of Bougainville.

3. **"She had been hung up by one arm in the sun for two days and nights"**: Koho's treatment of these women from his own tribe is an example of his depravity even among cannibals. In the Papuan region, as elsewhere in the Pacific where cannibalism was reported, in no case were people eaten who were tribal kin. As to the tenderizing of the living flesh, Papuans did traditionally break their victim's limbs and leave him alive, tied to a tree, until the children would finally dispatch the captive by stoning him to death. The body was dismembered and the flesh cut into strips, then wrapped in bark with vegetables. Finally, the meat was cooked in a pit specially dug for the feast. (See Bjerre, *The Last Cannibals*.)

4. **"McTavish was the first . . . the little, dried up Scotchman"**: William MacGregor was the first British administrator of British New Guinea, noted for the effectiveness of his handling of island populations. London also used this image of unlikely empowerment in his short story "Yah! Yah! Yah!" He appears to have been fascinated with the idea of the alienated Scot, possibly triggered by his visit to Tasman in the *Snark* during the autumn of 1908. There they met, Charmian recalled, "Mr. McNicoll, a small, hardbitten Scotsman, who holds power of life and death over the rapidly diminishing handful" of islanders who lived there.

5. **"He's down on Malaita now"**: This large Solomon Island is east of Guadalcanal. From 1871 until 1903 Malaita had been a principal target of the blackbirders, but the islanders were so savage that the whites dared not put down any permanent posts until 1909, when the British Protectorate was finally able to open a district office in Auki, on the northwest edge of the island. As late as 1920 the government confessed that there was still constant internecine warfare on Malaita, despite every effort of the white lawbringers to arrange peaceful conditions. The experiment itself was doomed to failure; on October 4, 1927, a group of Kwaio bushmen fell upon District Officer William Bell, dashing his brains out with the butt of a Snider rifle—the very item Bell had come to confiscate.

London's short story "Mauki" is an entertaining, compelling, and frightening tale of a Malaitan native, kidnapped as a boy by the chief of a tribe living in the bush and eventually traded to blackbirders for a few trade goods.

6. **"to the right are the copra-sheds"**: Copra is the dried meat of the coconut. After aging in sheds, the copra was processed into oil before being shipped to Europe and America, where it was (and still is) used in the manufacture of soap and other products. Coconut plantations were the primary employers of indentured native workers in Melanesia.

7. **"Koho had arisen, like a Kamehameha"**: Kamehameha I (1737?– 1819) was the first monarch to unify all the Hawaiian islands under a single, autocratic, and ruthless leader.

8. **"I knew a chap . . . who used a hammer and a ten-penney nail"**: London talks about his own adventures in tooth extraction in chapter 17 of *The Cruise of the Snark*: "I did not know anything about dentistry, but a friend fitted me out with forceps and similar weapons, and in Honolulu I picked up a book upon teeth. Also, in the sub-tropical city I managed to get hold of a skull, from which I extracted the teeth swiftly and painlessly. Thus equipped, I was ready, though not exactly eager, to tackle any tooth that got in my way. It was in Nuku-hiva, in the Marquesas, that my first case presented itself in the shape of a little, old Chinese. The first thing I did was to get the buck fever, and I leave it to any fair-minded person if buck fever, with its attendant heart-palpitations and arm-tremblings, is the right condition for a man to be in who is endeavouring to pose as an old hand at the business. I did not fool the aged Chinaman. He was as frightened as I and a bit more shaky. I almost forgot to be frightened in the fear that he would bolt. I swear, if he had tried to, that I would have tripped him up and sat on him until calmness and reason returned.

"I wanted that tooth. Also, Martin [Johnson] wanted a snapshot of me getting it. Likewise Charmian got her camera. Then the procession started. We were stopping at what had been the club-house when Stevenson was in the Maraquesas on the *Casco*. On the veranda, where he had passed so many pleasant hours, the light was not good—for snapshots, I mean. I led on into the garden, a chair in one hand, the other hand filled with forceps of various sorts, my knees knocking together disgracefully. The poor old Chinaman came second, and he was shaking, too. Charmian and Martin brought up the rear, armed with kodaks. We dived under the avocado trees, threaded our way through the cocoanut palms, and came on a spot the satisfied Martin's photographic eye.

"I looked at the tooth, and then discovered that I could not remember anything about the teeth I had pulled from the skull five months previously. Did it have one prong? two prongs? or three prongs? What was left of the part that showed appeared very crumbly, and I knew that I should have to take hold of the tooth deep down in the gum. It was very necessary that I should know how many prongs that tooth had. Back to the house I went for the book on teeth. The poor old victim looked like photographs I had seen of fellow-countrymen of his, criminals, on their knees, waiting the stroke of the beheading sword.

"'Don't let him get away,' I cautioned to Martin. 'I want that tooth.'

"'I sure won't,' he replied with enthusiasm, from behind his camera. 'I want that photograph.'

"For the first time I felt sorry for the Chinaman. Though the book did not tell me anything about pulling teeth, it was all right, for on one page I found drawings of all the teeth, including their prongs and how they were set in the jaw. Then came the pursuit of the forceps. I had seven pairs, but was in doubt as to which pair I should use. I did not want any mistake. As I turned the hardware over with rattle and clang, the poor victim began to lose his grip and to turn a greenish yellow around the gills. He complained about the sun, but that was necessary for the photograph, and he had to stand it. I fitted the forceps around the tooth, and the patient shivered and began to wilt.

"'Ready?' I called to Martin.

"'All ready,' he answered.

"I gave a pull. Ye gods! The tooth was loose! Out it came on the instant. I was jubilant as I held it aloft in the forceps.

"'Put it back, please, oh, put it back,' Martin pleaded. 'You were too quick for me.'

"And the poor Chinaman sat there while I put the tooth back and pulled over. Martin snapped the camera. The deed was done. Elation? Pride? No hunter was ever prouder of his first pronged buck than I was of that three-pronged tooth. I did it! I did it! With my own hands and a pair of forceps I did it, to say nothing of the forgotten memories of the dead man's skull.

"My next case was a Tahitian sailor. He was a small man, in a state of collapse from long days and nights of jumping toothache. I lanced the gums first. I didn't know how to lance them, but I lanced them just the same. It was a long pull and a strong pull. The man was a hero. He groaned and moaned, and I thought he was going to faint. But he kept his mouth open and let me pull. And then it came.

"After that I was ready to meet all comers—just the proper state of mind for a Waterloo. And it came. Its name was Tomi. He was a strapping giant of a heathen with a bad reputation. He was addicted to deeds of violence. Among other things he had beaten two of his wives to death with his fists. His father and mother had been naked cannibals. When he sat down and I put the forceps into his mouth, he was nearly as tall as I was standing up. Big men, prone to violence, very often have a streak of fat in their make-up, so I was doubtful of him. Charmian grabbed one arm and Warren grabbed the other. Then the tug of war began. The instant the forceps closed down on the tooth, his jaws closed down on the forceps.

Also, both his hands flew up and gripped my pulling hand. I held on, and he held on. Charmian and Warren held on. We wrestled all about the shop.

"It was three against one, and my hold on an aching tooth was certainly a foul one; but in spite of the handicap he got away with us. The forceps slipped off, banging and grinding along against his upper teeth with a nerve-scraping sound. Out of his mouth flew the forceps, and he rose up in the air with a bloodcurdling yell. The three of us fell back. We expected to be massacred. But that howling savage of sanguinary reputation sank back in the chair. He held his head in both his hands, and groaned and groaned and groaned. Nor would he listen to reason. I was a quack. My painless tooth-extraction was a delusion and a snare and a low advertising dodge. I was so anxious to get that tooth that I was almost ready to bribe him. But that went against my professional pride and I let him depart with the tooth still intact, the only case on record up to date of failure on my part when once I had got a grip. Since then I have never let a tooth go by me. Only the other day I volunteered to beat up three days to windward to pull a woman missionary's tooth. I expect, before the voyage of the *Snark* is finished, to be doing bridge work and putting on gold crowns."

9. **"Worth frowned at sight of the Snider"**: By the middle of the nineteenth century, even the most conservative European military man had become convinced that the muzzle-loading rifle had had its day and that the breech-loading weapon, which allowed greater accuracy and speed, was the inevitable wave of the future. In 1864 American Jacob Snider won a competition over the best design for an adaptive mechanism that would allow a mass conversion of the muzzle-loading Enfield rifle. Moreover, in this conversion, a new kind of bullet, called the Boxer cartridge, came into use. It incorporated a firing device within the cartridge itself. Within the next five years, all of the old Enfields had been converted, and the Snider rifle went into production in its own right. Before long, hundreds of thousands of Sniders were in use, primarily in Canada and Turkey, but also throughout Asia and into Australia. When at last the Snider achieved obsolescence, they were readily and cheaply gathered together by enterprising traders to unload on the natives living in occupied colonized areas, especially the South Pacific. In the New Hebrides and the Solomons, the Snider soon became the emblem of masculinity and empowerment; even when the rifles were too dirty to fire safely, they served as very effective war clubs. For decades after Jack London visited the Pacific, the Snider continued to maintain its status value among the islanders.

10. **"*Tambo* along black fella"**: The word "tambo" shows a linguistic connection to Polynesian languages: In the Solomons, this is the way "taboo" is pronounced. One of the first capitalistic impulses of the white invaders of the Pacific was to sell rum to the islanders, despite the vociferations of the teetotalling Protestant missionaries. By encouraging dependency and even addiction, the whites more easily secured influence

and power over the natives, and the missionaries fought hard to see that
their island charges kept away from intoxicants. Grief thus displays his
integrity—however patronizing it may be—by denying Koho access to alcohol.

11. **"At Guvutu . . . to examine the grass lands back of Penduffryn"**:
Ghavutu is an island to the south of Nggela Sule, one of the Florida Islands between Guadalcanal and Malaita. Tulagi (pronounced "Too-LAR-
gee") was the former capital of the Solomons, located just to the west of
Ghavutu. World War II left Tulagi in ruins. Penduffryn plantation, located
on Guadalcanal fourteen miles west of Lungga Point, was one of the most
prosperous copra centers in the Pacific, and Jack and Charmian knew the
area well. (In fact, his hobnobbing with the rich and decadent exploiters
of island people and resources has since earned the socialist writer criticism for his apparent hypocrisy.) After the destruction of Tulagi in 1943,
American soldiers built Honiara to serve as the new capital for the British
government, near the former location of Penduffryn.

12. **"'I was able to recover the heads. . . . They'd make excellent curios'"**: McTavish displays a grisly but practical streak in suggesting that
the heads might have considerable financial value, reminding us that head-
hunting in the area was actually stimulated by white men a hundred years
before this story takes place. At the end of the eighteenth century, Europeans found examples of smoked, dried heads from New Zealand to be irresistible curios, and they were glad to pay a premium price for any they could
get. This drove the market value up and encouraged islanders throughout
the Pacific to revive a practice that had by then nearly disappeared. Jack
London purchased a shrunken head himself, bringing it back to California, where it remained among his artifacts until some time in the 1990s,
when a conscientious person persuaded the California State Parks Department to return it for proper burial.

"A LITTLE ACCOUNT WITH SWITHIN HALL"

1. **"Leu-Leu Atoll is sunk"**: This unidentified island may be fictitious,
but it apparently lies near the Banks Group, south of the Solomons and
north of the New Hebrides (Vanuatu). Some Pacific islands have actually
disappeared, and some—especially atolls—are so close to sea level that
they may be visible at one time, not at another.

2. **"my easting"**: Navigational term referring to eastward departure.

3. **"Many shelves of books lined the walls"**: Swithin Hall's collection, as Grief notes, reflects a man with a wide range of interests, and there
is no doubt that Hall must have been an interesting character, whatever
his ethical lapses in business. Here are some of the areas in which he reads:

Tolstoy: Count Leo Tolstoy (1828–1910). Russian mystic, philosopher, and novelist, author of *War and Peace* and *Anna Karenina*.

Turgenieff: Ivan Sergeyevich Turgenev (1818–83). Russian novelist, author of *Fathers and Sons, Smoke*, and many short stories.

Gorky: Maksim Gorky, penname of Aleksey Maksimovich Peshkov (1868–1936). Russian essayist, dramatist, and short story writer.

Cooper: James Fenimore Cooper (1789–1851). American Romantic novelist, author of the Leatherstocking series, including *The Last of the Mohicans*.

Mark Twain: Penname of Samuel Langhorn Clemens (1835–1910). One of the world's best-known humorists and perhaps the most popular American novelist of the late nineteenth century. Twain had died shortly before this story was composed, and it may be as a kind of tribute to a contemporary master that London placed a set on Hall's shelves.

Hugo: Victor Hugo (1802–85). French Romantic novelist, author of such familiar works as *Les Miserables* and *The Hunchback of Notre Dame*.

Zola: Emile Zola (1840–1902). French novelist and inspiration for the American Naturalist movement in fiction. California novelist Frank Norris is credited with bringing Zola's influence into American literature —the same movement to which Jack London's work is generally assigned.

Sue: Eugene Sue (1804–57). French novelist, author of the multi-volume series *The Wandering Jew* and *Mysteries of Paris*.

Flaubert: Gustave Flaubert (1821–80). French author of the contro-versial first novel *Madame Bovary*, the daring topics and unrelenting real-ism of which scandalized midcentury readers and precipitated a court trial over its alleged immorality.

De Maupassant: Guy de Maupassant (1850–93). French short story writer, specializing in ironic plot twists.

Paul de Koch: Probably London meant Robert Heinrich Hermann Koch (1843–1910). A key figure in the development of modern medicine, Koch is identified as one of the first to outline the germ theory of illness. Koch discovered the causes of tuberculosis (1882) and cholera (1883). (Paul de Kruif [1890–1971], the American bacteriologist and popular writer, is ineligible as a candidate for London's conflation; De Kruif was only twenty-one when this story was composed, and his famous book *The Microbe Hunters* would not appear until 1926.)

Metchnikoff: Elie Metchnikoff (1845–1916). Author of several phil-osophical studies, including *The Psychology of Science and Morality in the Internal Evolution of Man, The Psychology of Pessimism and Opti-mism and Its Effects upon Literature, The Prolongation of Human Life*, and *The Nature of Man: Studies in Optimistic Philosophy*. Metchnikoff won (jointly with Paul Ehrlich, the famous scientist who discovered a treatment for syphilis) the Nobel prize for physiology in 1908, in recogni-tion of his discovery of phagocytosis, the process by which some cells can surround and destroy harmful bacteria. The discovery became the founda-tion for the subsequent understanding of immunology.

Weininger: Otto Weininger (1880–1903). Author of *Geschlect und Charakter* (*Sex and Character*, 1903). A troubled theorist who rejected Judaism for Christianity then denounced Judaism as weak and without a legitimate moral foundation, Weininger shot himself to death at the age of twenty-three, soon after his book came out. Some of his ideas were later used to support anti-Semitic agitation.

Schopenhauer: Arthur Schopenhauer (1788–1860). Philosopher, author of such works as *The World as Will and Representation* (1818) and *On the Will in Nature* (1836). Schopenhauer is associated with the elaboration of philosophical pessimism and takes as his major theme the individual's struggle to escape or defeat the demands of the will. Significantly, London also mentions Schopenhauer in the first paragraph of *The Sea-Wolf*.

Ellis: Havelock Ellis (1859–1939). At the time Swithin Hall was collecting Ellis, the British scientist had yet to complete his major work, *Studies in the Psychology of Sex*, which he began to publish in 1897, ultimately to occupy seven volumes by 1928. Ellis was among the first to analyze the main features of what he called "inversion," or homosexuality. He remained a somewhat scandalous figure all his life for holding opinions quite at odds with the prevailing views of his time, and until 1935 his works were restricted by law from readers who were not physicians. In our day, he is more likely to be lionized as a hero of the sexual revolution, a pioneering ethicist of prison reform, and a vigorous supporter of women's rights.

Lydston: G. Frank Lydston was an American expert on penology and crime. Author of *The Diseases of Society: The Vice and Crime Problem* (1906), he estimated that the world at the time devoted five billion dollars to the establishment and maintenance of prisons.

Krafft-Ebbing: Richard, Freiherr von Krafft-Ebing (1840–1902). Author of *Psychopathia Sexualis* (1886), a detailed and lengthy study of unusual sexual practices and obsessions drawn from his study of case histories of psychiatric patients.

Forel: Auguste-Henri Forel (1848–1931). Forel specialized in the study of the anatomy of the brain, pioneering in the identification of the functions of certain brain structures. He was also interested in social reforms and concerned himself with treatments for such diseases as alcoholism and syphilis.

Woodruff's *Expansion of Races*: Charles Edward Woodruff (1860–1915). Author of a study (1909) examining the migrations of racial groups within the United States, Woodruff was an anthropologist interested in the relation between race and environment.

Hudson's "Law of Psychic Phenomena": Thomson Jay Hudson (1834–1903). Though his title, *The Law of Psychic Phenomena* (1893), seems to indicate an emphasis on the paranormal, in fact, Hudson was trying to provide a theoretical foundation for the understanding of all psychological events in light of the evidence for hypnosis, telepathy, and clairvoyance. To fully appreciate the boldness of Hudson's design, it is important to realize that the Society for Psychical Research was formed in 1882 and that the first university psychology laboratory only opened in 1885; all Hudson's data were fresh and as yet unsystematized. Though the book was one of the most successful in its field, going through forty-five editions by 1922, it seems to have made little or no impact on either psychical research or psychology proper.

Zola's "Paris": The concluding volume of Zola's *Trilogy of the Three Cities, Paris* appeared in 1898.

Mahan's "Problem of Asia": Alfred Thayer Mahan (1840–1914). U.S. admiral. The most important figure in late nineteenth-century military thinking about the role of the navy in establishing and maintaining international power, Mahan convinced President Theodore Roosevelt that a strong navy was essential to the outward expansion of America. Other nations tried to follow suit, resulting in a worldwide naval buildup. Mahan's major work was *The Influence of Sea Power in History* (1890).

"A GOBOTO NIGHT"

1. **"Goboto"**: The first difficulty for analysis of this tale lies in the title. "Goboto" apparently doesn't exist. All we learn from the text is that the island is "a quarter of a mile in diameter" and that it is not located in the Solomon group. After an extensive inquiry, the editors are betting on the island of Ranongga, in the Western Province, south of Vella Lavella Island. It is a small island of the right proportions, without a considerable history of European habitation, and it was once known as Vesu Ghoghoto, which could easily be corrupted into Goboto. Subsequent mention of a nearby place named Karo-Karo may be a corruption of Kolokolo, a lake on Vella Lavella. Given London's accuracy of detail in his fiction, the point is of some interest. Some of the characters, too, are likely to be based on actual people. "Captain Jensen, the wildest of the Blackbirders" is no doubt a version of Captain Jansen, the skipper of the recruiting vessel *Minota*, whom the Londons knew well. After the sailing adventure with Jansen described in our introduction to this story, they returned on the *Snark* to a place Charmian called "Guvutu" in her log. She meant, of course, Ghavutu, a small island near Tulaghi in the Florida Islands, near Guadalcanal. That Jack also calls it Guvutu and contrasts it to Goboto suggests that Goboto may be a similar corruption.

2. **"a few tons of coal have lain untouched for twenty years"**: That the coal supply on Goboto has lain untouched for twenty years suggests that the station's importance to the company by now has been significantly marginalized. The admiralty's warships were often steamers; they had for many decades patrolled the Pacific to see that no laws—particularly blackbirding restrictions—were being broken; occasionally, these ships also were

called upon to "punish" rebellious islanders by firing on villages. That was in the now-past heyday of island exploitation.

3. "'It's David Grief,' Peter Gee remarked": Dale L. Walker (1981) draws our attention to London's allusions to Sherlock Holmes in the deductions of Peter Gee, as Gee explains to the green Australian, Deacon, how he "knows" that it is David Grief's vessel that has just anchored at Goboto. Conan Doyle's short stories about the master detective had begun in 1891, with the British magazine *The Strand* gambling on the success of a "serial" character who appears in a group of otherwise independent stories. As Conan Doyle later reminisced, "They began to buy the magazine, and it prospered, and so, I may say, did I" (see Homer and Roden, "The Movietone Interview"). Wearying of his character, Conan Doyle had already killed off and then reluctantly resurrected his hero, to more or less universal approbation. The importance of Conan Doyle's success was an inspiration for other career writers, and London's own asking prices for his work were directly related to the higher wages Holmes's creator was able to command.

4. "It was the stolid integrity of the Chinese blood": London's attitudes about racial and cultural characteristics were not unusual in his time. The narrator apparently believes, for example, that Chinese are universally people of integrity, while the English are both reckless and licentious. Australians are known for their racial prejudice; station clerk Jack Andrews says, "They're daffy down there on colour." And the boorish Deacon has, according to the station manager McMurtrey, "'all-white Australia' on the brain." David A. Moreland, in the only thorough critical examination of this story, "Racism in 'A Goboto Night'" (1999), points out that the bully Alfred Deacon is a "thinly disguised" characterization of the real-life Alfred Deakin, the Australian racist prime minister who supported the "Australia for the Australians" movement, which sought to keep all people of color from entering the country. The political movement calling for the establishment of an all-white Australia had become so urgent by the first decade of the twentieth century that it had the unforeseen positive result of virtually halting all "recruitment" of Melanesians for Australian plantations. Though most people who studied world cultures viewed with alarm the interbreeding of races, which seemed the inevitable outcome of the erasure of racial divisions in society, London seems to have favored miscegenation. Note, for example, the tone of sympathy directed toward characters who are racially mixed in his other Pacific fiction, including the Grief story "The Pearls of Parlay" and particularly "The House of Pride" and "The Seed of McCoy." London's racial theories are currently the topic of considerable scholarly attention. For example, Moreland points out that the racism at the core of this story is quite complicated. At the same time that the story is about the insensitive racism of the Australians at the beginning of the twentieth century, pointing out the

need to value every man for his unique gifts regardless of race, there is as well an undercurrent of apparently unintentional racism in the narrative voice. On occasion, we see the narrator's propensity to qualify positive statements about people of mixed blood in terms of the individual's proximity to a white ideal: "Peter Gee was that rare creature, a good as well as clever Eurasian," observes the narrator. One of the other characters, Mc-Murtrey, also admires Gee: "We can't permit any bullying, especially of a man like Peter Gee, who's whiter than most white men." Moreland goes on to point out that this story "exemplifies the difficulties inherent in any attempt to deduce London's racial belief from his fiction, for herein he denounces a racism which relegates an exceptional person to the darkness, while simultaneously validating the negative racial stereotyping . . . which is responsible for the initial injustice" (9). Interested readers may wish to refer to two works from the decade after London wrote these stories: Carl Campbell Brigham, *A Study of American Intelligence* (Princeton, N.J.: Princeton University Press, 1923); and Lothrop Stoddard, *Racial Realities in Europe* (New York: Scribners, 1925).

5. **"I spoke to Grief, on the *Gunga*, in Sandfly Passage, day before yesterday"**: Grief is between Sandfly Island and Nggela Sule, within ten kilometers of Ghavutu Island. The Nggela Islands (or Florida Islands) lie between Guadalcanal and Malaita. If Goboto is indeed Ranongga, it would be easy for Grief to sail the distance in two days.

"THE FEATHERS OF THE SUN"

1. **"Fitu-Iva"**: Fatu Hiva is the southernmost island of the Marquesa Group, northeast of Tahiti and north of the Tuamoto Archipelago. The Spanish explorer Mendana was the first European to see this lush paradise, in 1595. Jack and Charmian London first visited the Marquesas on December 6, 1907.

2. **"fight like Maoris"**: The Maoris are indigenous people of New Zealand. Their daunting reputation as cannibals discouraged colonization for almost seventy years, from Captain Cook's initial visit in 1769 until the 1830s, when British colonists, made foolhardy by their desire to grab more land, decided to attempt to settle the islands. The Maoris put up a fierce resistance, which the British answered with mixed results. Finally, superior British firepower was able to crush all resistance.

3. **"Pillar Rocks at the entrance"**: Hanavave Bay, on the western part of the island, boasts twin natural columns, causing the early sailors to call it "Baie des Verges," or Bay of Penises. Blushing missionaries later provided a more chaste image by adding an *i* in the right spot, transforming it to "Baie des Vierges," or Bay of Virgins.

4. **"Willie Smee, the supercargo"**: "The Feathers of the Sun" has many of the features of fantasy, and the presence of Grief's colleague named

Peter and an officer named Smee suggests connections with Sir James Barrie's *Peter Pan*. Though the play began its popular run in 1904, the book, under the title *Peter and Wendy*, appeared only in 1911—the same year the Grief stories were serialized in the *Saturday Evening Post*. We do not know whether Jack London saw the play before he wrote the story.

The supercargo is an officer of a merchant ship whose duty it is to manage the commercial affairs of a voyage.

5. "**clad in *ahu's* and *lava-lavas***": *Ahu* is Hawaiian for "garment," and the term suggests a cloak made of tiny feathers. A lava-lava is a simple cloth wrapped around the waist and extending to the knees.

6. "**old hymns taught them by forgotten missionaries**": The French Catholic Picpusien fathers had the responsibility of establishing a mission in the Marquesas in 1838. The priests were brought to the islands on the ship *Venus* under the command of Captain Dupetit-Thouars. *Himine* is Marquesan for "hymn."

7. "**the prophet Jeremiah**": Jeremiah, the Old Testament seer who weighed in against superficiality in religion, incautious political alliances, and the dangers of daily immorality, is best known erroneously as a weeping prophet of doom, probably arising from a mistaken attribution of him as the author of the Book of Lamentations.

8. "**those smart Levuka boys**": Levuka, on the small island of Ovalau, which in turn is located just to the east of Viti Levu, was the captial of Fiji until the shift to Suva in 1832. Levuka was the main collection point for the copra trade for the entire South Pacific region until 1957, when a new facility was built in Suva.

9. "**Squarefaces**": A popular term derived from the manufacture of cheap, ginlike liquor in South Africa, sold in square bottles.

10. "**Kai-kanak**": man-eater [note in 1st ed.].

11. "**runnin' over to Yap**": Yap lies in the Caroline Islands, between the Solomons and the Philippines.

12. "**to charge the demurrage**": Demurrage is a fee charged to someone who detains a vessel from expeditious loading or unloading while in dock.

"THE PEARLS OF PARLAY"

1. "**Kanaka**": Name given to native islanders of Polynesian blood.

2. "**Paumotus**": Today called the Tuamotos, this is a chain of some eighty atolls, located east of Tahiti and south of the Marquesas. Ferdinand Magellan first stumbled into these islands in 1521, and some years later Bougainville also found the chain. Noting the navigational hazards surrounding the area, the Frenchman named it the "Dangerous Archipelago." Jack and Charmian London tried to find the chain in mid-December of 1907, but they "missed it," so the *Snark* sailed on to Tahiti.

3. "**Pearls**": Christian missionaries both established copra planta-

tions and introduced pearl diving in the middle of the nineteenth century. Pearl production remained an important part of the Paumotos economic life until late in the twentieth century. It has been replaced by an active tourism industry.

4. **"Narii Herring"**: This is an example of London's in-joking: Narii Salmon (1856–1906) was an islander sea captain who had died just before the voyage of the *Snark*. By changing his name from one sort of fish to another, London effects a meiosis that allows him to apply all the defects of character necessary for his villain.

WORKS CITED

Baird, James. *Ishmael*. Baltimore: Johns Hopkins University Press, 1956.

Berkove, Lawrence I. "Les derniers nouvelles de Jack London." *Europe*, nos. 844–45 (August-September 1999): 99–107.

———. "London's Developing Conceptions of Masculinity." *Jack London Journal* 3 (1996): 117–26.

Bjerre, Jens. *The Last Cannibals*. New York: Morrow, 1957.

Bridgwater, Patrick. *Nietzsche in Anglosaxony: A Study of Nietzsche's Impact on English and American Literature*. Leicester, England: Leicester University Press, 1972.

Bristow, Joseph. *The Oxford Book of Adventure Stories*. Oxford: Oxford University Press, 1994.

Harvey, Anne-Marie. "Sons of the Sun: Making White, Middle-Class Manhood in Jack London's David Grief Stories and the *Saturday Evening Post*." *American Studies* 39, no. 3 (fall 1998): 37–68.

Homer, Michael W., and Christopher Roden. "The Movietone Interview." *ACD: The Journal of the Arthur Conan Doyle Society* 6 (1995): 18–24.

Johnson, Osa. *Bride in the Solomons*. New York: Garden City, 1944.

Kaufmann, Walter, ed. *The Portable Nietzsche*. New York: Viking Books, 1982.

Kingman, Russ. *Jack London: A Definitive Chronology*. Glen Ellen, Calif.: Rejl, 1992.

———. *A Pictorial Life of Jack London*. New York: Crown, 1979.

Labor, Earle, and Jeanne Campbell Reesman. *Jack London*. New York: Twayne, 1994.

London, Jack. *The Complete Short Stories of Jack London*. 3 vols. Edited by Earle Labor, Robert C. Leitz III, and I. Milo Shepard. Stanford, Calif.: Stanford University Press, 1993.

———. *The Letters of Jack London*. Edited by Earle Labor, Robert C. Leitz III, and I. Milo Shepard. Stanford, Calif.: Stanford University Press, 1988.

———. *Martin Eden*. New York: Macmillan, 1909.

———. "A Preliminary Letter from Jack London, Who Is Going Round the World for the Woman's Home Companion." *Woman's Home Companion*. November 1906, 19.

———. *The Sea-Wolf*. New York: Macmillan, 1904.

————. *A Son of the Sun*. New York: Doubleday, Page, 1912.

Moreland, David. "Racism in 'A Goboto Night,'" *The Call: The Newsletter of the Jack London Society* 9, no. 2 (fall-winter 1999): 3–4, 8–9.

Nietzsche, Friedrich. *Thus Spoke Zarathustra: A Book for Everyone and No One*. Trans. R. J. Hollingdale. Baltimore: Penguin Books, 1961.

Oliver, Douglas. *The Pacific Islands*. Cambridge, Mass.: Harvard University Press, 1958.

Parkay, Forrest Winston. "The Influence of Nietzsche's *Thus Spoke Zarathustra* on London's *The Sea-Wolf*." *Jack London Newsletter* 4 (1971): 16–24.

Qualtiere, Michael. "Nietzschean Psychology in London's *The Sea-Wolf*." *Western American Literature* 16 (1982): 261–78.

Reesman, Jeanne Campbell. *Jack London: A Study of the Short Fiction*. New York: Twayne, 1999.

Stasz, Clarice. *American Dreamers: Charmian and Jack London*. New York: St. Martin's Press, 1988.

Tietze, Thomas R., and Gary Riedl. "Jack London and the South Seas." Jack London Collection, Sunsite.Berkeley.edu/London/Essays/southseas.html. (August 21, 1996).

————. "'Saints in Slime': The Ironic Use of Racism in Jack London's South Seas Tales." *Thalia: Studies in Literary Humor* 12 (1992): 59–66.

Walker, Dale L. *Jack London and Conan Doyle: A Literary Kinship*. Bloomington, Ind.: Gaslight, 1981.

Watson, Charles N., Jr. "Nietzsche and *The Sea-Wolf*: A Rebuttal." *Jack London Newsletter* 9 (1976): 33–35.

Williams, James. "The Composition of Jack London's Writings." *American Literary Realism* 23 (1991): 64–83.

SUGGESTIONS FOR FURTHER READING

Cameron, Ian. *Lost Paradise: The Exploration of the Pacific*. Topsfield, Mass.: Salem House, 1987.

Day, A. Grove. *Jack London in the South Seas*. New York: Four Winds Press, 1971.

Grattan, C. Hartley. *The Southwest Pacific to 1900*. Ann Arbor: University of Michigan Press, 1971.

———. *The Southwest Pacific since 1900*. Ann Arbor: University of Michigan Press, 1963.

Harcombe, David. *Solomon Islands*. 1st ed. Singapore: Lonely Planet, 1988.

Heyerdahl, Thor. *Fatu-Hiva: Back to Nature*. New York: Doubelday, 1974.

Honan, Mark, and David Harcombe. *Solomon Islands*. 3d ed. Hong Kong: Lonely Planet, 1997.

Johnson, Martin. *Through the South Seas with Jack London*. New York: Dodd, Mead, 1913.

Keesing, Felix M. *Native Peoples of the Pacific World*. Washington, D.C.: Infantry Journal, 1945.

Kessing, Roger M. *Kwaio Religion: The Living and the Dead in a Solomon Island Society*. New York: Columbia University Press, 1982.

Kessing, Roger M., and Peter Corris. *Lightning Meets the West Wind: Malaita Massacre*. Melbourne: Oxford University Press, 1980.

London, Charmian. *The Book of Jack London*. 2 vols. New York: Century, 1921.

———. *The Log of the Snark*. New York: Macmillan, 1915.

London, Jack. *The Cruise of the Snark*. New York: Macmillan, 1911.

———. *The House of Pride*. New York: Macmillan, 1912.

———. *On the Makaloa Mat*. New York: Macmillan, 1919.

———. *The Red One*. New York: Macmillan, 1918.

———. *South Sea Tales*. New York: Macmillan, 1911.

———. *The Turtles of Tasman*. New York: Macmillan, 1916.

Purdon, Charles J. *The Snider-Enfield Rifle*. Alexandria Bay, N.Y.: Museum Restoration Service, 1990.

Sherry, Frank. *Pacific Passions: The European Struggle for Power in the Great Ocean in the Age of Exploration*. New York: Morrow, 1994.

Stanley, David. *South Pacific Handbook*. Chico, Calif.: Moon, 1996.

Wheeler, Tony, and Jean-Bernard Carillet. *Tahiti and French Polynesia*. 4th ed. Hong Kong: Lonely Planet, 1997.